FORGET ME NOT, ELIZABETH

A PRIDE & PREJUDICE VARIATION

JENNIFER JOY

D1253135

CONTENTS

FREE BOOK

Want a free novelette?
Join Jennifer Joy's Newsletter!

rs. Fitzwilliam Darcy. Elizabeth Bennet wrinkled her nose at her signature. Much too commanding and formal. Dipping her quill into the inkwell, she tested another variant.

Mrs. Lizzy Darcy. She twisted her lips. That was not quite right either. Far too inelegant, informal … no matter how lovely the "L" swooped and curled on the page.

Mrs. Elizabeth Darcy. She sighed contentedly, signing her forthcoming name once more, exaggerating the loop on the "Y" with flourish. Nearly perfect.

She filled the cream surface with the surname she would forever use once she signed her name beside her husband's in the marriage register that morning.

Her husband. Elizabeth's heart hummed. The three previous weeks, during which the banns had been read, were a torture, forcing her to be patient when she would rather not, but today was her reward. Finally, she would marry the man she truly, deeply, madly — nay, not madly. Never that! — ardently … Yes, *ardently* loved.

"Sit still, if you please, Miss. I am nearly done," Sarah repeated. The maid had spent the past hour braiding and twisting Elizabeth's hair into submission, carefully poking bunches of bishop's lace between sprays of pink and white roses from Mama's garden — the first blooms of summer.

Daydreaming of her Mr. Darcy, Elizabeth traced her finger over her favorite signature, and attempted to be still while her emotions twirled and rejoiced. Today was the day.

"There," Sarah said, stepping back and clasping her hands at her chin to admire her handiwork. "You are lovely, Miss. As beautiful as ever."

Elizabeth was grateful. She was not given to vanity, but for days she had dreaded waking on her wedding day to an uncontrollable mane and a face full of unsightly blemishes.

"Sarah! Oh, where is that girl?" Mama called from her rooms.

Sarah pinched her eyes closed with a forbearing sigh.

Elizabeth stifled a laugh. Her mother was renowned for her nervous spasms, and today being the day which would go a long way in alleviating the source of her nerves — that of seeing two of her daughters married well and settled — she had been particularly demanding that morning and would remain so until vows were exchanged, their unions official. "Thank you, Sarah. Your nimble fingers accomplished what I could not have dared."

Pleased, Sarah bobbed a curtsy. "I will see to Mrs. Bennet," she said, her step lighter than her usual trudge.

For the first time since waking, Elizabeth was alone. She knew it would not last for long, nor would she wish it to, so she enjoyed the moment, the calm before the storm ... or, more appropriately put, the celebration.

Billowing curtains and the soft, sweet breeze beckoned Elizabeth to the window. Even the weather cooperated, adding to the perfection of the wedding day she and Fitzwilliam would share with her sister Jane and Mr. Bingley. A double wedding.

Her father came into view from the direction of the orchard behind the house. He was difficult to miss with his white, wide-brimmed hat and long, damask coat joined with a frothy veil of the finest lace. Elizabeth smiled, remembering how Mama's rapture when Papa had brought the delicate lace home had turned to horror when he cut a big circle out of the center and had Mrs. Hill stitch it onto his old hat and stiff coat. What she had thought to be a rare, thoughtful gift was the start of Papa's latest obsession — bees. Mama did not approve, but she was relieved enough that he had moved on from collecting beetles — they all were —

that she did not object so long as the hive's residents stayed in their dwelling ... and far away from hers.

Mama's shrill voice traveled the length of the hall. "Mary, do not dawdle. Fordyce's sermons are not so enthralling you cannot resume your reading until after the service. Kitty, if you insist on this incessant coughing, you shall have to watch the ceremony through the stained glass window. I will allow for no interruptions on this glorious, blessed day." A clap of her hands, and Elizabeth imagined her mother raising her face heavenward when she continued in one breath, "We are saved! A few more hours, and we are saved! Such clever girls, my Jane and Lizzy. They will put you in the way to marry well, Kitty, and I daresay, even your chances of making a match are much improved, Mary, with such handsome, wealthy gentlemen as your brothers-in-law."

Elizabeth rolled her eyes. She had never been Mama's favorite, but her engagement had covered over all of her sins so far as her mother was concerned.

Jane drifted into the bedchamber, golden tendrils framing her porcelain cheeks, an English rose in full bloom.

"You are beautiful, Jane."

Ever the modest, soft-spoken one of the five Bennet sisters, Jane looked down, a becoming blush gracing her features. When she looked up again, her eyes beamed brightly, her smile wide. "As are you, Lizzy." She crossed the room, clasping Elizabeth's hands in her own. No embraces. Not yet. Easily crushed muslin and wrinkled silk did not allow them. However, once their new gowns had been properly and dutifully admired, Elizabeth planned to hug her sisters, her mama, and papa until her arms grew heavy.

"Can you believe this day has finally arrived? I thought it would never come," Jane said with as much impatience as Elizabeth had ever heard her sister express.

"I have been pinching myself all morning to be certain this is not a dream. It is all so perfect, so wonderful."

"To think I shall be the mistress of Netherfield Park before the day's end, and you of Pemberley. I can hardly believe our good fortune." Jane plucked at the satin ribbon tied at her waist. "I almost wish Charles had not invited so many relatives and friends for the ceremony and wedding breakfast." She dropped her voice. "I am happy to share my joy with those who are important to him, but I hope it is not selfish of me to wish to have those first precious hours after we are wed to ourselves. Just my husband and me."

Elizabeth chuckled in commiseration. "I should worry more if you did not wish to spend more time with your new husband." More comfort than that, she could not offer, for unlike Bingley, Fitzwilliam had invited no one from his side of the family at all. Elizabeth had agreed it was for the best. His aunt Lady Catherine de Bourgh would only stir up trouble. His little sister, Georgiana, was busy preparing Pemberley for their arrival with the help of his uncle and aunt Matlock. And his cousin Colonel Richard Fitzwilliam, the only other relation besides Lady Catherine and Miss de Bourgh of Elizabeth's acquaintance, would dine with them that evening at Darcy House in London.

Each of them had sensible excuses. Completely comprehensible, given the shortness of their engagement. But a little niggle of suspicion — fed by the repeated and indisputable proofs Fitzwilliam had given that his love was stronger than his aversion to her sometimes offensive-but-always-well-meaning family — spurred her to expect that his side of the family would not be so poorly represented.

As constant as Fitzwilliam had always been, he was a man of surprises. The depth of his attachment had been tested to the full. Not only had she rudely refused him once, accusing him of the cruelest, ungentlemanly behavior toward a man undeserving of her sympathy, but when her youngest sister, Lydia, had run away with that same ne'er-do-well, Fitzwilliam had hunted them down and covered over their transgressions with a layer of respectability. He had arranged their marriage and saved her family from ruin.

And still, after all that trouble, he chose her. Shame at how wrongly she had misjudged him heated her cheeks. However, those same formidable obstacles which had so nearly prevented them from seeing each other for who they, in reality, were, also convinced Elizabeth that their love would endure. Theirs was not a love easily won ... and, therefore, just as easily lost or neglected. No, they had fought for each other, longed for each other when hope was gone, changed their views and refined their characters. There was nothing left but for them to be splendidly happy.

Jane tried to smile, and Elizabeth reeled her wandering thoughts back to her sister. Of what use was it to lament the present or ponder the past when a delightful future awaited both of them? Elizabeth squeezed Jane's hands. "We have the rest of our lives to spend with our husbands."

"That is what I keep telling myself, but I still envy you for being able to depart for London after the feast when I shall have a houseful of guests."

"You, envious?" Elizabeth teased, then groaned inwardly when she observed her usually serene sister chewing on her lip and furrowing her brow. She ought to sympathize with her. After all, she would be equally displeased had she been in Jane's position, having her capabilities as a hostess tested so soon and under the critical eyes of Mr. Bingley's pernicious sisters. "Oh, Jane, you will rise to the occasion as you always do."

"It is not only that. I will own I am nervous, but..." She paused, searching for the right words. "It is that ... I hope I shall always be kind ... but neither do I wish for others to take advantage of my kindness or that of my husband."

Shaking her head, Elizabeth lifted Jane's chin, looking her firmly in the eye. "You will make Mr. Bingley an excellent wife and an exceptional mistress of Netherfield Park, and I have no doubt that you will both be very happy."

Creaky floorboards and the uneven rhythm of Mrs. Hill's arthritic footstep announced Longbourn's housekeeper. "I had hoped to catch both of you," she said, squinting her eyes and clucking her tongue at Sarah's handiwork before expressing her approval with a firm nod. Her purpose seen to, her face softened. Brushing her rough fingers over Elizabeth's cheek with one hand and Jane's with the other, Mrs. Hill said tenderly, "I wish you all the happiness in the world on this blessed day. Longbourn will not be the same without you."

Elizabeth reached up, placing her hand on top of Mrs. Hill's, leaving Jane to express the gracious words the elderly woman needed to hear. While fewer ladies in the household would certainly lessen the housekeeper's workload, Elizabeth was certain her mother would have little difficulty finding other ways in which to occupy Mrs. Hill's time.

Mrs. Hill dropped her hands to dab at her cheeks. With a sniff, she turned toward the window. "As many times as I have shut this window for you, Miss Lizzy, I daresay I shall miss chastising you for leaving it open so often."

As unapologetic as Mrs. Hill was forgiving, Elizabeth merely smiled. She hoped Pemberley's house-keeper was as caring as Longbourn's.

A heavy tread caught Elizabeth's attention, and she looked out to the hall to see the new footman stand beside the doorway. Thatcher cleared his throat and tapped on the door frame. "Mrs. Hill, if I might beg a moment."

Mrs. Hill rolled her eyes. Elizabeth bit her tongue. Thatcher was her mother's pride and joy ... and the bane of the Hills' existence. Men of a certain age suitable for service were scarce while the country was at war. They preferred to seek their fortunes in the Navy or satisfy their obligations to nation and family by enlisting in the regulars. The few who remained behind were usually unfit in some way, and Thatcher was no exception. However, his deficiency was not visible, and being young and handsome in his livery, Mama was quick to praise her find. So long as he was not given too many instructions, he showed her choice to advantage.

"What is it, Thatcher?" Mrs. Hill asked through an exasperated sigh.

He scratched his head. "I am sorry to disrupt you, ma'am, but I cannot find Mr. Hill. I thought I saw him going out to the carriage house, but when I followed him there, I saw nobody. And by the time I returned to the house, I could not recall why you had sent me to find him. I swept the flagstones outside the kitchen, hoping the activity would help me remember." Bowing his head, he added quietly, "I regret to say it did not work."

Good-naturedly, Mrs. Hill suggested he reserve his mental exertions for the wedding breakfast and leave Mr. Hill to her.

"Mrs. Hill! Mrs. Hill, I need you!" shrieked Mama.

With a parting glance, the housekeeper disappeared down the hall with Thatcher, no doubt repeating the same instructions she had been instilling in him since the first reading of the banns.

"Poor Mrs. Hill. Mama will run her off her feet by the end of the day," said Jane.

Elizabeth had not added her sympathy to Jane's before their mother burst into their bedchamber.

"It is a disaster! I am at my wit's end, and Mr. Bennet is nowhere to be found. He is not in his study." Mama flailed her arms in the air, adding, "The father of the brides is missing, we will be late unless we depart soon, and I just now realized that we cannot all fit into the carriage without crushing your gowns beyond reparation." She flicked her fan open, waving it fitfully at her flushed face. "My poor nerves. If Mr. Bennet does not return soon, I shall have to send the footman out to fetch him. I daresay he is dawdling with his bees."

Suspecting her father's absence had as much to do with avoiding Mama's nerves as the inevitability of Elizabeth's departure to a far-away estate, she suggested, "Mama, why do you not go in the carriage with Jane, Kitty, and Mary? I will send Thatcher to find Papa, and by the time the carriage returns, he will be ready to accompany me."

Mama shook her head. "I should rather the brides arrive at the same time."

"The distance is short, and the delay will only be minutes. However, our dresses and slippers will be pristine, and you will be allowed to ensure everything else is arranged by the time I arrive. If you depart now, the ceremony will start on the appointed hour."

Elizabeth saw her mother was still unconvinced. She added, "Nothing will go wrong, Mama. What could happen on such a perfect day?"

Mama huffed. Tapping Elizabeth on the shoulder with her fan, she added, "Never tempt fate aloud, Lizzy. Until your names are signed beside Mr. Bingley's and Mr. Darcy's, I will have no rest. There is nothing else to be done. We shall have to make two trips." In a flurry of eau de parfum, she gathered her daughters and herded them out to the waiting carriage.

Alone once again, Elizabeth stood in the center of her room, taking a deep breath and spinning in a slow circle.

Today was real. She and Jane had spent their last night together in the bedchamber they had always shared. The faded floral wallpaper, the scarred chair by the window, the collection of candle stubs by which she read at night, the dressing table which had belonged to her great-grandmother, the armoire with the squeaky door, the rug Mrs. Hill had knitted to keep the chill from her feet when she woke in the morning. Longbourn had been a wonderful, comfortable home.

As much as Elizabeth looked forward to exploring Derbyshire with Fitzwilliam, she was certain she would miss her childhood abode … eventually. Just not today.

Today was for unbridled joy and hard-won celebration. The excitement of exploring her new home (and her new husband) sent tingles of anticipation through her limbs.

She would leave this room for the last time as Miss Elizabeth Bennet. When she next returned, she would be Mrs. Elizabeth Darcy.

CHAPTER 2

Fitzwilliam Darcy checked his pocket watch again. The seconds did not tick any faster for his constant scrutiny. Fifteen minutes had never felt so long. Longer than the last year and half during which he had met, felt himself in danger of, and fallen in love with Elizabeth Bennet.

He glanced through the open entrance door to the carriage which would convey him and Bingley to Longbourn's chapel. The horses pawed impatiently. Darcy resumed pacing.

After another turn about the hall, he paused by the doors. Pulling out the ring he had selected especially for Elizabeth, he held it up to the morning sun, appreciating how the light gleamed crimson reflections off the polished garnets. Five glistening, red gemstones shaped into a forget-me-not encased with gold stretching around the band symbolized everything he had already promised in his heart to give Elizabeth: faithfulness, dependability, constancy, love, his very self.

He had fallen in love with her despite his best efforts to the contrary. Despite her better judgment, he thought with a chuckle. How proud he had been — insulting her, leaving her vulnerable to others' self-serving lies, and demeaning everyone she held dear in a madcap declaration of his undying love. Of course, he had expected her to throw herself at his feet, grateful he would condescend to make an offer for her when he had so graciously overcome all the obstacles he had taken pains to enumerate. What a fool he had been.

Thank goodness their worst troubles were in the past, the valuable lessons learned and applied. It was easy — even for Darcy — to laugh at their faults now.

He had won Elizabeth's heart, and he would cherish it all the more, knowing she gave her his hand in full understanding of his weaknesses (of which she was foremost). While Darcy was tempted to believe his lessons learned and his pride conquered, his character was too firmly formed to believe such deeply ingrained tendencies entirely subjugated. But he would always exert himself for Elizabeth.

He loved her so much. She demanded as much from him as he demanded from others, forcing him to soften his expectations and leaving more place in his heart for her. Would that she remained the same always.

Tucking the ring back into his pocket, he glanced again at his pocket watch.

Two minutes passed. With a grimace, he resumed his pacing.

Were it up to him, he would have applied for a common license and married Elizabeth weeks ago in a small, private ceremony. However, Elizabeth's eyes had sparkled like flutes of champagne when Bingley had suggested a double wedding. Blast Bingley.

Darcy was not so cruel as to separate Elizabeth from her family before she was ready, and so he had been forced to develop patience as he waited for the banns to be read, contenting himself that he would not have to share her once they were wed. He had dutifully informed his family, his invitation lackluster in an attempt to discourage them from attending for that very reason. Otherwise, his relatives (except for his aunt Catherine) would descend on them and he would have to share Elizabeth, and he had waited long enough. Surely, a gentleman ought not be deprived of his wife after the ceremony and the wedding breakfast.

Soon, this same morning, he would give his name to Elizabeth. Mrs. Elizabeth Darcy. He would swear before God, her family, and friends that he would never part from her side from that day forward. He would love her and cherish her so long as they both lived. The blessed day had finally arrived, and Darcy was impatient to begin his life with the woman he adored.

He checked his pocket watch again and groaned. Ten minutes. The longest ten minutes of his life.

CHAPTER 3

George Wickham grimaced at his wife, as he often did. Why did she have to be so loud?

"Good morning, Lucas!" she exclaimed, her voice carrying across the square. Extracting her handkerchief, in case she had not drawn enough attention since they had descended from the coach at Meryton, she waved the white linen frantically at the gentleman whose name she had squealed.

The young lady with Mr. Lucas gripped him by the elbow and pulled him inside the haberdasher's shop, pretending not to have heard the excited cries of Lydia Wickham.

Wickham imitated the lady's example, gripped his wife's arm, and tugged her along with him. "Come, Lydia, we do not have much time."

She whined, "I do not understand why you cannot stay longer, George." She ran her hand over her stomach. She was probably hungry. Again. She was always hungry.

Wickham's own stomach churned. Would that he had never set eyes on Lydia Bennet.

Pouting out her bottom lip, she looked up through her eyelashes at him. "Why do you not stay with me, George? Surely, the regiment will understand."

Releasing his clenched jaw, careful to soften his voice, Wickham said, "It pains me greatly, my love, but I am not one to doubt the wisdom of your doctor, and his suggestions for your nerves run contrary to the demands put upon me as an officer. I have leave long enough only to see you safely to your family and to return to my post."

Her bottom lip protruded further.

Before she grated on his nerves and he, as a consequence, did something he might later regret, he held up his hand to prevent his wife from speaking. "The doctor insisted you must be in a calm setting, somewhere with fresh, country air. You know as well as I do that the miasma at the barracks is not suitable for your agitated nerves, nor is the company we must keep suitable to your needs." He stopped walking, took her hands in his, and peered into her petulant eyes. Gently, he said, "I am only concerned for your welfare, my love. A brief spell with your family at quiet Longbourn will soon set you right, and by then, my regiment will be reassigned away from the factories and smoke. I have it on good authority we are headed to the coast next." He had heard no such thing, but he would do anything to appease Lydia and make his departure easier. "Salty breezes and all the sea bathing you could wish for. What think you of that, my love?"

The peevishness pinching her face weakened at the mention of the pleasures awaiting her. She wrapped her arm around his, holding him tightly. Possessively. It was all Wickham could do not to recoil.

Just a few minutes more.

"Of course, George, I ought to have known. You are always so good to me. It is only that I have not been apart from you since we were wed, and I cannot bear the thought of being separated for any length of time."

He resumed walking along the road to Longbourn, leaving Lydia no choice but to stumble along beside him. She did not loosen her hold on his arm, though his pace was brisk. They were near Longbourn.

An approaching carriage set his heart racing. It could not yet be the cart he had arranged to convey her luggage to Longbourn. Slowly, as though he had not a care in the world, he glanced over his shoulder to see who it was and instantly relaxed. Just a farmer driving his cart. He raised his hand in greeting, ensuring the man a good look of his face. He needed to be seen, just not by the wrong people. He prayed all of them were at the wedding by now.

"You walk too fast, George."

He snapped. "I would walk faster if you did not slow me down."

Lydia bunched her chin like a toddler. "La, you are disagreeable today. You will not stay when I want you too, and you insist on leaving me at Longbourn instead of the church to see my sisters marry. I have as little desire to see stuffy Mr. Darcy as you do, but I do so wish to see Jane's and Lizzy's gowns." She patted her stomach again, and Wickham struggled against the urge to tighten his grip around her fleshy elbow. Only the knowledge of his plan granted him solace.

A few more minutes. Then Lydia would be her father's problem, not his. It was for her own benefit. The doctor had said so.

He mumbled, "I am sorry, my love. Knowing I must leave you has made me cross."

She snuggled against his arm, giggling. "I ought to have known. My poor, dearest George, missing me already."

He forced a smile and continued walking.

"Let us peek through the windows, at least," she pressed. "Now that my sisters are married to rich men, they will have no use for their old gowns, and if I am not there to claim them, they will all go to Kitty and Mary."

Wickham did not slow his pace. "As I told you before, we must arrive at Longbourn while your family is away."

"But why?"

He took a deep breath. "Consider how your sudden, unexpected arrival at the church would affect your sisters. This is their grand day, but you would be certain to overshadow them with your presence. Then, they would resent you and you would not benefit from their kindness."

Lydia gasped. "No! I had not considered that before, but I daresay you are correct. What with all the news I have to share, I would be certain to get all the attention. You are so clever, George. So what if Kitty and Mary get their dusty, old gowns? Lizzy is sure to invite us to stay at Pemberley, and she will be rich enough to spare me several new gowns. And Jane is generous to a fault. I know she will not refuse me when I ask her to lend me money."

Wickham, too, hoped his wife's sisters would be as generous as Lydia believed. He was in desperate need of funds. However, he thought it best not to point out the futility of Mrs. Darcy ever inviting them to Pemberley to his wife. It would sooner freeze in late June than Darcy allow the Wickhams to set foot on his precious estate.

Carriage wheels rattled and harnesses jingled behind them. Wickham tucked his head down and pulled Lydia closer to the side of the road. The foolish girl turned and waved openly.

Wickham prayed it was not her family. It ought not to be. He had deposited his wife at the inn with a plate of cucumber sandwiches while he crept behind the carriage house to ensure the Bennets had departed. It had taken him longer than he had wanted, but the family had made two trips in their carriage, he supposed, to save the ladies' gowns or to save the carriage from suffering an accident with its heavy burden. Accidents happen all the time. And when one least expected.

He had not seen Darcy.

If only Darcy knew what he planned, he would thank him.

Miss Elizabeth must have bewitched him completely for the grand gentleman to willingly attach himself to such a family. Mr. High-and-Mighty with his fortune and connections would be grateful to him once he realized the burden from which Wickham planned to free him.

Perhaps, in the future, he would look upon Wickham with more favor. With more generosity.

Longbourn came into view and, with his relief imminent, it became easier for Wickham to think more kindly of his wife. Slowing his pace and pressing her hands against his heart, he looked upon her with the charming regard which had won him the hearts of many maidens. "It distresses me greatly to depart so suddenly, my love. I think only of your welfare. I must stay on good terms with my commander. It simply cannot be helped." He stroked her smooth cheek, trailing his fingers down to trace the outline of her lips.

She rose up to her toes and leaned against him.

This had always been Lydia's most redeeming trait.

She was affectionate. He crushed his mouth against hers, kissing her as though it might be their last.

When he released her, she stepped away, her hand over her heart and her chest heaving for breath. "My sisters would be shocked to be kissed with as much passion as I am accustomed to."

Her constant comparisons between herself and her sisters had grown tiresome months ago, but Wickham prided himself that in at least one area he was superior to Darcy with his cold manners and repressed emotion. Even when Wickham had nearly managed to elope with Darcy's little sister, he had suppressed his anger. He had not called Wickham out, nor had he challenged him to a duel. Not one blow or shove. Darcy was the personification of passionless self-possession. And he was soon to be in Wickham's debt.

Resting his forehead against Lydia's, Wickham said, "I must depart before your family returns. They will be delighted to see you, and I hope you will give them my best regards as well as explain the difficulty of my position suitably." Dragging her by the shoulders, he turned her around and sent her down the path to Longbourn when a thought occurred to him. Calling after her, he said, "Wave to me from your bedchamber window once you gain entrance."

Lydia smiled at him and skipped toward her house. Minutes later, a window toward the front facing the carriage house slid open, and his wife leaned perilously over the edge so carelessly Wickham held his breath.

Only when she retreated inside did he turn around and begin his sojourn back to the village.

He made certain to greet the villagers he passed all the way into Meryton. He made certain he was seen hopping onto the back of a cart on the road to London. And he made certain nobody observed him hop off the cart a couple of miles down the lane and cut across the fields.

CHAPTER 4

*E*lizabeth looked across the carriage at her father. They were partway to the church now, and every turn of the wheels taking her closer to her new life also reminded her of how much she would miss her father.

Unwilling to give in to sad sentiments, she teased, "Your bees are bound to be happier than Mr. Collins' and shall reward you with more honey for your exertions on behalf of their hive."

Papa chuckled. "I have not yet devised a manner by which to collect their honey without destroying their habitation, but I hope to hear from the Polish beekeeper soon. As for Mr. Collins … I will own that his negligence is a powerful incentive for me." He rubbed his hands together, adding with a twinkle in his eye, "I believe I shall send the very first of this summer's honey to him and Mrs. Collins."

"As a gift?" Elizabeth arched her eyebrow, watching her father. "Or as proof of your success over your distant relative?"

He shrugged. "I will take what victories I can." His smile tensed. "The truth of the matter is that Mr. Collins is bound to live longer than me, and he will eventually inherit my estate. Your mother and sisters remaining at Longbourn, who depend on me for their security, might very well be cast out of their home. Unless some miracle happens, I am bound to fail them."

Elizabeth sighed. So much for avoiding sad sentiments. "I doubt Mr. Collins will send them to the hedgerows as Mama often worries. Charlotte would never cast her friends out, nor would she insist Mama, Kitty, and Mary leave unless they had somewhere to go."

Papa dabbed at his eyes, his voice gravelly. "Both of my sensible daughters are leaving me today." He waved his hand at Elizabeth. "Do not trouble yourself, my dear girl. These are not tears of mourning but of joy."

Hardly convincing. "Perhaps with fewer daughters underfoot, you will have more time to guide Mary and Kitty. Mary does not suffer from want of sense, only, perhaps, an excess of righteousness. And Kitty is bound to continue to improve without Lydia's constant influence."

"I almost wish Lydia was still with us at Longbourn rather than with that scoundrel, Wickham. What kind of life can he give her? He will soon grow impatient with her ... if he has not already." He sighed deeply, rubbing his hand over his face, seemingly determined to be gloomy on her happiest of days.

Elizabeth leaned forward. "Fitzwilliam would never have insisted they marry if he believed Wickham truly unkind. I daresay they are well enough." She hoped. Truth be told, Elizabeth tried not to think of her youngest sister too often, for her thoughts never led to anywhere pleasant.

This was not the conversation Elizabeth had meant to have with her father. This melancholy exchange simply would not do. Turning the conversation to a pleasanter topic worthy of the day, she added, "Besides, Mama's nerves will settle significantly once Jane and I are advantageously married to our gentlemen of fortune."

Papa chuckled. "Your mother has made such a habit of nervousness, she shall not know how to occupy herself. It is a good thing she found that new footman, so she has someone else to fret over."

"And you have your bees to keep you busy. They are soon to swarm, are they not?"

Bees always made her father smile, and this mention accomplished no less. "It is the right time of the year. I have done everything to lure them away from their hive in the apple tree to my straw skips, but I am content to allow them as much time as they decide to take until I can perfect the design."

Elizabeth settled against the squabs, ready to hear

more about the practices of Polish beekeepers, the brood comb melted and spread over cloths to lure bees to a new dwelling, and the vertical trays another gentleman (she could not remember where he was from) had designed to facilitate the collection of honey without endangering the residents of the skip.

"Is there anything you regret about today, Lizzy?"

She started, taken by surprise at the unexpected question, and startled herself even more when she blurted the truth. "I dearly wish some of Fitzwilliam's family might have chosen to join us … But I understand his wishes and their reasons … so … while I regret their absence and our hasty departure for London, I would not change it."

"Do you suspect he is ashamed of us still?" her father asked with a disconcerting grin.

"Not at all! He is merely eager, as I am, to begin our life together."

"True. For a moment, I forgot he is not deprived of his proper allotment of embarrassing relatives in the form of Her Esteemed Greatness, Lady Catherine de Bourgh. Who could be embarrassed by us with such a creature as an aunt? A woman with expensive fireplaces who descends upon humble residences to insult the size of their gardens and impose her wishes on a young lady whose courage rises at every attempt to intimidate her?"

Elizabeth laughed. "I ought to thank Her Ladyship. Had she not made the journey to Longbourn to secure my promise that I was *not* engaged to, nor would I ever agree to enter such an agreement with her nephew, Fitzwilliam would not have learned of my change of heart."

Elizabeth had unwittingly frustrated Lady Catherine's scheme to marry her nephew to her own daughter. Elizabeth had won Fitzwilliam's heart ... and Lady Catherine's hatred. Now that Elizabeth gave the matter more consideration, she was grateful Fitzwilliam had not pressed his family to join them. Aside from Georgiana and Colonel Fitzwilliam, she did not know his family at all. What if they resembled Lady Catherine? Elizabeth shivered at the thought and her narrow escape orchestrated thoughtfully by her betrothed to shield her from the disapproval of his relatives.

Papa sighed. "There will always be tensions between our families. It gives us a sense of purpose, a means to ease our consciences by exaggerating the faults of those considered loftier than ourselves, reminding us of their humanity and vindicating our own deficiencies by paltry comparison."

"How can you say that? Fitzwilliam is a constant man. He is not the sort to unite himself to a family unless he wished to."

"That only proves the depth of his devotion to you, Lizzy. The rest of us, he will forbear for your sake. However, I hope that with our improved circumstances — after all, we boast a footman now — and Lydia's departure, we will improve in his sight."

Elizabeth rolled her eyes. Better his usual nonsense than the melancholy which had plagued him earlier. "If the footman does not sway his opinion more in your favor, then Lydia's absence is certain to do so."

"And so it will be. You are a clever girl. As your mother is fond of saying, 'Jane cannot be so beautiful for nothing.' Well, I have always thought you could not be born so clever for nothing."

Elizabeth smiled. She was grateful for her quick mind. She would need all of her wits about her in the days, weeks, months, years to come as the wife of a man of privilege and fortune with an immense household to run and the first circles to win over.

Keeping her tone light, she asked, "Do you have any further words of wisdom to impart to me?" They were only a couple of curves away from the church.

He considered, rubbing his cleanly shaved chin. "Had your courtship been less troubled, I might have more wisdom to impart. However, your attachment was forged in fire and I am convinced you love each other as you ought to."

"It is a comfort to know the worst is behind us," she teased. "We may marry and simply be happy."

"Does there exist a life without trouble?" Papa quipped.

"I suppose not, but I hope to have learned enough from my past mistakes to know better than to repeat them."

The carriage creaked and dropped.

Elizabeth's heart jumped into her throat, smothering her cry.

Papa leaned toward the window, reaching to lower the glass.

A deafening crack pierced the air, and before the echo throbbing in Elizabeth's ears quieted, she was thrust to the side, her father's shout the last sound she heard before blackness overcame her.

CHAPTER 5

*M*other whacked her cane against the roof of the carriage, and Anne de Bourgh retreated deeper into her corner. She wished she could disappear. Wished she were somewhere else. Wished she were someone else.

"Do not dawdle! We must not be late," her mother commanded.

Anne had no doubt the coachman heard her demands over the beat and jingle of the horses in their harness and the rumble of the shaking carriage. She heard the snap of his whip with his shouts, urging them onward.

She wished they would arrive too late, then nothing could be done.

Mother said she would never forgive Darcy for marrying another when he had been promised to Anne since birth. But Anne had never held any particular regard for her cousin and, therefore, had no desire to marry him for any reason other than to satisfy her mother.

Resting her head against the cushion, Anne closed her eyes and inhaled through her nose slowly, exhaling out her mouth, to control the nausea. Her mother would be unwilling to stop. Any delay would only add to her ill-humor. Mother was always in an ill-humor of late. More so than normal.

Anne wished she were at Rosings, at the bend in the stream beyond the grove where the water pooled and warmed and where she had watched tadpoles darting about with Patrick.

Her heart stirred the way it always did when she remembered those days. Days when her father was still alive and Patrick's mother was charged with Anne's care. Happier days.

Father had allowed Anne to play out of doors, had encouraged it. And Mrs. Gibbs had charged her youngest son, the youngest of her brood of ten and who was only a few years older than Anne, to ensure she did not come to any harm or get into too much mischief. Anne frowned. Nobody looking at her now would believe how she would turn up in the Rosings kitchen, her feet muddy, her dress torn, and her hair disheveled. Her father would pinch her chin and smile at her. "Did my little girl have an adventure today?" he would ask, and she delighted in reliving her explorations and discoveries to eager ears while Cook and her assistant made her more presentable.

Patrick had shown her the joys of tying her skirts around her legs and taking off her shoes to wiggle her toes in the bed of the stream. To sit with her back facing the sun, letting it warm her through. Laying in sweet fields of freshly cut grass. Weaving crowns of daisies. Anne had worn the crowns he made her with pride, feeling every inch the princess. Papa had said she looked charming, beautiful. Mother had made her toss her crown into the fireplace. For days after, she blamed every insect daring enough to enter the house on Anne.

Where was Patrick now? Or, rather, Mr. Gibbs as she must think of him. Had he made his fortune? Was he married, with several children of his own? Anne's heart squeezed, but she smiled despite the ache. Patrick would make an excellent father. He had been so patient with her, tracking ladybirds through the garden and making wishes on dandelions.

Her mother snorted angrily, waking Mrs. Jenkinson who had the remarkable ability to sleep in jostling, tumultuous conveyances.

Anne pulled open the shade.

"You will ruin your complexion," her mother said, pulling the shade down.

Retreating into the pleasanter memories in the recesses of her mind, Anne pretended she lay in the grass gazing up at the puffy clouds changing shapes. The only enjoyment she was allowed now was her pony and cart. She lived for her daily drive. Papa had planned to teach her, but it was Patrick who had taken on the task after her father had died. He had taught her how to brush the horses after their exertion, a chore in which Anne indulged when her mother would not notice. The groomsman kept her secret.

What would Patrick and Papa think of the woman she had become? Pale, frail, excessively meek.

Anne swallowed hard, tears swelling behind her eyelids.

Mother thwacked the top of the carriage again.

Again, Anne prayed they would arrive too late.

CHAPTER 6

*D*arcy looked down the length of the aisle, holding his breath and willing the doors to open, allowing him a glimpse of his bride. From that day forth, he never meant to part from her.

But the Bennets were late.

He pulled the forget-me-not wedding ring out of his pocket, the whispers fading as he focused on the fastenings gripping the gemstones. The pews were packed with Elizabeth's family and friends, Longbourn's tenants, several of Bingley's intimate acquaintances... Even Mr. Collins was present where Elizabeth was not.

While other brides had been known to increase the suspense of the occasion by appearing late, Elizabeth was neither so vain nor cruel. Some obstacle must have delayed her, some accident befallen her or one of her party.

With a nod at the vicar, Darcy stepped down the aisle, intent on resolving the evil keeping his Elizabeth from his side.

The door creaked open, and Mrs. Bennet scrambled to meet him. Her eyes squinted, her face flushed, and her general manner flustered. Addressing him as much as the assembled waiting, she smiled and said, "Our apologies for the delay. One of the brides has torn her gown, and it must be repaired before the service. We thank you for your presence on this glorious, blessed day … and your patience. Pray allow us a few minutes more."

If Mrs. Bennet's manners were not so often agitated, Darcy would have discredited her explanation that instant. He looked over his shoulder where Bingley stood beside the vicar.

The clergyman nodded. "It is early yet. There is sufficient time to perform the ceremony."

Darcy ought to join Bingley, but he was nearer the entrance doors. He just needed to see Elizabeth. One look to allay the dread churning in his stomach.

Miss Bingley's sharp whisper to her sister, Mrs. Hurst, reached Darcy in the aisle where he stood directly beside them. "Perhaps Miss Eliza had a change of heart."

Darcy's jaw clenched. He did not envy Miss Bennet her sisters-in-law. He had hoped they would not be present, but it appeared that Miss Bingley would hold out hope until there was no more to be had, and Mrs. Hurst would encourage her.

Mrs. Hurst mumbled, "She is as flighty as Mrs. Wickham."

He forced his shoulders to relax and exhaled slowly. He was marrying the woman he loved — Elizabeth — and that was that. She was worth the attachment he would have to endure. Yes, Wickham would be his brother, but nothing of value ever came without a cost, and Elizabeth was as precious as Wickham was worthless.

Darcy grimaced at the memory. He had had to drag that ingrate to his London parish with a common license and, with the girl's uncle also serving as a witness, stand behind Wickham until their inked signatures dried in the register.

One disaster averted and effectively patched over. The Bennets' reputation saved.

The smile on Elizabeth's face, the tenderness with which she had regarded Darcy from that moment on had made his exertions worth the sacrifice. It went beyond gratitude, beyond obligation. Elizabeth was too strong-willed, her mind too firm, to agree to marry him for anything less than the deepest love. Miss Bingley's spite was borne from jealousy.

Mrs. Bennet looked over her shoulder at the doors closed behind her, then back at him. She occupied all the space she possibly could in the middle of the aisle, preventing him from taking another step forward. She probably feared he would bolt at the first hint of complication, that if she blinked or breathed wrong, her house of cards would collapse.

Darcy could have reassured her, but he had not yet learned how to converse with the matron without provoking her nerves or his impatience. He would learn, but today his aim was to marry Elizabeth, and every second that ticked by without her beside him was a second wasted. He stepped forward, but Mrs. Bennet refused to budge.

"Mr. Darcy, you cannot see the bride before the wedding! It is not done!"

A foolish custom if ever there was one.

She shoved his arm, pushing him away. "Now, you go and stand by Mr. Bingley, and allow me to see to Lizzy's gown. Just a few more minutes is all we require."

He was tempted to pick his soon-to-be mother-in-law up and move her out of his way, but he did not suppose that would foster good feeling between them. Elizabeth had teased him for his skeptical tendency. And so, he followed the direction of Mrs. Bennet's nudges back down the length of the aisle and resumed his place beside Bingley, ignoring his misgivings.

CHAPTER 7

*E*lizabeth blinked, her vision blurred. Voices echoed through a hazy fog. A face loomed in front of her, and she recognized the pungent scent of her father's pipe tobacco.

"Lizzy? Lizzy, wake up, dear girl."

What had happened? Elizabeth tried to speak, but her words stuck together, escaping in a moan. She tried to sit up, but her limbs did not respond.

She felt her father slip his arm under her head and, very gently, he helped her to sit.

Elizabeth's heartbeat pulsated, pounding up to her skull. She winced against the brightness of the sun. Pressing her fingers against her temple, she winced when they met with tender, rising flesh.

An injury. Had she hit her head? How?

Papa sat beside her, his arm wrapped around her shoulders, holding her to him on a grassy knoll on the side of the road. The carriage sat twisted and unmoving on the lane, the axle on the side of the coach where Elizabeth sat broken and littered over the compact dirt.

The evidence was before her — they had been in a carriage accident — but she could not connect the pieces. "What happened?" she asked.

Her father held up his hand, tucking his fingers into his palm. "How many do you see?"

She gave him a face. "Three."

"What is your name?" he pressed.

She humored him with a reply. "Elizabeth Bennet."

"What is my name?"

"Thomas Bennet, although I only ever call you 'Papa.'"

He embraced her so tightly, she felt him tremble, and she did not have the heart to complain that she could not breathe. "I have never been so worried. You took a blow to the head and lost consciousness for a spell."

She reached up to her forehead again, carefully testing the size of her injury. "How long?"

"Two or three minutes. Quite possibly less, but it felt like an eternity until you woke."

"What happened?"

"The rear axle broke, and you smacked your head against the edge of the window. It knocked you out cold in an instant, and when the carriage toppled over, you fell like a rag doll along with it." He rubbed his

41

hands over his eyes. "It was awful, Lizzy. I thought—," his voice cracked. "I thought you were gone."

She snuggled against him, taking comfort in his warmth. "I am perfectly well. Aside from a headache."

He stroked her cheek, his fingers catching in her hair. She did not care.

"Do you think you are able to stand?" he asked.

"I will only know if I try." Elizabeth did not feel completely recovered, but a sense of urgency did not allow for her to remain on the grassy knoll. She had a sense there was somewhere she needed to be....

"That is my girl." He grabbed her elbows, assisting her up and watching her with lingering concern etching his face.

Determined to prove her wellness, for her father's benefit as well as her own, Elizabeth released her hold on his forearms. Once she stopped swaying, she picked her way to the road.

The footman and coachman watched her by the horses. Papa nodded at them, explaining, "Thatcher will ride into Meryton to fetch the blacksmith. If it is not too much trouble, I suggest we walk the rest of the way. It is not far, and Jane will be worried if we tarry. We are already late."

Clarity came to Elizabeth like a parting of the clouds. They were late for the wedding!

Tugging on her father's hand, Elizabeth hastened her pace. "We must hurry. I will not ruin the happiest day of Jane's life. If I know her at all, she will delay the service to wait for us."

Papa furrowed his brows. "I am only sorry I am unable to spare your slippers from the dust. Your dress is stained beyond repair. If I were younger and stronger, I would carry you, but I fear that I am rather taxed at the moment."

Elizabeth's laugh softened to a chuckle which quickly died out when her head threatened to split in half. Contenting herself with a smile, she said, "A gallant offer, indeed."

Her smile faded when Papa cleared his throat and motioned down the lane. Mama charged toward them, fists clenched stiffly at her sides, her face flushed a brilliant red. "Where have you been? I have stalled the best I can, but I was hard-pressed to convince Mr. Darcy not to leave! And in such a state! Grass stains all over your beautiful gown," she wailed.

Elizabeth shrugged. "So long as Mr. Bingley does not leave, I do not see the trouble. Nobody will notice me or the condition of my gown."

She heard her father catch his breath, his mouth agape as he turned to face her.

"What?" Elizabeth asked, looking between her mother and father.

"Oh dear," he said.

Before Elizabeth could inquire into his strange reaction, her mother latched on to her hand and pulled her at a brisk clip down the lane and up the step into the Longbourn parish church. "Come, Lizzy! I will not allow for any more delays," she chirped.

Jane met them at the entrance, her concern changing to delight. "What happened? Are you well? We are all so worried."

Caressing her sister's cheek, Elizabeth said, "You are a dear for waiting for us."

Jane's eyebrows met. "I could never suggest continuing without you." She glanced at Papa.

What did all these sideways glances mean? Elizabeth wished they would stop worrying about her. Other than a bruise on her forehead and a headache, she was perfectly well.

Papa sighed heavily. "We must send for Mr. Jones immediately."

The apothecary? Elizabeth protested, "My headache is not so bad I cannot wait until after the wedding."

"There is no time for that now anyway," Mama hissed, opening the doors wide and shoving Elizabeth forward.

The pews were packed. Mr. Bingley stood beside the vicar. He smiled brightly at Jane.

Another young man stood beside Mr. Bingley. Tall, dark, strong. Very handsome. His smile and firm gaze made Elizabeth blush.

Papa whispered into Elizabeth's ear. "Do you know those gentlemen?"

She turned to him, her agitation mounting when

she felt the watchful stares of dozens, if not hundreds, of eyes on her.

He signaled the gentlemen to join them, further provoking Mama's nerves, and asking Elizabeth, "Does the name Darcy mean anything to you?"

Why was he speaking in riddles? Frustration growing, she replied, "Is it supposed to?"

The gentlemen stood before them now, their wide shoulders blocking the onlookers' view and lending them a measure of privacy. It was considerate of her father, but Elizabeth did not understand why they were having this conversation when Jane ought to be exchanging vows with Mr. Bingley.

Papa inclined his head. "Mr. Bingley." Slower, and with his gaze fixed on Elizabeth, he said, "Mr. Darcy."

The handsome man smiled at her as though he knew her. His eyes were dark and captivating. But the intimacy in his gaze perplexed her. Mr. Darcy. Mr. Darcy, she repeated in her mind until her head whirled, and the ground spun under her feet.

The man named Mr. Darcy caught her in his arms, his silk cravat brushing against her cheek. He held her close, as though he had embraced her before. Her skin burned and tingled at his nearness, as though she had allowed it. Enjoyed it.

Not liking this helplessness, Elizabeth shook herself free of him as soon as she gained her footing. All three gentlemen looked at her expectantly, eyebrows drawn, mouths gaping.

She knew she needed to say something, but what?

Papa prompted her, "Mr. Darcy..." He waved his hand in front of him, prompting her to finish his sentence.

Mama finished for her. "Of course, she knows who Mr. Darcy is. We are wasting time, and the vicar is waiting."

Freeing Elizabeth from her mother's grip, Papa repeated, "Mr. Darcy ... your betrothed?"

Elizabeth's gaze flickered over to Mr. Darcy. The horror in his semblance mirrored her own sentiments. Stepping back, shaking her head, she gasped. "I am sorry, but I have never seen this gentleman before in my life!"

CHAPTER 8

*D*arcy could not breathe. He could hardly stand.

Mrs. Bennet swooned. "I am so vexed, I shall faint. In all my life, I have never been so sorely vexed. Such spasms taking me over!"

Mr. Bennet held her up. "I know you are overwhelmed with concern for our daughter's welfare, as any loving mother would be, but our Lizzy needs us to keep our senses, my love."

"You only say that because she has lost hers!" Mama wailed and sobbed.

Elizabeth shook her head, her jaw stubborn and defiant. It was a look Darcy had come to adore over the past months, and it gave him hope. Her memory loss was temporary. It had to be.

She whispered her letters before moving on to the more challenging intellectual task of naming

England's monarchs as she ticked them off her fingers. Her cheeks were a feverish red when she finished, her eyes imploring as she continued, "My name is Elizabeth Anne Bennet. This is the Longbourn chapel where Mr. Brown has christened me and my four other sisters." Motioning to her parents, she added, "You are my father, Thomas Bennet. My mother, Fanny Bennet." She continued through their group, "You are Mr. Charles Bingley, who let Netherfield Park, and will soon be my brother when you marry my dearest sister, Jane." Her eyes finally landed on Darcy.

He would almost prefer for her to look at him in anger than this empty, emotionless confusion.

She squinted her eyes, concentrating … to no effect.

Mrs. Bennet, now standing quite well on her own, stammered. "You are to marry Mr. Darcy, today, Lizzy. Come, now! We must not disappoint all of your guests."

"How can I marry a man I do not know?"

"Do not know! How can you say such a thing? Can you not remember anything? His name? The name of his estate? The amount of his fortune?" Mrs. Bennet questioned frantically.

Miss Bennet tried to calm her mother, but her vexation only grew with each question Elizabeth did not — could not — answer.

Darcy's throat pinched and swelled, making speech difficult. "What happened?" he asked.

Mr. Bennet replied, "We had a carriage accident,

and Lizzy was knocked unconscious. It appears she is suffering from amnesia."

Darcy felt Bingley's hand on his shoulder, offering comfort, but what comfort could be found when his bride did not remember him?

Mr. Bennet added, "Her mind is strong, and I have no doubt she will be well on the morrow."

"The morrow!" wailed Mrs. Bennet.

"If not sooner," Mr. Bennet added quickly. "We must be patient. Her mind is too sound to suffer such a privation of memory for long. You are much too important to her to remain forgotten, Darcy."

Darcy supposed he ought to take some comfort in Mr. Bennet's reassurances. But the one dominating fact stared him unwaveringly in the face. She had forgotten him. Him. If he was so important to Elizabeth, why was he the one person she had forgotten?

The vicar joined them, bringing with him an echo of whispers. "I fear we will not finish before noon if we do not begin the ceremony soon."

Though Elizabeth held her head high, her shoulders slumped. Darcy saw the tears swelling in her eyes, and he had to resist the urge to pull her into his arms. She had shoved him away quickly enough earlier, rejecting his comfort.

Turning to the clergyman, Darcy asked, "Please, only one minute more, I beg you."

He reached for Elizabeth's hand as he had grown accustomed to do, only to be reminded once again that all of their history had been erased when she stared at him and withdrew her hand. Another blow.

Gritting his teeth and stiffening his shoulders, Darcy said, "Let us give Elizabeth some space. Mr. Bennet, will you please join us for a moment?"

When the three of them stood just outside the building, Darcy sucked in a breath and asked, "How long was Elizabeth unconscious?"

"No more than a minute or two. Only long enough for the footman and I to carry her to the side of the road."

Darcy did not know much about head injuries, but he knew that the shorter the loss of consciousness, the better. A minute or two was not too bad, was it?

Elizabeth twisted her fingers in front of her. Darcy wished there was something he could do to reassure her, but until he understood the extent of her injury, he refused to draw conclusions. She would be well, and that was that. He would make sure of it.

Softly, he asked, "Do you remember anyone else?" he gestured to the seated assembly, most of whom were twisted in their pew to look at them.

Darcy tried not to place too much significance on her reply, but he held his breath all the same.

One by one, starting with the nearest row, she named every guest sitting inside the cold, stone church … excepting a few who had recently come from London, friends of Bingley.

When she finished, she asked, "Do you wish for me

to continue? Or will you believe me when I tell you I know everybody? I could tell you how I met them as well as my general impression of their characters." Her eyelashes fluttered and she chewed on her lip. "But I do not remember anything about you. I am sorry. I know I must, but I feel as though I am seeing you for the first time, Mr. Darcy."

Mr. Darcy. Not Fitzwilliam. She did not even know his name, or if she did, she no longer felt free to pronounce it. This was much worse than he had thought possible. How could his bride — his Elizabeth — not know him?

Mrs. Bennet would not be consoled, insisting between gasps of breath and ultimatums that Elizabeth marry him anyway.

Elizabeth heard her. She could not help but hear her, and her reaction broke Darcy's heart. Elizabeth was stubborn for the people she loved. It was one of the traits he most appreciated, her unwavering loyalty, her eagerness to defend others. But it was not so endearing when he was no longer included in her circle.

He watched her stiffen in determination, he heard the tremble in her breath, and he saw her blink back her tears, and he knew in that instant he could do nothing to add to his bride's distress. She may not remember him, but he loved her still, and he would do whatever it took to help her recover.

Addressing Elizabeth and her father, Darcy said,

"May I suggest we postpone our wedding until a more favorable time?" To Elizabeth, he added, "I would never force you to do anything you do not wish to do. I will wait." The words were painful to choke out, but Darcy was grateful he had said them when Elizabeth's expression softened.

"Thank you," she said.

Mr. Bennet wrapped his arm around her shoulders. "That is very generous of you, Mr. Darcy."

Darcy's heart ached when she leaned against her father for support instead of him. "I could do nothing less for the woman I love. I mean it, Elizabeth. I will wait for you. As long as it takes."

Her eyes searched his face. Darcy watched, praying she would find what she searched for, waiting for the moment when her face lit up with recognition.

But the moment did not come, and while Darcy could have stood there all day waiting for it, he did not wish to delay Bingley and Miss Bennet's happiness any longer.

Mrs. Bennet's vigorous exclamations had weakened to whimpers. Even the buzz of the curious onlookers had dulled into a thick silence. Like a wake.

Forcing a smile, Darcy turned to Bingley. "Let us not detain the vicar any longer."

Miss Bennet accepted Bingley's arm, and together they took their positions in front of the vicar.

Darcy sat beside Elizabeth, close but not too close,

all the time hoping her memory would return to her before the ceremony began.

"We are gathered together here..." the clergyman began.

Darcy looked askance at Elizabeth.

Nothing.

His heart dropped to his toes. He wanted to enjoy Bingley's joyous day, but he did not have it in him. He was too numb.

His seat in the front row gave him the perfect view of the two lovers peering at each other, their hearts in their eyes, their happiness written all over their faces too great to conceal.

He sat erect though heavy thoughts weighed on him. He ought to be standing there with Elizabeth. When he had seen Elizabeth enter the chapel on her father's arm, beautiful in her cream gown and her wild brunette curls, Darcy had wondered how his heart could hold so much joy. So much tender longing.

How quickly his happiness transformed to hurt.

Quiet consumed the congregation, but Darcy's every thought shouted his heartbreak.

CHAPTER 9

The sorrow in Mr. Darcy's eyes, the absolute dejection in his furrowed brows and crestfallen expression, haunted Elizabeth. That she had a strong connection to the man sitting beside her was undeniable. She felt his hurt as acutely as if it were her own, so much so, she could not distinguish which emotion belonged to her and which originated from Mr. Darcy.

He was equally aware of her. She saw it in his ready posture and the way his legs were poised under him, ready to act. For her.

It pierced Elizabeth to the core. She had hurt him deeply, and still, Mr. Darcy was ready to act on her behalf. She had no doubt that if she asked him to run to London, he would do it.

She squeezed her eyes closed, shutting out the alternating whimpers and sighs of her mother, the hushed voices of the assembled, and leaving only the image of the man who filled her awareness beside her. Peeking through her eyelashes, she glanced at him, memorizing his features, holding the picture in her mind closely in the hope it would spark a memory.

Tighter, closer. She clenched her hands. Any memory would do.

The bump on her head fought back, pounding against her concentration like a cricket bat. However, her body warmed at his nearness, feeling what her mind refused to remember.

Her mother leaned against Papa, muttering behind her handkerchief. "Mr. Bennet, you must make her marry Mr. Darcy."

Elizabeth considered. What if she went through with it anyway? True, the sadness in Mr. Darcy's eyes was undeniable, and she hated to disappoint anyone in whom she had entrusted something so important as her heart, her future, her happiness. She had always believed she would never agree to marry for anything less than the deepest, most steadfast love. Surely, she must have loved Mr. Darcy dearly. Surely.

But … a little voice whispered from the recesses of her mind … was it possible to forget someone you truly loved?

Papa whispered to Mama, "It is better for one daughter to marry than for both to remain unattached. The wedding license remains valid for three months, and you may trust that our Lizzy will recover in time.

Of all her strengths, her mind has always been the strongest."

Until today, Elizabeth thought.

Mr. Darcy looked at her fully and nodded his head slowly. The intensity in his gaze sent coils of electric shocks through her, spiraling out from her center. It was both thrilling and maddening. Why did her brain refuse to cooperate with what her body craved?

"Pray do not be troubled. I will help you. My affections and feelings have not changed," he whispered, his voice deep and raw.

His compassion twisted like a knife in Elizabeth's gut, and as the vicar's droll monotone echoed in the background, she was overwhelmed by the urge to cry.

She sucked in her breath, but her emotions were too strong. One tear escaped.

Elizabeth forced herself to smile. It was a happy tear. For Mr. Bingley and Jane. This was their day, and Elizabeth would not be guilty of lessening their joy. She felt guilty enough.

Unable to gaze directly upon the happy couple, Elizabeth looked about her.

Mr. Collins listened with his face uplifted to the heavens and his eyes closed in deep meditation. William Collins, Papa's nearest relation and Charlotte's husband. Had he not dabbed his face so often with his handkerchief, Elizabeth might have suspected him asleep and not in a reverie.

Behind him, Miss Bingley whispered to her sister,

her expression smug and haughty. Caroline Bingley and Louisa Hurst.

Elizabeth pounded her fist against her leg. How could she remember such disagreeable people when she could not remember her groom?

She peeked at him askance again. He wore a blue coat, fine kerseymere with gilt buttons and a high collar, a high-buttoned blue and fawn silk damask waistcoat topped with an elegantly knotted cravat, and nankeen pantaloons. His picture could have been printed on a fashion plate, a tasteful, understated Beau Brummell. A man of the first circles who did not wish to call attention to himself.

Tracing his features along the firm lines of his wide forehead, down his defined jaw to the dark curls softening the sharp edge of his high collar, Elizabeth tucked her fingers under her thigh. She could not very well stroke his curls in the front row of the church in the middle of the vicar's speech, could she?

Biting her lips, she continued her inspection. He was tall, and his tanned complexion bespoke of a love of the out of doors. Just like her.

What else did they have in common?

Not a crease or fold was out of place, nor a thread loose or button askew. His breeches fit like a second skin, his high boots polished to a smooth sheen. She wore a new dress, the finest found in her wardrobe, and yet the cloth and cut of his coat was superior. He was clearly an individual of wealth — unlike her.

However, she took comfort that his dress tended to elegance rather than extravagance. Like her. Elizabeth believed in the magic of a well-made, perfectly fitted gown, but she was not one to pile on jewels and fripperies merely to call more attention to herself.

Sneaking another brief glance over her shoulder, she glanced over the crowded room, but while she recognized most of the faces in the room, she could not associate one of them with Mr. Darcy ... aside from Mr. Bingley and his scornful sisters.

Either Mr. Darcy did not have much in the way of family and friends — Could he be an orphan? — or he had not seen fit to invite them.

Elizabeth frowned. Wealthy gentlemen of the highest circles were too often in demand to believe him without friends. And orphans in his position were rare enough with family names and legacies to maintain.

She sighed, mulling over the apparent facts. They did not have family, fortune, or connections in common. Which left interests and intellect. Such love matches were rare, and Elizabeth hardly dared to hope she had been fortunate enough to secure one.

But what else was there?

Her elation was short-lived, her summations leading to one unsettling conclusion: If they had been intellectual equals before, they were no longer. Her mind was altered. What if she never remembered him? What if, instead of improving, she got worse?

The vicar addressed the assembly. "Therefore, if any

man can show any just cause, why they may not lawfully be joined together, let him now speak, or else hereafter forever hold his peace." He clasped his hands together and looked from one end of the room to the other.

Elizabeth held her breath, her suspense mounting with each passing second. Must he pause so long? Why was she nervous? Surely, nobody opposed Mr. Bingley and Jane's union. Or was it her union to Mr. Darcy which might have been opposed?

Oh, if only she knew! Every question she could not answer added to her consternation.

She bent her mind on what little facts and observations she had amassed. They were few enough, but it was plain that Mr. Darcy was from the upper echelons of society ... whereas her family lingered on the fringes of respectability. He was a gentleman of fortune while she was accustomed to economizing to secure the treasures (mostly books) she could never afford.

Before Elizabeth convinced herself that her attachment to Mr. Darcy had been nothing more than a fluke of good fortune, the vicar continued.

She released her breath. This was foolishness. She had not lost her mind completely, only her memory of one person. Only one. And who was she to doubt that she would recover her memories of Mr. Darcy as quickly as she had lost them?

Resolve straightened her back and elevated her chin. She would remember Mr. Darcy before the day was through or her name was not Elizabeth Bennet. Papa was right. She had a strong mind, and where she could bind determination with wit, she was certain to succeed.

DARCY FELT Elizabeth's gaze on him, watching, exploring. He fixed his eyes forward. It took every bit of his self-possession not to pull her into his arms and cover her mouth with his, filling her senses with the love that overwhelmed him until she remembered him.

How could she have forgotten him? He was certain he could never forget her. Was his love greater than hers? Had his stubborn determination to win her over been too much for her to resist? Had she merely succumbed? Lord, let it not be that.

Gluing his vision on Bingley until it blurred, Darcy attempted not to scowl. But his loss was too great. He and Elizabeth should be standing in front of the vicar, too.

Having already addressed the assembled, the vicar now spoke directly to the bride and groom. "I require and charge you both, as ye will answer at the dreadful day of judgment when the secrets of all hearts shall be disclosed, that if either of you know any impediment, why ye may not be lawfully joined together in Matrimony, ye do now confess it."

Did the man want someone to protest? Darcy held

his breath despite himself. Nobody had replied earlier, and the couple themselves were unlikely to do so. Only his attachment to Elizabeth had met with intense opposition from certain members of his family. His aunt Catherine had already exposed her scandalous, self-serving behavior once. Darcy did not think her so selfish as to insist again.

Squeak bang — the entrance door slammed open, and the tap-step tap-step Darcy recognized all too well echoed through the stone chamber.

"I am Lady Catherine de Bourgh, and I have come to stop this abomination!"

CHAPTER 10

*A*nne clasped her hands in front of her and studied the stone step under her feet. She had never felt more mortified. If Mother had thought she could bully Darcy to her will by interrupting his wedding, she had forgotten Darcy's character.

He bolted down the aisle, chased by thunderclouds, eyes flashing with lightning. Anne had never seen him so livid, and as quickly as she had peeked up, she cast her eyes down again.

She said nothing, hating how her silence lent her mother support when she was ashamed of her behavior. But what could she say to make her mother — or anyone else, for that matter — listen? Anne was as invisible as a carpet on the floor.

Darcy escorted Mother out, both of them brushing past Anne, neither sparing her so much as a glance. Worse than a carpet. She was stagnant air.

Miss Elizabeth turned in her seat, her eyes meeting Anne's. Seeing her.

Anne's cheeks burned. There was no accusation, no reprimand in Miss Elizabeth's look. To the contrary, there was kindness, and just as she had been struck with Miss Elizabeth's bold confidence during her brief stay at Hunsford, Anne was again struck with the lady's strength of character. She did not look away.

Anne envied her.

Wait. Miss Elizabeth was not standing in front of the vicar. And Darcy had already steered Mother out to the churchyard. Why was he not standing with his betrothed?

Anne blinked, not believing her own eyes. The vicar continued, forcing her to hear what her other senses doubted.

Nausea rippled in Anne's stomach. Had Mother somehow succeeded in preventing Miss Elizabeth's union to Darcy?

Dread chilled her to the bone. What had Mother done?

Mr. Collins approached, and Anne stepped out of the doorway to allow him to pass. He bowed as he always did, his eyes fixed on the patroness on whom he doted. They fed off each other's vanity — he with his indelicately arranged, blatant compliments; she with her condescension on one so eager to praise her. It was a pity. Anne thought highly of Mrs. Collins. Charlotte was a sensible woman. She would be a good influence over her husband, if only he would allow her more consequence over him than he allowed The Great and Highly Esteemed Lady Catherine de Bourgh.

With a sigh, Annie joined the party hissing at each other beside her father's carriage. She suspected Mr. Collins' presence signified he had greater devotion to his family than she had believed him to possess, but his easy abandon the moment her mother appeared only confirmed that he wished to reestablish himself in his patroness' good graces.

Anne did not understand it. Mr. Collins' living was secure. He need not kowtow to her mother's every whim when only the Archbishop of Canterbury had the authority to strip him of his living … and then only after conviction of gross sin. Impossible.

Still, Anne hoped Mr. Collins would prove his character right then. Just once she would like to see someone stand up in opposition to her mother. Just as Miss Elizabeth had done.

Mother did not like to discuss it, but Anne remembered how infuriated she had been when she returned from Longbourn. Like a banshee in the night, making demands which did not belong to her to make on a young woman's heart — a lady over which she held no influence or authority.

Mr. Collins bowed, his squeaking corset and unwanted presence interrupting Darcy and Mother's verbal battle. "How extraordinary Her Ladyship should arrive when divine intervention has already interrupted that which most displeases her."

Darcy looked fit to jab the clergyman squarely on the nose, but he had always possessed remarkable restraint. Ignoring Mr. Collins, Darcy said, "I have never given you leave to suppose I would subject myself to your wishes. My father never supported your scheme. I wish to marry the young lady I love, and that young lady is Elizabeth Bennet. She is my choice."

Mother narrowed her eyes at him, her nostrils flaring. "And yet you are out here speaking with me instead of inside marrying that insolent girl." After all these months, she still would not address Elizabeth by her name.

Darcy ran his hand over his face. "She suffered an accident which has delayed our union."

Anne gasped.

Mother snapped at her. "You had best wait in the coach, Anne."

Anne did not budge. Could not move. Her shock was too great, her unexpressed concerns too heavy. She watched Darcy, praying he would explain.

"A blow to the head has given her temporary amnesia," he said.

"Temporary?" Mother arched her brow, already calculating, scheming.

Darcy's jaw clenched, and he spoke through his teeth. "Her mind is sound. She only suffered a minimal loss of her memory."

"Minimal? How so?"

"She remembers almost everything."

"Stop speaking so vaguely, Darcy. What or whom does she fail to remember?"

"She only lacks memory of me. However, I have every reason to hope she will recover soon."

"She remembers everyone else?"

"Yes."

"Everyone *but* you?" Mother gloated. She had been searching for a weakness, and she had found it. "That girl must not love you very much if she cannot remember you."

Anne saw how deeply her mother's cruelty pierced her cousin. She reached out to him but thought better of it. Mother would think more of it than Anne meant to express.

Darcy remained silent. Anne could think of nothing to say which might spare him from the pain inflicted upon him. And Mr. Collins was of no use at all.

With nobody to stop her, Mother continued, "This incident is proof of her low birth. She is not worthy of our family."

Darcy seethed. "How dare you—"

"Her mind is as unsound as those of the rest of her family if she is so easily taken with an illness of the mind. That girl is bound for the asylum."

Surely, she could not believe that! "No, Mama—"

"Hush, Anne! You will hold your tongue while I arrange your future."

This was not the future she wanted at all. Anne turned to Darcy. He would fix this horrible situation. He fixed everything. She held her tongue and waited for him to put everything right.

He took a step toward the church. "You have traveled here for naught, Aunt. I must ask you to leave."

Anne wanted nothing more.

Mother called after him. "I think not. It is plain to me that you are in sore need of my superior counsel and wise guidance."

"Mama, he is right. We ought to go."

Darcy continued walking, and Anne followed suit in the direction of the carriage. Only, her mother did not follow. Instead, she raised her voice. "Anne is fatigued and requires rest. I will take rooms at the Meryton Inn. It is my intention to stay there until we reach a satisfactory arrangement."

That would never happen. She would never be satisfied until Darcy agreed to her scheme, and Darcy would never be happy without his Elizabeth. What a mess.

"Mr. Collins, has a doctor seen that girl yet?" Mother asked quietly, one eye on Darcy, who stood near the entrance, making certain they departed.

The clergyman nodded. "Longbourn does not boast a doctor as Hunsford does, Her Ladyship. Its residents must content themselves with nothing more than a simple apothecary, Mr. Jones."

"He has not examined her, then?"

67

"No, though I saw him enter the church minutes before your arrival. I daresay he will see her as soon as the ceremony is done."

"You will send him to me after he has seen her."

Mr. Collins bowed. "Of course, I would be honored to be of service to—"

"You cannot know how helpful you have already been," she said, leaving him to alight the carriage, a rare smile stretching her lips.

Anne did not know what to think. She liked Miss Elizabeth. She was not intimidated by her mother, as most were. As Anne was. Her forehead tightened. Now, that was not exactly correct. Anne was not intimidated by her mother. Just … tired. Worn.

And, right now, watching her mother smile, Anne was sorry. Sorry Miss Elizabeth was injured. Sorry to learn Darcy was not already married and no longer an option. Sorry because she knew that her mother would stop at nothing to prevent him from marrying the woman he loved.

Anne's disappointment deepened — at circumstances beyond her control, but mostly in herself. It was a good thing Patrick was not here to see her. He would not approve of the woman she had become. He certainly would never want her. He was probably married with several children of his own by now. And happy. As happy as he deserved to be, which was a great deal. Anne prayed that at least he was happier than she was.

Years of bound emotions loosened, stirring within her. Sadness she would very likely never achieve contentment, anger at herself for allowing it, and the smallest shard of hope. Not for herself. She was beyond that. But she would hope for Darcy and Miss Elizabeth … and Patrick.

Anne clenched her hands in her skirts. From that day forward, she refused to be a tool in her mother's arsenal.

The bold thought overwhelmed her. Strong words for a weak woman. What could she do? Anne pondered the question, but even as the carriage jolted into motion, the wheels turning in her mind produced nothing. She was absolutely useless.

CHAPTER 11

*M*ama wavered between ecstasy and despair, success and failure. When she considered Jane, the joy in her smile and the joviality in her voice expressed the approval of a mother fully contented with her daughter. When she looked at Elizabeth, she frowned and fretted.

Elizabeth might have laughed off her mother's vexation had she not been so frustrated with herself.

Once the ceremony was complete and the marriage register signed and witnessed, the newlywed couple graciously remained to accept the felicitations of their guests.

Elizabeth wanted nothing more than to return to Longbourn. She craved solace and silence, time to sort her jumbled thoughts and put herself — her life — to rights.

Mama clucked her tongue. "I do not understand why Mr. Darcy could not marry you anyway. You will remember eventually. Why not act upon the decision you made before the incident?"

What bothered Elizabeth most about her mother's complaint was the unexpected rationality of her reasoning. She had agreed to marry Mr. Darcy, that much was plain. So, why did she hesitate to follow through with a decision she had already made? Why this waffling indecisiveness?

Her mother continued, waving her fan frantically. "We shall have to dismiss the footman … and just when he was catching on to his duties so well."

Despite the silliness of her mother's grievances, Elizabeth felt guilty. And as she watched Bingley and Jane, her regret grew, seeped into her bones. She had lost something of much more import than a new footman — a piece of her Elizabeth feared she might never recover.

She glanced at Mr. Darcy standing alone along the edges of the congratulating crowd. Was he her missing piece? Had she truly loved him so much, he had become a part of her?

Miss Bingley sauntered over to them, neck arched and eyes sparkling. Looping her arm through Elizabeth's, as though they were the dearest of friends, she said, "My poor Eliza, this must be such a tragedy for you. I cannot imagine how I would feel if I lost the one thing I most prided myself in." She was far too pleased to evidence genuine sympathy.

Elizabeth raised her eyebrows, unwilling to supply Miss Bingley with a reply the lady would only use against her.

Lacking proper inducement, Miss Bingley continued without encouragement. "Surely, one so clever, a lady known for her quickness of wit, would rather suffer any loss other than that of her mind."

Word had spread fast, and as was usual with malicious gossip, had worsened Elizabeth's condition. Not that she needed anyone, especially Miss Bingley, to rub salt in her wound.

Elizabeth felt rather than observed Mr. Darcy shift closer to her.

"I am convinced that the very qualities you rightly credit to Elizabeth will assist her in a full recovery," he said. He stood so near, his warmth radiated to Elizabeth's right side, and she so naturally leaned against him, she startled herself (and nettled Miss Bingley) with her intimate, unmeditated gesture.

Mr. Darcy brushed a curl over her shoulder, sending shivers feathering over her skin and burning a trail where his fingers lingered. He had calluses.

Elizabeth liked calluses, especially on a gentleman's hands. They were the trophies of determination and exertion and, for Elizabeth, they offered reassurance. He had said he would wait for her, and she believed him.

Whether the gesture was out of habit or for Miss Bingley's benefit, Elizabeth did not know. What she did know was that Mr. Darcy undeniably stirred her senses, and maybe, just maybe, what her body knew, her mind would soon recall.

Awakened by his touch or a caress or a kiss.

Elizabeth was willing to try. She did not even blush at her thoughts.

Miss Bingley released her hold on Elizabeth and with a sniff, spinning on her heeled slippers, left to join her sister amidst the throng of ladies admiring Jane's gown.

Jane's eyes met Elizabeth's, her concern holding her until Elizabeth nodded and smiled. Mr. Darcy's quick defense and bold admiration had gone to her head, and if anyone were to ask Elizabeth how she felt that moment she would have answered, "Quite divine."

She would have turned to him had her mother not waved her fan in front of her face. "Do you see? Mr. Darcy believes you will fully recover, so why delay the inevitable?"

Mr. Darcy stepped away, disturbing Elizabeth with the cold he left behind. "Mrs. Bennet, my feelings remain unchanged. Elizabeth must be allowed to recover."

Elizabeth dashed back to reality and the cold church.

"To force such a union right now would be unfair to her, and I would forever regret treating her unjustly when I would vow to cherish her." His promise was a thawing ray of sunshine ... which silenced Mama for all of five seconds, wherein she resumed her original arguments with greater appeal.

Mr. Darcy held up his hands, speaking with the patience of one who had made peace with the inevitability of such dealings with her mother. "I do not intend to go anywhere."

They continued back and forth, her mother's complaints growing increasingly unreasonable and Mr. Darcy's forbearance displaying itself to accentuating advantage, though he must have been agitated. His posture was stiff where his words were soft.

Elizabeth rested her hand over her mother's arm. "Mama, let us not dwell on that which encourages dissatisfaction. Look at Jane." She stepped aside, allowing her mother a better view of the bride. "Is she not lovely? Do she and Mr. Bingley not make a fine match?"

Tears filled Mama's eyes, and she clutched one hand over her heart. "She is beautiful. And he is amiable and rich."

Elizabeth rolled her eyes. Hardly the thing she wanted her mother to say in front of Mr. Darcy.

Papa joined them. Nodding at Mr. Darcy, he took Mama's arm. "I suggest we return to Longbourn to oversee the wedding feast before our guests descend upon us." To Elizabeth, he said, "Mr. Jones is waiting to see you in the vestry. I have already spoken with him, and he suggested that Mr. Darcy be present."

"Here? Now?" Elizabeth asked.

Father nodded, his wordless reply reminding Elizabeth of the seriousness of her injury. Of the severity of her loss.

CHAPTER 12

*M*r. Jones, Meryton's apothecary, was a short, rotund man with a pink complexion and an inveterate smile. The man appeared in a constant state of joviality, an appearance which he no doubt attempted to remedy with long, lamb chop whiskers ... to no effect.

He was not an easy man to take seriously, and Darcy was not convinced his opinion was the most appropriate to seek. Mr. Jones had, however, requested Darcy's presence, and the apothecary's invitation allowed for a greater degree of tolerance.

The vicar had cramped three chairs into the vestry, and at Mr. Jones' gesture, Darcy and Elizabeth sat opposite him.

"I came as soon as I could," he began, pulling out several papers from the case on the floor beside his chair. "As you know, the care I offer as an apothecary

differs quite drastically from a doctor of the mind —
such men are rare and often contradictory. Too little is
understood of the workings of the brain."

Darcy crossed his arms over his chest. This was not
a promising beginning. He would rather not waste his
time when a trip to London to search for a qualified
physician awaited him. "Are you capable of helping
Miss Elizabeth, or not?"

Mr. Jones shuffled through the pages, replying
absentmindedly. "I believe I can. Not through any
treatment, mind you, but with this information in my
possession." He lifted one page up in triumph, then
placed it on top of the pile on his leg, smoothing
them carefully. "I subscribe to all the medical journals available, and I believe I may offer some guidance by way of facts. That was why my arrival was
delayed."

"Do not trouble yourself, Mr. Jones," Elizabeth said.
"I would not have missed my sister's wedding for an
examination anyway."

His smile widened. "I thought as much, Miss
Bennet. Now, your father told me the details of the
accident, but I would like to hear what you recall from
the time leading up to the incident and immediately
after."

Darcy would not let Mr. Jones near Elizabeth unless
he proved his qualifications. It was a point in the
gentleman's favor that he did not offer treatment by
means of a miraculous tonic. But Darcy needed a

degree of certainty that Mr. Jones' advice would not do more harm than it would help.

Before Elizabeth could reply, Darcy asked, "Which medical journals did you consult?" He did not boast any particularly profound knowledge in science and medicine, but he enjoyed deep conversation with thinkers more sagacious than himself. He knew which sources they trusted, and which they discredited.

"Oh, of course. How thoughtless of me. My apologies, Mr. Darcy."

Darcy marveled at the gentleman's ability to smile and apologize while giving every appearance of sincerity.

Mr. Jones tapped his papers. "I have consulted with *The Philosophical Transactions of the Royal Society of London*, for one."

"Recent journals?"

"Their older articles are hardly worth consulting. I appreciate the attention their present-day writers give to details, and I find their inclusion of failed experiments convincing of an unbiased study — the work of the medical members on their committee, no doubt."

Darcy remained skeptical. "I have spoken with several studied men who criticize their caution as excessive. *Philosophical Transactions* is well-known for not stating any opinion without saying *perhaps it is so* or *it may seem apparent* or *it is not improbable*."

Mr. Jones chuckled. "They do, at that! You keep good company, Mr. Darcy. I am relieved you are not ignorant regarding the source of research I must rely upon. Allow me to assure you that I do not consult their findings to instruct me on how to proceed but rather to enable me to come to my own conclusions for the benefit of my neighbors, with whom I have the advantage of intimacy." He nodded at Elizabeth as a father would.

Elizabeth returned his smile, then turned to Darcy, a mischievous twinkle in her fine eyes. "Are you satisfied Mr. Jones is reputable enough to see to my injury, Mr. Darcy, or do you have any more questions?"

Darcy's heart lightened, overjoyed at her display of humor. She was not as altered as he had feared. Playing along, he teased, "I am nearly satisfied. Perhaps Mr. Jones would tell us what other works he consulted?"

Mr. Jones was happy to oblige. "I brought a study in which the methodology is emphasized with admirable clarity. The experimental description is second to none. Were it my field of medicine, the detail would allow me to replicate the study." He pulled out another paper, pressing it to his breast before extending it to Darcy. "This is the one."

"*Edinburgh Medical Journal*," Darcy read aloud. This was the source his personal physician most often cited.

"Yes, the author, a renowned doctor of the mind, the foremost authority in the nation, focuses on the disease..."

Darcy cringed. Elizabeth was not diseased. Just injured.

Unaware of the effect his choice of words had on his audience, Mr. Jones continued, "... I find his descriptions professional and methodical. The work of a doctor and scientist with a great deal of experience."

Speaking over the lump lodged in his throat, Darcy said, "I thank you for allaying my doubts, Mr. Jones."

"Any sensible gentleman would require the same, Mr. Darcy. Now, if I may, I have several questions for Miss Bennet."

Over the next quarter of an hour, Darcy stewed in silence while Elizabeth answered every question the apothecary posed to her.

Mr. Jones was visibly pleased. "Very good. Very good, indeed. Now, I would like very much to hear how you met this gentleman." He gestured at Darcy.

The confidence with which she had spoken disappeared. Just as Darcy had feared it would.

"I do not know," she whispered.

"What is his name?"

"Mr. Darcy."

"His given name?"

She paused, and Darcy's hope rose.

"I cannot recall."

Hope plummeted. Shattered against the pitiless flagstones.

Her fine eyes, so often vivacious and gleeful, brimmed with melancholy ... and guilt. "I am sorry."

Darcy would do anything to rid her of this sadness, to shield her from ever feeling anything but happy again. It felt impossible to smile, but he made himself do it. "I have always regretted the poor first impression I gave, and now, I find myself with the rare opportunity to amend the past." A panicked thought quickened his pulse. "I do hope I have not reflected poorly on my character. I had not thought to request an introduction."

Mr. Jones came to his aid. "Miss Elizabeth Bennet, it is my honor to present Mr. Fitzwilliam Darcy of Pemberley in Derbyshire." He watched her closely, as did Darcy, for any sign of recognition.

There was none.

But Elizabeth's smile returned. "I am happy to make your acquaintance, Mr. Darcy," she said. "I am curious to know what you could have done to give such a poor impression when I consider your every action despite the shock of changed circumstances as considerate and ... gentlemanly."

Gentlemanly. A sweeter word she could not have uttered when he had acted so ungentlemanly toward her and her family in the past. Had Mr. Jones not cleared his throat, Darcy would have kissed her.

Perhaps it was for the best. This Elizabeth had no reason to welcome his kisses. He would have to be careful. He crossed his arms and feet and restrained his affections.

Mr. Jones steepled his fingers under his chin. "There is still much to learn about amnesia, and your case is unique in that it is remarkably selective, but I will explain it as well as I can." He held up his hands. "According to French scientist, Francois Bichat, the brain is made up of two hemispheres. These hemispheres act in synchrony — one side mirrors the other. He calls it the Law of Symmetry." He squeezed one hand into a fist. "You see, when one hemisphere is injured, it throws the whole of the brain off balance, causing a general confusion." He waved his other hand around the fist. "Like this, see?"

"How can the hemispheres be brought back into symmetry?" Elizabeth asked.

"Before I tell you that, I must explain why symmetry is so important. If balance is rectified, no permanent harm is done. That is what we want for you. However, if the imbalance continues, derangement progresses." He stopped.

Derangement was such a hopeless word. Darcy cleared his throat, gently nudging the conversation down a more propitious path. "How long before recovery is impossible?"

"Most people achieve this balance within a few hours. A few cases recover by the following day. After that, the derangement sets in."

He calculated the time. About two hours had passed since the accident.

The apothecary continued, "Sadly, those patients lose their minds altogether."

Elizabeth gasped. "Insanity?"

"I am afraid so. But that is the worst of it. I hold every hope that you will recover any minute."

Damage to one hemisphere. Symmetry. How, exactly, was symmetry supposed to be restored? A sick feeling seized Darcy. "Are we to conclude that this Law of Symmetry suggests injuring the other side of the brain's hemisphere to restore equilibrium?"

Elizabeth's eyes widened. "You mean to suggest that a blow to the other side of my head will put me right?"

The doctor had grace enough to look sheepish. "It is the commonly accepted treatment at the moment."

Elizabeth pointed at his case. "And I suppose you are carrying a club in there with which to bash your patients on the head?"

Mr. Jones blushed and blustered.

Darcy rubbed his temples. This was ridiculous. "While I appreciate your clear explanation of this law of the mind, I have to question the theory's soundness. If one blow causes injury, surely another would only worsen the harm. I cannot allow it."

"Nor will I permit it," exclaimed Elizabeth.

Tapping his papers, Mr. Jones said, "It is only senseless to those who have not studied the complexities of the human brain. These scientists have. Many have met with success after this … treatment."

Darcy exclaimed, "My concern is with those who have not met with success, sir."

Elizabeth nodded in agreement.

The apothecary opened his case and returned the

papers inside. No club was visible, nor did the man's round figure permit him to hide one on his person. Darcy relaxed.

Shaking his head, Mr. Jones said, "I have known you your entire life, Miss Bennet, so I will spare you from further inquiry. There are other determinants proven to provoke amnesia, but I know them not to be an option."

"I pray you would tell me what these determinants are, Mr. Jones. I wish to understand everything I can about my injury. Perhaps we might find the missing piece to solve this puzzle."

He sighed. "They are not the habits of a lady."

"I will hear them all the same."

Another sigh. "The only other known and studied causes for amnesia besides a head injury are drunkenness, loose morals, and affectation. Please do not ask me to explain further."

"Are you suggesting I am pretending — faking my loss of memory?" Elizabeth gasped, then, just as quickly, softened her manner. "Not you specifically, Mr. Jones, but the committee of scientists and medics who dedicate their lives to the study of the brain. This is the best they can do?"

Mr. Jones dabbed his face with a handkerchief. "It is not unheard of for a young lady to imagine herself affected before … entering a marriage. Not you, of course," he added hurriedly, "but others have certainly used it to … justify their … change of heart."

Darcy heard Elizabeth inhale sharply, saw her eyes sparkle with tears, her chin tremble, felt her fear. In this, he could console her. Addressing Mr. Jones, he said, "Like you, I do not believe Elizabeth capable of such disguise. Not when she accepted my second proposal as vehemently as she rejected my first."

Being a decent sort, Mr. Jones pretended not to hear Darcy's admission, but the brilliance in Elizabeth's surprise made his divulgence less humiliating. A tear dripped down her cheek, not from her upset but from release. Darcy handed her his handkerchief.

She dabbed her face dry. "Really? I refused you?"

Darcy nodded.

"How can I not remember a terrible first impression and a refused proposal? Vehement, you described it. What on earth did you say to deserve that?"

Darcy groaned. He had had his fill of humiliation for one morning. "That is a conversation for another time."

"I wait on tenterhooks."

Mr. Jones closed his case and stood. "It is not improbable that there will be no need for Mr. Darcy to tell you your story, Miss Bennet. You have always been clever and quick-witted. Perhaps you will recover before the end of the day. And if, by chance, you do not … it is my genuine hope you will reconsider the treatment."

He sounded like an article straight from *Philosophical Transactions*.

CHAPTER 13

*E*lizabeth watched Mr. Darcy by the path leading to Longbourn where he arranged for Mr. Jones to provide him with a list of the foremost experts on the mind in the country.

While the apothecary's views disclaimed logic and reason, he merely reflected the attitude most accepted among those supposedly capable of helping her.

Not an encouraging prospect. Derangement and insanity never were.

But Mr. Darcy was relentless. He would stop at nothing until he had exhausted the knowledge of every expert and the effectiveness of every treatment in the country. Elizabeth was grateful for his concern as it proved the depth of his concern. Surely, it was the best way to proceed. The wisest course.

And how she dreaded it.

Mr. Darcy was, however, determined.

He was a confounding man. He bore all the distinctions of a proud man. What man with wealth, good looks, a high standing in society, and a mind half as sharp would not be proud?

Mr. Darcy, it would seem, for she could not rightly accuse him of pride. Not only had he exposed himself to criticism in front of Mr. Jones, but he had done so with humor. He had put her at ease at his own expense.

Frustration fanned the flames of Elizabeth's determination. She would remember Mr. Darcy by the end of the day.

If knowledge was the key to understanding, then learning about Mr. Darcy would unlock her memories of the gentleman.

Feeling better having a plan of her own, Elizabeth let the sun warming her bonnet melt her fears and carry it away in the soft June breeze. Tilting her head up to warm her face, she heard bees buzzing, leaves rustling, and the gentlemen's conversation fade into footsteps. She opened her eyes to see Mr. Darcy in front of her.

He held out his arm. "May I walk with you to Longbourn?"

She arched an eyebrow. "Without a chaperone?" He did not have the flash or flirtatious manner of a rake, nor could she imagine herself agreeing to marry one.

"We are engaged … if you wish to remain so." His dark eyes captured hers, and she sucked in a breath when they flickered to her lips. She caught herself leaning into him, acting on her earlier, brazen thoughts of Mr. Darcy's kiss awakening her and leaving Elizabeth uncertain as to the perspicacity of them walking alone. It was one thing to spin fantasies in the confines of one's mind; quite another to act upon them.

She regained her balance. "I do ... I think."

Would a kiss restore her memory? She shook her head. Information first, then ... maybe ... a kiss. As a last resort.

Mr. Darcy smelled pleasant. She would wager he tasted pleasant.

His velvety voice broke the ensuing silence. "You look lovely."

Elizabeth blushed furiously. Mr. Darcy could not have known the topic of her musings, but she felt as though he had caught her. As though he could read her mind.

She looked around, shocked to see they were already half-way to Longbourn. How long had she been pondering inappropriate displays of affection with the same man with whom she walked? Her ears burned.

He watched her, expecting a reply.

Right. Lovely. She looked down. The front of her wedding gown was wrinkled, the hem dirty. She knew grass stains smudged the back. The silk roses matching the ribbon tied around her waist — blue like Mr. Darcy's waistcoat — were crushed and coated in dust.

She did not feel lovely; and the evidence she wore proved she did not look it either.

"Are you too vain for spectacles, Mr. Darcy?" she teased.

He had a brilliant smile. It reached his eyes. "No, although my vision will always cast you in a favorable light."

"You do me more favor than you do yourself. I recall you admitting to giving a poor first impression at our first meeting."

He groaned, such a wince of displeasure twisting his features as to spur Elizabeth's compassion and humor.

"You could tell me a more favorable account, and I would not know it," she said, smiling up at him.

He did not smile. Clutching her arm more firmly to his side, he stopped, his eyes not once wavering from hers. "I could never take advantage of your ignorance. Disguise of every sort is my abhorrence."

Elizabeth believed him. They resumed walking.

She felt his chest expand, then his deep exhale before he began. "I had much to learn before I could even attempt to deserve you, and I pray you see my continued efforts to improve myself for your benefit as I relate those events which are now my most painful memories."

"Events? There have been more than one?" She bit her tongue, chastising herself for speaking before giving her words proper thought. He had mentioned her refusing. That certainly qualified as a painful event.

Another wince and groan. "Regrettably, there have been several."

Elizabeth frowned. She did not like being the source of his discomfort when he had done so much to comfort her that morning. "Then I must insist that for every difficult memory, you also share a pleasant one. I would very much like to know how we met. Perhaps, it will jog my own recollections."

He sighed. "I insulted your vanity to your face, then refused to dance with anyone not in my party … at the public assembly."

Swallowing her shock, Elizabeth listened as he described that evening from his perspective. His posture stiffened and his tone sharpened with every insult he confessed. Then, to her surprise, he gave the version she had previously told him from her point of view, until the disappointment of reliving these past events moved Elizabeth to intervene.

"Pray, speak not another word of the matter. I have heard quite enough for the present and am wondering what pleasantness could possibly have proceeded from such a beginning."

His shoulders relaxed, and the corners of his lips curled upward. "When I did finally condescend to ask you for a dance, you refused me."

Elizabeth gasped. "And that gave you pleasure?" It

was a wonder they had agreed to marry at all with such a dreadful start.

His smile spread. Gracious, he was handsome. "It was after the Meryton Assembly. Sir William Lucas invited us to Lucas Lodge and, being of a merry sort, he insisted we dance. I recall his precise words to you: 'Who would object to such a partner?'"

Mr. Darcy chuckled. "I accepted his favorable appraisal of my person, my character, as a matter of course … until you looked at me archly and turned away to join another party, leaving me with a gaping Sir William and my own injured pride."

She glanced at him askance. Was the man mad?

"No lady had ever put me so effectively in my place. Your refusal to place my gratification above your own esteem won my respect."

"Were you really so haughty?" While Elizabeth had suspected him proud, she had not thought him arrogant.

"It pains me to admit it, but I saw nobody but you the rest of the evening. There being nothing subtle about our exchange, word spread and Miss Bingley joined me, eager to benefit from your dismissal. She assumed to know the subject of my reverie."

"How did she fare?"

"I told her she could not possibly imagine the subject of my contemplations, and it was when she attempted to guess that I got a glimpse of the offensiveness of my behavior."

When he did not immediately speak, Elizabeth prompted, "What did she say?"

"She assumed I was considering how insupportable it would be to pass many evenings with such society. She complained of the insipidity and the noise, of the self-importance of the people she considered to be nothing. She pressed me to express my strictures on them. So certain was she of my disapproval, of my judgment, she expressed her approval of my opinions without any need of me giving them voice. I assured her that her conjecture was totally wrong, that my mind was more agreeably engaged."

The way he looked at Elizabeth confirmed that she was the subject in which he his mind had been so agreeably engaged, but she wanted to hear it anyway. "Oh?"

"I told her I had been meditating on the very great pleasure which a pair of fine eyes in the face of a pretty woman can bestow. And then, I named you."

"You said you admired me? To Miss Bingley?" How delightful! Elizabeth would have loved to have observed Miss Bingley's set-down.

Elizabeth frowned. Surely, had she known of this conversation, she would remember it. "Did I know this before today?"

Mr. Darcy thought for several moments. "If you did know, I do not believe I was the one to tell you. We rarely spoke of Miss Bingley, having many better topics to discuss."

She sighed her relief. She could not recall what she had not known.

Longbourn came into view, and Elizabeth's attention was caught by the curtain billowing through her open window. Strange. She often left it ajar, but she was almost certain Mrs. Hill had closed it.

Elizabeth tried to remember what had happened before leaving Longbourn. The footman had lost Mr. Hill, Mama had been beside herself, Jane had been beautiful and calm. Mrs. Hill had seen to everyone's agitations and troubles. But the details of what Elizabeth had been doing were blurry. Something with a letter? She clenched her fists, trying harder, asking herself more questions and her frustration mounting when she simply could not recall.

They were close enough to Longbourn to hear the commotion inside.

Taking a deep breath, she stepped into the narrow entrance hall, Mr. Darcy following closely behind her.

Mrs. Hill bustled by, face flushed and carrying a tray laden with wedding cake sitting atop Mama's best china, into the drawing room.

That was not quite right. The wedding feast was supposed to be held in the larger dining room. Mr. Darcy sensed it too. The offness.

Raucous laughter and a voice Elizabeth had not heard in several months — a voice she had not thought to hear for at least several more — whined, "This cake is not as delicious as what I am accustomed to in the north. My dear Wickham always ensured I had the best, what with me being with child and all."

Elizabeth froze this side of the doorway. On the other side, she heard her father say under his breath, "Lord help us."

CHAPTER 14

*D*arcy peeked over Elizabeth's head. Mrs. Wickham occupied the entire settee. One hand rested over her stomach, the other held a plate of cake of which she had already eaten the greater portion, despite her complaints of its inferiority. Several cushions were propped behind her back, but Mrs. Bennet seemed to think that was not enough. She took the pillow from Mr. Bennet's chair before he could sit in it and stuffed it behind her youngest daughter before she refilled Mrs. Wickham's teacup, generously doling sugar into the steaming liquid and stirring as she gushed, "It was very considerate of Mr. Wickham to see to your comfort. Hurry and eat your cake so that we may join the rest of our party in the dining room."

Wickham, considerate? Of anyone besides himself?

Darcy squeezed his eyelids closed to keep from rolling his eyes.

"Darcy! Lizzy! Come in!" Mr. Bennet exclaimed, waving them in and looking grateful for their arrival. "You have heard Lydia's news, I presume?"

Darcy stepped further into the room, looking about, preparing himself for Wickham's company.

Much to his mollification, only Lydia, Mr. Bennet, and Mrs. Bennet were present. Darcy had known that his nemesis' company would eventually be forced on him, but he had hoped it would not happen so soon.

What Elizabeth had said, he knew not, but given the satisfaction on Lydia's face, it had been pleasant enough. It now fell to him to say something. "It seems I must offer you both my felicitations. Where is Wickham?"

Lydia beamed brightly, rubbing her hand over her plump middle. "He deeply regrets that he could not stay, but George is such a good soldier and so responsible, the regiment could not spare him a day beyond his leave."

"He is not here?" Darcy asked, part relief, part disbelief. If George Wickham was responsible, then Fitzwilliam Darcy was a scullery maid. What sort of a man left his wife with her family at the other extremity of the country when she was with his child?

Her bottom lip protruded. "It is the regiment's fault. They are so demanding, you know. The sacrifices I must make as an officer's wife is appalling, which was why George insisted I have all the comforts of home during my confinement. He could not give me the attention I require while attending to his duties, being so much in demand and too often sent away on regimental business."

Dalliances, more likely.

"Surely, his commanding officer gave him enough time to see you safely settled," Elizabeth said, her lips pressing into a thin, disapproving line.

Did she remember that lout? Darcy tried not to feel insulted. It was dashed difficult.

Lydia picked at her cake. "I suspect he is in London by now. I had wanted him to leave me at the chapel so that I might see my sisters marry, but we would have arrived too late, so he saw me settled here instead." Abruptly, she set her plate on the nearest table, her full attention on Elizabeth. "But Lizzy, what is this? Why are you not on Mr. Darcy's arm? You are acting as though he were a stranger and not your husband."

Elizabeth opened her mouth to reply, but Lydia continued, "I am sure Mr. Darcy will wish to congratulate me. After all, I will give him a new nephew to dote on and spoil soon…"

Darcy winced, as did Elizabeth, though Darcy suspected for vastly different reasons. As Lydia continued chattering, Darcy fell into his own contemplations.

The reality of having Wickham as his brother-in-law was punishment enough for Darcy's lenience with his former friend, but this proof that Wickham cared more for himself than his own unborn child lit a fire in Darcy's chest. Men such as Wickham should never be allowed to father children.

Why was Lydia here? And at such a delicate time? Years of Wickham's appalling behavior triggered Darcy's skepticism.

She bore no evidence of bruises or cuts, none visible to the eye anyway. Wickham had a special talent for teaching the girls with whom he meddled the harsh realities of the world. As immature as Lydia was, Darcy did not wish that sort of education on her.

Had he done right by forcing Wickham to marry Lydia? Darcy's motive had not been entirely selfless. Then again, it had not been wholly selfish either. He had only thought of Elizabeth.

And she did not remember him.

Lydia's boisterous voice interrupted his thoughts. "But, really, Lizzy, did you marry today or not?"

Mrs. Bennet clucked her tongue. "I will allow for no more unpleasantness today. Thank goodness my Lydia is with us. This is the happiest day of my life! Jane married so well, and Lydia with child!" She bustled out of the room, no doubt to fetch her beloved daughter another plate of food.

Mr. Bennet raised his eyebrows at Elizabeth. "You are blessed with a mother whose emotions waver from one extreme to the other as quickly as the wind turns."

Darcy's lips flinched. Oftentimes Mr. Bennet's

humor carried a bite, but Darcy supposed it was a preferable means of coping with disappointment than bitterness or indifference. Darcy was relieved that he and Elizabeth were intellectual equals ... or, he hoped they still were. He had not yet noticed anything untoward ... aside from her inability to remember him.

Elizabeth chuckled softly. "It is a comfort, I suppose. Not long ago, she was vexed with me for ruining the happiest day of her life."

There it was again. Her quick wit and nimble humor. It was only a matter of time before she was fully recovered. Before the end of the day, Darcy would wager.

Hill appeared in the doorway with an apologetic look. "You have another visitor, sir. Mr. Collins."

"He has a lot of nerve," Lydia said.

For once, Darcy agreed with her. Since marrying Charlotte Lucas, Mr. Collins had little reason to show his face at Longbourn until the sad day he would eventually inherit the estate upon Mr. Bennet's death. Any other man would understand the undercurrent of tension his presence provoked, the tremendous loss he represented to them. But Mr. Collins was boorishly daft.

The clergyman, looking somber in his black wardrobe, bowed deeply in the center of the room. He reminded Darcy of his aunt and cousin. He needed to deal with them. Later. His primary concern was Elizabeth.

"Mr. Collins, what a surprise to see you." Mr. Bennet stood, gesturing at the door. "Will you join our party for the wedding feast?"

Deftly, he steered Mr. Collins out of the drawing room and down the hall. Lydia heaved herself off the settee, dragging Elizabeth along with her and leaving Darcy to follow behind. When Mr. Bennet saw them into the dining room, he stopped Darcy before he continued after Elizabeth. "I take it your conversation with Mr. Jones did not go well?"

Darcy swallowed. "No."

Laughter filled the room, spilling out into the hall. Bingley praised his wife, and glasses clinked together toasting their health and happiness. Darcy was not given to envy, but every cheer and compliment added to his misery. Today had been meant for him and Elizabeth to celebrate — instead, he got blank stares and the prospect of a cold bed that night.

Mr. Bennet rubbed his whiskers. "Ah … well … that is … unfortunate."

A tremendous understatement from a man possessing an ample vocabulary.

"Join me in my study, Darcy. There is a good deal we must discuss, and I daresay our company will not be immediately missed."

Having no desire to join the merrymakers, Darcy followed Mr. Bennet to his inner sanctuary.

CHAPTER 15

*E*lizabeth could not ruin Jane's celebration. Dwelling on Mr. Jones' most positive outcome, she told her sister and Mr. Bingley, "I am perfectly well besides this bruise on my head."

Jane's eyes searched her face. "And what of the amnesia?" she asked quietly.

Holding Jane's hands, her gaze unwavering, Elizabeth declared, "I shall be recovered by the end of the day. Mr. Jones found no reason to believe otherwise, nor do I have any reason to doubt him."

Mr. Bingley cried, "Another wedding on the morrow!" to the applause of the crowded room.

She sat with the newlywed couple, wishing Mr. Darcy was near and understanding why he was not. Papa would wish to hear Mr. Jones' assessment, and though Elizabeth did not understand why she trusted Mr. Darcy to give a thorough and reliable report, she did. As convinced as she was that he would disapprove of the reassurances she had given to her relatives and their guests.

Merriment became onerous, but Elizabeth was determined to endure as long as she could for Jane. Whether it was due to the stifling lack of air in the room or Mr. Collins' frequent stares or the weight of Elizabeth's own concerns, she could not swallow a bite, though the cook had prepared a feast to tempt the most fastidious consumer. Even to Miss Bingley, who was not predisposed to show favor of any table not her own or her social superior.

Thatcher passed in and out of the dining room, disappointing Elizabeth every time he was not Mr. Darcy. She found herself watching the entrance more than she attended to the conversation. Mr. Darcy had been away for quite some time. Just how much did he have to discuss with Papa? And without her? If they were discussing her condition, her treatment, her future, ought she not be present? Or, perhaps they were not speaking of her at all and were, instead, chatting about bees or books or the best brandy while she was suffering from an overdose of her company's cheer?

Did she really wish for Mr. Darcy to return? Elizabeth pondered. She had noticed how intently he had watched Lydia, his expression grave, his disapproval marked. He must know how closely Lydia's senselessness had come to scandalizing their entire family.

What did Mr. Darcy think of her family? If he knew Mr. Wickham, was he willing to tolerate becoming his brother when ... if ... he married her?

Not only had Elizabeth forgotten her own thoughts, but she no longer knew his.

Elizabeth looked at the door again, wishing for quiet, wanting to converse with Mr. Darcy, needing to understand. Needing her memories.

The clock on the mantel ticked mercilessly, taunting her with the passing time. It had been four hours since the accident. Four hours with nary one recollection of Mr. Darcy.

Laughter bubbled around the table, and Elizabeth returned her attention to the banquet. She smiled often and commented occasionally, but when she could smile no more, she dismissed herself, claiming a headache and the need for some fresh air and quiet.

Papa met her in the hall. "In search of your betrothed?" he asked.

"He is not with you?"

"Not for the better part of an hour. He has a great deal to consider."

About them? Without her? Elizabeth was not so vain to assume Mr. Darcy's every thought centered around her, but neither did she wish to be discounted and brushed aside so easily.

Gently settling his hand on her shoulder, her father said, "Be gentle with him, Lizzy. You are no longer in possession of all the facts. Do not repeat the same mistakes."

"I do not remember the mistakes to avoid repeating them." Her voice quivered, her fingernails biting into her palm, angry at the barrier blocking her brain.

Papa squeezed her arm. "Do not be too hasty to think the worst of Mr. Darcy."

Had she been so dreadful to Mr. Darcy? It was a wonder he still loved her.

He continued, "He has been very patient with us, and I daresay he will continue to be so."

Elizabeth blinked, her eyes burning. "Patience has its limits," she mumbled. Mr. Darcy had assured her he would wait for her, but what if she never remembered him? What if his patience was undeserved? From what he had told her, he had exerted himself to improve his character to win her heart, but what had she done for him?

"Have faith, Lizzy. Darcy loves you deeply. He has proved it over and over again."

His encouragement brought Elizabeth little relief.

Papa took her hand, tugging her down the hall toward the entrance door. "I have not checked on my hive since early this morning. The queen has sent her scouts out several days now to select their new home."

"Have you seen them inspecting your skips?"

"I have seen them buzzing about. If they accept one of my skips, it will be because of the brood comb I melted and coated over the inside of the straw. I am curious to see which of my three skips they select for their new home … if I can coax them to accept it, that is."

They were out of doors now and walking along the side of the house. Her window was still open, the curtain billowing above them. She followed her father, her concerns lightening with every step until he stopped short and muttered, "Bother and abomination."

She followed his line of vision to see the coachman approaching.

Sighing deeply, Papa said, "I ought to have known he would report on the state of the carriage the moment I stop waiting to tend to my favorite daughter and my bees." Grimacing, he added, "The damage must be extensive, or he would not have tarried."

Elizabeth patted his hand. "Better damage to the purse than to the person."

He looked at her hopefully. "Have you remembered anything?"

She smiled at him just as she had at Jane. "I am on the brink of it, I know it."

Papa did not accept her dismissal as easily as Jane. Elizabeth ought not to have expected him to — not when he had dragged her unconscious from the crippled carriage.

Before he could insist she join him inside or insist anything at all, Elizabeth added, "I would be delighted to check on your bees." Nodding at the house, she said,

"That hive is much too busy, and I am in need of quiet contemplation."

Reluctantly, he released her hand to join the coachman, pausing before he turned the corner as though he doubted she remembered the way to the grove bordering the apple orchard or feared she would get lost on the property she knew as well as the back of her hand.

Elizabeth waved, her footsteps deviating from their intended course when she saw a gentleman sitting alone on the bench under the willow tree by the pond.

Her heart fluttered. She had thought Mr. Darcy would have departed for London by now in search of another medic.

He looked up when she sat beside him. There was a melancholy in his bowed head and brown eyes that made her want to run her fingers down his cheek. She resisted the urge.

They sat in comfortable silence, watching the ducks and geese glide over the glassy water, sending ripples over the smooth surface. A burst of laughter broke the silence from the house.

"They will be happy together," Mr. Darcy said.

Elizabeth's fingers tingled. She would have run them through his dark, curly hair had she not shoved them under her legs. "Would we have been as happy?"

His gaze met hers, holding hers firmly. "Happier."

They sat facing each other, Elizabeth's heart racing while her mind chased evasive remembrances.

"Your father sent an urgent message to a friend of his from Oxford. A Mr. Sculthorpe."

"I know him. He is a gentleman of confidence, a doctor and scholar, who has been kind to us over the years."

"Mr. Bennet claims he is well-informed, an expert on the mind, though of a more theoretical bend than the others of whom Mr. Jones recommended."

Elizabeth answered the question he was too polite to ask outright. "His knowledge of medicine and science is extensive, far greater than most."

"Is he truly an expert?"

"In theory. He does not see patients, but he is a doctor and highly respected among scientists for his research and experiments."

"Do you trust him?" There was desperation in Mr. Darcy's voice.

"I do. He would never do anything to worsen my injury."

Mr. Darcy's shoulders relaxed. "That is what your father said, too."

"Does this mean you will stay on at Netherfield Park?"

He ran his hands through his hair. Would that she could do the same. She clenched the bench under her leg, her fingernails scratching against the wood.

"I do not wish to leave, but I must do something. I cannot rest until you are returned to me."

Was she so altered he spoke of her as if she were

lost? Elizabeth braced herself, determined to ask him to share another bit of their history when boots scuffled on the gravel path behind them.

Her father rushed toward them, his white hair wisping with each long stride. Elizabeth had never seen him walk so fast.

Mr. Darcy sat on the edge of the bench, ready to stand, poised for action.

Papa spoke between gasps of breath. "I am grateful you are still here, Mr. Darcy. The coachman has recently returned from the blacksmith. He bears bad news."

Elizabeth wondered what her father expected to gain in sharing the woes of repairing his conveyance to Mr. Darcy. "Papa?"

He glanced at her, then back to Mr. Darcy. His breathing did not calm. "Alarming news." Another gasp, then he leaned a hand against the back of the bench.

"Pray, sit for a moment and rest, Papa."

He shook his head fiercely. "The back axle did not break." Another heave of his chest. "It was cut."

"Cut?" Elizabeth repeated under her breath.

Mr. Darcy's voice snapped. "Sabotage?"

Papa nodded, his voice low and his face grave. "Someone did not wish for us to arrive at the parish on time. Someone was willing to kill you to prevent you from marrying."

CHAPTER 16

*A*s any lady who has ever lost one glove from a set knows, the only way to find the lost item is to stop looking. Elizabeth had concentrated so much of her attention on what she had lost, she had forgotten this simple truth until her father presented another puzzle to solve.

Confusion and uncertainty, her constant companions that morning, dwindled at the prospect of a tangible problem with which to engross her mind. The sooner she began, the sooner her memories would return.

"You said the axle was cut?" she asked.

"About a third of the way through, which explains why the coachman did not notice it."

Elizabeth nibbled on her lips, thinking aloud. "The wood is hard. Whoever did it would have to be strong … and unless this person carried around their own cutting tool, he or she would need to know Longbourn well enough to know where our saw is kept. It is a promising beginning."

Her father fell quiet, both he and Mr. Darcy regarding her quizzically. She tempered her smile. They must think her mad, but for the first time in hours, she felt in control. Capable. Competent. "It is an unfortunate discovery, but now that the danger is past, I cannot help but feel some relief. If I can piece clues together to find the saboteur, then I am certain to find my misplaced memories along the way."

Mr. Darcy's reaction was immediate and unyielding. "Absolutely not."

She crossed her arms. "Why not?" adding in her own mind, *And who are you to forbid me without explanation?*

To his credit, his eyes softened, but his posture remained stiff, his tone unrelenting. "You have suffered a terrible accident, and until your memories are recovered, surely you can see the advantage of not potentially exposing yourself to more danger. Someone purposefully sabotaged your family's carriage, knowing you would use it this morning. You must avoid trouble. You must rest."

You must. You must. Her back stiffened each time he told her what she must do. She was decided, and that was that. "We cannot assume I was the target of this attack. Otherwise, the saboteur would not have endangered all of my family in the hope of injuring only me."

Her father pinched his chin. "True. The accident might have befallen any or every one of my household. There was no guarantee Lizzy would be in the carriage when it happened, nor that she would hit her head and suffer amnesia."

Elizabeth took his reasoning a step further, glorying in the quickness with which her mind cooperated and drew conclusions. Blessed relief! "It seems increasingly possible that no sinister motive was implied at all, in which case, I am safe to investigate without any unnecessary concern for my safety."

Mr. Darcy snapped. "I cannot allow you to risk your life like this."

"It is more likely I am not risking anything at all — only my time and intellect. And if this exercise nudges my mind in the right direction, I stand to gain everything I lost. I see nothing but benefits."

"And I, the danger."

She wanted to hug Mr. Darcy … and strangle him. If this was what love was, then the contrary emotions plaguing her since the accident were proof of her heart's steadfastness.

Or — another possibility — this conflict of interest would reveal a side of Mr. Darcy she had not previously known. If her findings led to nothing more than testing his true character, then it was time well spent and effort wisely expended.

Lifting her chin, Elizabeth met his stare … glare. "I will not be intimidated, Mr. Darcy. Not by anyone, and certainly not by you."

His nostrils flared. "Well do I know it, dash it all. Your courage always rises to the occasion."

He did not say it as a compliment, but Elizabeth took great pleasure in understanding it as one anyway. Bobbing a curtsy, she said, "Thank you."

His eyes narrowed at her, and a growly sound emanated from his throat.

But the corners of his lips twitched.

DARCY PINCHED the bridge of his nose, a headache pressing against skull. The amnesia had not changed Elizabeth's character in the least. She was every bit as intrepid and bold and … and stubborn as she had ever been.

He wanted to strangle her … and hold her.

Elizabeth's determination to poke into the sabotage might stir up a hornets' nest. He could not leave her to investigate alone. It altered his plans. He would need to stay near to offer his protection when he ought to be riding to London in search of a treatment to heal her condition.

Blast the woman!

He would have to write to Richard. His cousin, the colonel, would request leave and join them from

London posthaste if the message was urgent. Darcy would ensure its urgency.

Elizabeth would not like having two bodyguards following her just as she had resisted every other suggestion he had made.

Headstrong woman.

He would make one more plea, then Lord help her. Holding his hands in front of him, he said, "Allow me to help you."

Her eyes flashed. "I assure you, Mr. Darcy, I am perfectly capable of solving this mystery on my own. I have not lost my mind … not yet. I am not mad or incapable."

One more plea. "I never meant to imply you were. I only want to keep you safe from harm."

She jutted out her chin. She was so stubborn.

And oh, how he adored her.

CHAPTER 17

arcy knew Elizabeth was upset. He ought to have asked her what she thought instead of assuming the full responsibility of her care. He winced. For treating her like a mindless invalid.

The damage was done.

If only she knew how helpless he felt. Had he been in the carriage, he might have protected her. Had he stopped by Longbourn before the ceremony, as he had yearned to do, he might have seen the damage and prevented the accident.

He ought to have prevented it.

Heaving a sigh, Darcy said, "I am sorry, Elizabeth. My eagerness to protect you from harm makes me presumptuous and imperious. Please understand I am only thinking of you."

Her confusion pained his heart. Knowing Elizabeth could no longer read his reactions and thoughts as clearly as she had the day prior robbed him of certainty.

He held his breath, waiting for her humor to shine through, and was rewarded. She teased, "How can I stay angry at you when you admit to your error so easily? It is impossible."

Elizabeth did not hold grudges as he did — thank goodness, or he never would have persuaded her to love him. She forgave as quickly as her anger flashed. As many times as Darcy had been the recipient of her clemency, he marveled at her ability to forgive and forget. Now that she was unable to recall him and his errors to mind, he appreciated even more how affection had allowed her to cover over his transgressions of her own volition. It was her gift.

He extended his hand to her. "I have some urgent letters to write. Do you wish to return with me, or would you rather remain here?" His fingers reached for her, aching for her touch.

She folded her hands together. "I have a great deal to consider and wish to be alone for a few more minutes."

Disappointed, he dropped his hand.

"Do not fear, Mr. Darcy. I will not be long," she added with an impish grin, "not with a saboteur lurking about."

Drat. In his eagerness to please her, he had forgotten. He looked about, tugging his fingers through his hair, unable to leave her after he had offered to do that very thing.

Arching her eyebrow and tilting her chin, she said, "My father's study overlooks this pond. I daresay he would not deny you the loan of ink and paper while you assure my safety from the window."

Maybe she *could* still read his thoughts. He bowed, reluctant to leave her. However, the letters would not write themselves, and Darcy would waste no more time without his Elizabeth.

He hastened up the path and down the hall, not slowing his pace until he reached Mr. Bennet's door. Had it been slightly ajar, he would have been tempted to barge in. But it was closed, and he was obligated to knock.

In the time it took Mr. Bennet to open his door, Darcy overheard Lydia touting the superiority of her northern physician to anyone who cared to listen. "He has the most scrumptious nerve tonic. Not like that horrible, bitter stuff Mr. Jones makes for you, Mama. It tastes like bilberries, and its effect is immediate. I shall let you try some when you need it."

Mrs. Bennet replied, as Mr. Bennet opened the door, that with one daughter so advantageously married and another with child, she could not imagine ever feeling vexed again.

Mr. Bennet peered over his spectacles at Darcy. "When the mistress of the house is happy, everyone is happy."

"Wise words I shall keep in mind."

Mr. Bennet chuckled. "Come to the window. The prospect is lovely."

As Elizabeth said, it faced the pond. Though the land slanted downward, he could still see the top of the bench and the chestnut curls caressing her profile from his perch.

"My Lizzy is as strong-willed as you are, Darcy." He chuckled. "If she has her way, which she often does, she will be well by morning."

"And if she is not?"

"It will be an obstacle I hope you will choose to contend with."

"Of course."

"If both of you are determined to be happy, then I have no doubt you shall meet with the greatest success." Leaning back in his chair, Mr. Bennet clasped his hands together over his stomach. "I do not suppose you came here to discuss my correspondence with my Polish beekeeper friend or to see my drawings for the panels I plan to insert in my skips?"

Politeness made Darcy glance at the drawings spread over Mr. Bennet's desk. "My land steward is a greater authority than I am. If you are able to extract honey without harming the bees, the scientific community will be eager to hear about it."

Mr. Bennet's eyes gleamed. "I suppose I could write a paper on it." He gazed off into the distance, his eyes resting on Elizabeth. Then, just as suddenly as he drifted off in his daydreams, he cleared his throat. "I suspect you have a reason for coming to my study. Is there a matter with which I might help you?"

"I have several urgent messages I must send."

Motioning to the small writing desk between them and the window, Mr. Bennet said, "You should find everything you need there. If there is anything else you require, I will be with my drawings."

Darcy pulled a sheet of paper closer. The first letter would go to his London housekeeper. She was expecting him and Elizabeth that evening.

The easiest letter seen to, he pulled out another piece of paper, dating it and addressing it to his personal London physician.

DEAR DOCTOR CHAMBERS,

I trust your delicacy and discretion to carry out a request of the utmost importance to me. The young lady I was to marry suffered an accident, a blow to the head resulting in amnesia. The local apothecary, an informed gentleman whose diagnosis I trust but whose methods I found wanting, deemed her condition selective. I am inclined to agree with him, as the only lack in her memories seem to be any and all pertaining to me. She does not know me at all.

My request is that you seek out the foremost doctors and scientists of the mind, those particularly knowledgeable regarding amnesia, available in London. Inquire into treatments and therapies. I am unable to travel to London imme-

118

diately, but I will do so at the first opportunity to discuss your findings. I trust you will have several, or at least a few.

ATTENTIVELY,

Fitzwilliam Darcy

HE FOLDED THE NOTE, confident in his doctor's assistance (for which he would make sure to reward him handsomely.)

The next letter was a struggle.

DEAREST GEORGIANA,

I am eager to join you at Pemberley with Elizabeth, but I fear we have been unavoidably delayed.

THE NEXT LINE was impossible to pen. *Accident* sounded too grave. As did *calamity* and *disaster*. *Little incident*, on the contrary, was too flippant. *Mishap? Misadventure?* That was it.

A MISADVENTURE BEFELL ELIZABETH, and I would not dream of insisting she travel until she is fully recovered.

. . .

HE WROTE at length about other matters between glances through the window, careful to keep his tone light so as not to cause his sister alarm. There was no need distressing her when, in all probability, Elizabeth's memories would return before the evening. Or, as Mr. Bennet suggested, on the morrow. That was the estimate Mr. Jones had given them.

Beyond that…

Darcy shivered. He would not allow Elizabeth to worsen. He would see to it she had every advantage she required.

His final letter was for his cousin.

RICHARD,

I need you immediately. The Bennets' carriage was sabotaged, and Elizabeth was hurt. She is sound in body, but she has no memory of me.

I am at my wit's end.

Please come directly. We have an enemy to expose, and I have a bride I am desperate to have restored to me.

MAKE HASTE,
Darcy

~

ELIZABETH COULD HAVE SAT by the pond for hours, but Mr. Darcy would not remove himself from his observational perch until she returned indoors.

She was pleased to hear him offering hearty congratulations to the rejoicing couple, and it was with a lighter heart Elizabeth crept up the stairs to her bedchamber.

Her room would feel empty without Jane. It already did. Elizabeth wrapped her arms around herself, a paper fluttering on the corner of the dressing table catching her eye.

Mrs. Fitzwilliam Darcy.

Mrs. Lizzy Darcy.

Mrs. Elizabeth Darcy...

Looped letters and swirls adorned the length of the page, bittersweet in their un-fulfillment. She had looked forward to taking Mr. Darcy's name. She had been on the brink of a new happy beginning.

A happy beginning an evil, unknown foe had stolen.

She would discover his or her identity. She would find him and expose his blatant injustice against her. She would demand satisfaction.

Filled with indignation, Elizabeth set to work, writing names along with means and motives, facts and potential clues.

CHAPTER 18

George Wickham tossed and turned, eager for morning to arise. After one night in the tenant hovel, he understood why nobody inhabited it. Fortunately, the night was warmer here than in the north, and the holes in the roof might have provided an exceptional view of the stars ... had the luminaries not been covered with clouds.

He also understood why the cot had not been reclaimed. Itchy, red welts spotted his flesh. The more he scratched, the more they itched.

Still, he was optimistic. If all went well, his misery would end, and he would return to the regiment that same morning.

But he must make certain first.

Sneaking over fields and sticking to the shadows, Wickham crept to Longbourn, not too close but close enough to observe the goings on.

The servants were up, and there was that new footman he had so narrowly escaped from noticing him the day before, sweeping the flagstones outside the kitchen.

The younger maid came out wielding a large tub. Wickham watched her closely. There was nothing different about her manner, and when Mrs. Hill summoned the footman to the kitchen, there appeared to be nothing out of sorts with her either.

No tears. No solemnity.

Maybe it was too early yet. Nobody had noticed.

What a bother. He would have to linger longer to be sure.

Wickham's stomach rumbled, and he cursed. Bitten, cold, hungry, and bored. Would that this misery would end.

He glanced at the house once more, determined there was nothing more to be learned, then returned to his hovel to partake of his meager breakfast — stale bread and hard cheese.

Belly mostly calmed and blood warmed, exhaustion claimed him, and he woke several hours later.

Donning a coat he had snatched from a clothesline, and shoving a farmer's hat down over his head, he walked gingerly to Longbourn. The family would be awake now.

He crept as close as he dared, listening, watching. But he heard none of the sounds he expected. No mourning. No wailing. No cries.

He lurked from his hiding place between the hedge and the carriage house, hoping to see evidence that his plan had met with success. But there was none.

Abomination! He was supposed to leave today, and now he would have to stay to help things along.

What could he do? He needed something quick. Something efficient. Something nobody could foresee or prevent. Not even him. There was no guilt in an accident.

Wickham's gaze scanned over the yard. What to do? What to do?

A door creaked and slammed, and Wickham clung to the side of the carriage house, holding his breath when footsteps grew louder and only peeking around the corner when they faded.

It was Mr. Bennet. At least, that was who Wickham supposed it was under the bizarre costume he wore: a broad-brimmed hat with what looked like a wedding veil fluttering around it and stitched to a long, white coat of coarse fabric and long sleeves with matching gloves.

Wickham lost precious time staring at the gentleman in his extraordinary ensemble, but when he came to his senses, he scrambled along the thicket for a better view.

Mr. Bennet wandered beyond the back of the house in the direction of his fruit trees.

Opportunity? Or another stalemate?

Having nothing better to do, Wickham followed.

CHAPTER 19

*D*arcy woke the following morning cautiously optimistic.

Perhaps he ought not to have alarmed Richard when, in all likelihood, a night's rest had healed the breach separating Elizabeth from him.

Mr. Bennet rose early to tend to his bees, and it had always been Elizabeth's habit to enjoy long walks in the morning. If he hurried, Darcy might see her walking over the fields. She would turn to greet him, her smile wide and her eyes bright with recognition. He would take her into his arms, and he would spin in circles and never let go of her again.

Eager to ride to Longbourn, Darcy crept down to the kitchen, wishing to break his fast and depart before the other residents of the house came downstairs.

Bingley's cook was not surprised to see him in her kitchen. Another would have insisted on sending a maid to serve him in the breakfast parlor, but she allowed him to sit at the table while she poached eggs and pulled freshly baked rolls out of the oven. She had placed a dish of butter in front of Darcy when Bingley tiptoed into her domain.

A light spattering of whiskers dotted his cheeks; his hair jutted wildly from his head. His nightshirt was tucked haphazardly into his breeches. He looked deliriously happy.

The fissure in Darcy's heart widened. He ought to have been slipping down to the kitchen at Darcy House for a tray to bring up to his bride that morning, too.

Grinning like a fool, Bingley sat beside Darcy. "I ought to have known you would be up." He nodded to the cook, who pulled out a tray and began piling it with dishes of jam and cream, rolls, scrambled eggs, ham, and strawberry tarts. Elizabeth favored tarts. His London cook would not allow the pastries Darcy had asked her to make to go to waste.

"Are you off to Longbourn?" Bingley asked.

"I am. I hope to find Elizabeth much improved."

Bingley nodded, his smile faded. "She is strong, and much too clever by half. Do not lose heart, Darcy. She will recover."

Darcy appreciated his friend's reassurance while recognizing the danger of allowing his hope to rise.

Bingley continued, "My sisters intend to depart for London today. But Jane and I discussed the matter and have decided to postpone our wedding tour until Elizabeth is fully recovered. You are welcome to stay here with us."

"I could not impose on your hospitality." Could not bear to see them so happily settled. "I will take a room at the Meryton Inn."

Bingley's back straightened. "With Lady Catherine taking over the establishment? I will not hear it. Pray do not leave on my account when this house is so big, and my wife and I have all the privacy we desire." His cheeks flushed fiery scarlet.

Darcy's heart pinged with envy ... and hope.

Twenty minutes later, he dismounted at Longbourn.

Hill opened the door before Darcy's feet touched the ground. The haste with which the older man saw to his duties, as well as the furrow creasing his brow and crinkling around his eyes, gave Darcy pause.

"Good day. Am I too early?"

Shaking his head slowly, his eyes drooping, Hill said, "Mr. Bennet suggested you would call early today."

Darcy thought his heart would burst if he waited a second longer. "How is Miss Elizabeth?"

"That, I cannot say, sir."

Tottering between despair and hope, Darcy followed the house servant into the drawing room where Elizabeth sat on the settee in front of the window, Mrs. Bennet positioned precariously on a chair opposite her.

The matron rose as soon as he entered the room. "Mr. Darcy, how lovely to see you so early. Does Lizzy not look fine?"

Soft morning beams glowed against Elizabeth's skin, shimmering against her silky curls. He wanted to twirl a tendril between his fingers as he had done before, but he clasped his hands in front of him, mourning the loss of the freedoms he had once enjoyed with his betrothed. With his Elizabeth.

Swallowing the lump in her throat, he answered, "She does."

Pleased with his reply, Mrs. Bennet guided him to the chair nearest Elizabeth, talking a flurry as she pushed him forward.

Elizabeth met his gaze then.

And he knew. He would not need the forget-me-not ring today.

ELIZABETH WOKE the following morning with images of Mr. Darcy's handsome face, tall strength, and unexpected humor fresh in her mind. Stretching under the warmth of her covers, her heart fluttered and loped in her chest. Surely, this was a promising beginning.

Slipping her hand under her pillow, she pulled out the piece of paper covered with his name and her many signatures. Mrs. Elizabeth Darcy. She rubbed her finger over the letters, the name rolling off her tongue.

As smooth as a worn book cover and as sweet as a strawberry tart.

Eager to reaffirm what she hoped to be true, she donned a wrap and ran out to the hallway, nearly stumbling into Mrs. Hill. Grabbing the housekeeper by the shoulders, Elizabeth asked, "Please, Mrs. Hill, ask me a question about Mr. Darcy. Anything you please."

After a few stammering starts, Mrs. Hill said, "What is his favorite meal?"

Elizabeth twisted her lips. "I hardly know." Was that something she was supposed to know? Had previously known?

Mrs. Hill patted her cheek. "I daresay it was not the right question to ask, Miss. I believe it was your mother who informed me of his preference for roasted pork."

Dashed hopes deflected, Elizabeth kissed Mrs. Hill's cheek before continuing down the hall to the first open door.

Lydia lounged in her bed with a breakfast tray teetering on her legs. With all she had eaten the day before, it was a wonder she could consume more. She had fallen asleep on the settee, and Papa had had to help Thatcher carry her upstairs to her bed.

"Lizzy," she greeted, slathering butter on her roll and spooning a blob of berry preserves on top.

"Ask me a question about Mr. Darcy," Elizabeth said, sitting on the end of Lydia's bed.

"Oh, that dreadful man," Lydia said, chewing and

swallowing. "After what he did to my poor, sweet George, you can hardly expect for me to wish to talk about him."

What had Mr. Darcy done to Wickham? Elizabeth tried to remember. She recalled a strong dislike between the gentlemen, but it was more of a sense than a recollection.

Lydia continued, "However, I am determined to overlook Mr. Darcy's displeasing temperament for your sake and for the sake of my child." She patted her stomach and shoved the rest of the roll into her mouth. "George was the given name of Mr. Darcy's father, was it not? I think that would make a fine name for a boy, do you not agree?"

Elizabeth did not know.

"His sister is named Georgiana, another variation," Lydia mused.

Elizabeth could not remember.

"Of course, on the chance the baby is a girl, I could name her after Mr. Darcy's mother. Anne is a fine name for a girl."

Elizabeth nodded, her disappointment complete. Sleep had not cured her mind.

"I do not know how you cannot recall your own betrothed. I could never forget George. The first time I saw him looking so handsome in his scarlet regimental coat with the gold braids and brass buttons..." Lydia sighed, leaning against her mound of pillows with one hand over her heart.

Her words struck their mark, weighing so heavily on Elizabeth, only the refusal to hear more of Lydia's taunts drove Elizabeth out of her sister's bedchamber and down the stairs to the breakfast room. She sat numbly while the maid arranged platters around the table and the footman hovered. Elizabeth could not bring herself to lift a lid.

How long she sat there alone, she could not say, but her mother's sharp voice interrupted Elizabeth's melancholia. "Mr. Darcy is here."

Half walking, half shoved by her mother, they crossed the hall to the drawing room where Mama pushed her onto a chair near the window. "You will appear to greatest advantage here ... and with space enough for you both," she mumbled while she poked Elizabeth into position, pinching her cheeks and fussing with her ribbons and running to sit an instant before Mr. Hill announced their caller.

"Mr. Darcy to see you, Miss Bennet."

Elizabeth kept her eyes averted. She could not look him in the eyes yet, but she was extremely aware of him. He watched her, a smile softening his face, his expression full of hope.

She wanted to weep. She was engaged to a pleasant gentleman with everything to recommend him, a man she must have loved dearly to have accepted his offer of marriage. A man who did not stand entirely on society's laws of propriety, given the early hour of his call

— a laxity she approved wholeheartedly given her love for solitary walks.

Mama was quick to fill the silence. "Mr. Darcy, how lovely to see you so early. Does Lizzy not look fine?"

The way he looked at her set Elizabeth's skin aflame.

"She does." He was so definite. So confident.

Elizabeth hated to disappoint him, but neither was she content to avoid the truth and its consequences. To delay the inevitable when he warranted her honesty.

She turned to face him, and she saw the moment — the shift in his posture, the strain in his eyes — when he knew.

His memory escaped her still.

Stepping closer to her, he reached out his hand, then dropped it uncertainly. "I trust you slept well?" he asked.

The rapidity with which Mr. Darcy replaced discouragement with awkwardness was so unexpected, Elizabeth found her humor and remembered her purpose.

Tucking her hand, which tingled in anticipation of his touch, into her skirts, she returned his smile. "I did, thank you," she replied, patting the empty spot on the settee in invitation, "though I found it difficult to quiet my mind long enough to rest properly. I have considered several suspects. There is, of course, Miss Bingley. She despises me, and I could not help but think that she would love nothing more than to take my place beside you at the altar."

Mama shrieked and grumbled.

Mr. Darcy sat beside Elizabeth. "I have never given her cause to entertain expectations."

"I know." How or why, Elizabeth could not explain, but she knew Mr. Darcy spoke honestly as certainly as she favored signing the letter "L."

But dwelling on such thoughts only led to frustration. She knew that, too. Returning to her preferred premeditated distraction, she added, "Cutting an axle seems far-fetched for Miss Bingley. I would sooner imagine her using a poison rather than exerting herself physically."

Mr. Darcy rubbed his chin. "I can ask the servants at Netherfield Park if any of them saw her leave the house the morning of the wedding."

"Perfect."

His chest heaved up and down; his voice carried a tinge of resignation. "Who else is on your list of suspects?"

He did not agree with her, but he consented to help her. *Another point in Mr. Darcy's favor,* thought Elizabeth. She said, "As much as I hate to say it, we cannot dismiss your aunt entirely."

"She did not arrive until after your accident."

"True. However, could her lateness have been an act?"

"Lady Catherine is many things, but she is not a liar."

Elizabeth chewed the inside of her cheek. She had been right to worry about his reaction.

He continued, "Speaking practically, I do not believe my aunt strong enough to cut hard wood with a saw."

Elizabeth had considered that. "What about her daughter?"

"Anne?"

"I do not know much of her character. Might she have assisted her mother?"

Mr. Darcy bunched his lips together and shifted his weight on the couch, away from her, Elizabeth noted. "My cousin is quiet, and when my aunt is present, she is known to fall completely silent for extended lengths of time."

"Would she do as Lady Catherine bid?"

"She usually does."

How sad. Elizabeth could not imagine living her entire life always being imposed upon. More out of pity for Miss de Bourgh than lack of suspicion, Elizabeth moved on. "I agree your aunt is too feeble to have cut the axle herself, and I do not know that Miss de Bourgh would be of much assistance either. What about a third party? Is there anyone your aunt might have requested to perform such a service?"

"You are determined to cast the blame on her?"

"Not at all. I merely wish to discuss the possibilities.

All of the possibilities. And you must admit, your aunt does not approve of me, which makes her suspect."

He frowned. "My aunt is opinionated and set in her ways, but she is not truly devious."

Elizabeth would have to take his word for it ... unless the evidence proved otherwise. She possessed a distinct impression of Lady Catherine's rudeness, but she could not recall her basis for such a belief.

"Very well," Elizabeth conceded. "Who does that leave, then?"

A tap on the door interrupted their conversation, and the announcement of Mr. Collins' arrival effectively ended their debate of suspects.

Mr. Darcy grimaced. Elizabeth would have done the same had his reaction not given rise to her humor.

Mr. Collins entered the room with a proprietary air, his bow deepening when he saw Mr. Darcy. "My dear Cousin Elizabeth, I took it upon myself to ensure your health before returning to Hunsford. Mrs. Collins would wish for me to ensure the welfare of her closest friend, as would my esteemed patroness, Lady Catherine de Bourgh, who condescended to inquire of your health to me only earlier this morning."

Elizabeth cut through the excessive fluff and pomp to extract the only worthwhile bit. "It is your aim to depart today?" she asked.

He bowed, taking the seat Mama must have recently vacated. "So long as your health has not suffered from the blow you suffered, I had hoped to return to Hunsford today."

"I daresay my memories will return soon enough without inconveniencing you, Mr. Collins."

His eyes widened, and he inhaled sharply through his nose. "You do not recall—" His gaze bounced to Mr. Darcy and back to her. Clearing his throat, he said, "— your betrothed?"

"Not yet, but it is only a matter of time," she said with a great deal too much cheer.

Mr. Collins extracted a handkerchief to dab at his face. "It is with immense sympathy I hear your bad news, Cousin."

He did not sound sympathetic. Just uncomfortable.

"Mrs. Collins will be greatly distressed," he added, returning the square to his pocket.

"Why did you come to the wedding?" Mr. Darcy asked.

Great question.

Elizabeth watched Mr. Collins. His face colored raspberry red. "Mrs. Collins had wished to attend the wedding, but her condition was too delicate to permit travel. She has been quite ill of late."

"I am sorry to hear it," Elizabeth said, truly sorry for her friend. She had hinted that she was in the family way in her last letter.

Mr. Collins nodded. "Lady Lucas insisted I retrieve a mixture of herbs she assures me will ease Mrs. Collins' malaise."

"Then, you must make haste, Mr. Collins, and return to her without delay," Elizabeth implored. She could not imagine a fate worse than a lifetime with Mr. Collins, but to suffer sickness to bring his offspring into the world besides was truly beyond the pale. Poor Charlotte.

Looking down at his boots, Mr. Collins said, "I would only add to her distress with the news of…" He looked up at Elizabeth and paled. "…recent events."

Mr. Darcy said, "That is what we are attempting to discern, Mr. Collins. We have had some unexpected guests arrive, not all of whom hold Elizabeth's welfare in high regard."

Elizabeth inhaled sharply. Did Mr. Darcy really suspect her bumbling cousin of sabotaging the carriage he would eventually inherit? Or was this retaliation for her questions about his aunt?

Clasping his damp linen in his thick hands, Mr. Collins said, "I take my duty toward my family seriously, Mr. Darcy, especially where it pleases my wife."

"At the risk of displeasing Lady Catherine?" Darcy scoffed.

Mr. Collins angled his head to the side. "I had not expected to see Her Ladyship at your wedding. I was as surprised to see her as I was to see Mr. Wickham."

Elizabeth sat taller in her chair. "Mr. Wickham, you say?"

Mr. Darcy met her eye, equally concerned.

"When was this?" she asked.

"I hardly think ... that is, I would have thought your memory—" Mr. Collins bumbled.

She simplified her question. "When did you see Mr. Wickham?"

"Yesterday, after I returned to Lucas Lodge to write a letter to Mrs. Collins, I walked to Meryton to see if Lady Catherine and Miss de Bourgh were well-settled at the inn. After ensuring their welfare, I posted my letter. That was when I saw him crossing a field."

Elizabeth met Mr. Darcy's shocked look. That was hours after Lydia had said Wickham had departed for his regiment. What had he been doing tarrying about? Elizabeth added his name to the list of suspects, though she could not fathom why Wickham would interfere with their wedding when he stood to gain from the connection.

Was Wickham the sort of man to injure another? Elizabeth had always considered him an opportunist, a lazy man lacking initiative and expecting a fortune. He would place himself advantageously to benefit from an accident, but she doubted he would provoke one.

But she could be wrong.

Mr. Collins looked between them, confused.

Mr. Darcy explained, "If Mr. Wickham is still in the village, he is likely to be the one responsible for Elizabeth's current state of mind."

The clergyman's mouth opened and closed several times before he produced any words. "Was the incident not an accident?"

"It was a deliberate, calculated act of sabotage, and whoever caused it will face the consequences when I bring them to justice for attempted murder." Darcy's tone was hard. Nothing in his manner suggested exaggeration. But ... murder? Was he serious? Sure, her father had suggested the same, but Elizabeth could think of dozens of other ways to more accurately and effectively end another's life. Not that she would enumerate on those now.

"Murder?" Mr. Collins wheezed.

Mr. Darcy must have read her thoughts. Turning to her, he asked, "Would you trust your sister's life, and that of her unborn child, with a man capable of cutting a carriage's axle for the sole purpose of crippling the conveyance and harming those inside?"

"But I did not die! I may not even have been the target of the attack!"

Mr. Darcy leveled his gaze at her. "I would prevent anyone from hurting you. I will protect you, and I will make it known to anyone who attempts to harm the woman I love that they will pay dearly for their stupidity."

"While I appreciate your protection, do you not think you might be overreacting?"

Mr. Collins rose from his squeaky chair, looking positively green. "I must return to Her Ladyship. I must warn her. This is dreadful."

Mr. Darcy snapped, "If you truly wish to be helpful, convince her to return to Rosings."

More to make a point of voicing her opinion than in slandering the esteemed lady's name, Elizabeth said, "Maybe it is for the best that Her Ladyship remains nearby. I do not believe her evil, only sorely entitled. She might know something."

Mr. Darcy did not look happy, but neither did he contradict Elizabeth.

Mr. Collins stumbled over his own chair, departing from the room with exceptional expeditiousness.

CHAPTER 20

$\mathcal{A}$s soon as Hill closed the door behind Mr. Collins, Elizabeth turned to Darcy. "Are you going to Meryton?"

Her eagerness made Darcy hesitant. "Yes," he drawled.

"I should like to go with you. If Wickham is in Meryton, we must find him."

Darcy was painfully aware that Elizabeth believed him overly cautious, but he would never forget the blank expression on his bride's face the day of their wedding.

He was at an impasse. He did not wish for her to involve herself in an investigation. However, he had little desire to leave her alone without protection. Would she be safer at Longbourn, surrounded by her family, or with him?

A carriage clattered and crunched down the lane, growing louder until it stopped.

Mrs. Bennet appeared in the drawing room. Darcy could not recall when she had left him alone with Elizabeth. For being so loud, she had an unnatural ability to vacate a room when it suited her purpose.

"It is Mr. Bingley's carriage," said the matron. "My dear Jane is so considerate. I just knew she would call today."

Elizabeth bit her lips and wrinkled her nose the way she did when she had to resign herself to something she would rather not. Darcy loved how expressive she was, how transparent. Leaning closer to her and lowering his voice, he said, "I am sorry to leave, but you are right. If Wickham is in the village, we must find him."

She bunched her cheeks. "I cannot disregard my sister's call when it is made out of concern for me."

"I promise to inform you the moment I learn anything new."

Taking his leave from his beloved before Bingley could hand his wife and Miss Bingley from the carriage, Darcy exchanged a few pleasantries with them while he waited for his horse.

Bingley pulled him aside. "I will look after Elizabeth's welfare as though she were my own sister."

"She *is* your sister."

"You know what I mean. Mr. Bennet told me about the carriage. I have not burdened Jane with this information, but I hope you know that I am ready to offer my assistance however I might be of use."

Darcy clapped his friend on the shoulder. "Thank you, Bingley." As he rode into Meryton, he marveled at the contrast between his true friends and his worst enemies when the sickening realization smacked him with all of its ugly, brunt force.

Elizabeth had not possessed any enemies before she had agreed to marry him.

ELIZABETH PEERED at her visitors through the window, groaning when she saw Miss Bingley. Was not the lady supposed to return to town with her sister today?

Her mood threatened to sour. Their timing was abominable, and while Elizabeth would always be kind to Jane and Bingley, knowing their motives to be selfless, she could not say the same for Miss Bingley.

She would simply have to mind her tongue lest she distress her sister needlessly.

Miss Bingley flounced in behind Jane, her face pinched in an expression Elizabeth had never seen before. Not scorn. Not disgust. Not boredom.

Rushing over to her side, Miss Bingley patted Elizabeth's arm. "Oh, you poor thing. You must be terribly distressed at this turn of events." She examined Elizabeth's face as though searching for proof of Elizabeth's disappointments. "Oh, yes, you are quite altered. I am so sorry for you."

False sympathy. That was the look. It did not flatter Miss Bingley.

Arching an eyebrow, Elizabeth tilted her chin toward her consoler. "I assure you I am quite well."

Miss Bingley was not easily convinced. "Of course, you must say that. You would never do anything to upset dear Jane nor to inconvenience your family, but the fact remains that you are as yet unattached, and unless you remember Mr. Darcy, you might remain unmarried for some time."

Bingley laughed. "Darcy? Wait?"

Miss Bingley huffed, struggling to maintain her sympathy while grasping for the opportunity she thought was available to snatch.

He continued, "Darcy is the most constant gentleman I know. If anything, he will be more determined than ever to win Miss Elizabeth again."

Elizabeth had always liked Mr. Bingley. She beamed at him, next giving his sister the benefit of her full smile.

Miss Bingley was not impressed. She took a seat on her brother's other side, putting him between her and Jane. Making him choose to whom he would lean closer and direct his conversation.

It was a foolish move.

If Miss Bingley expected him to favor her, she was

instantly forced to adjust her expectations when her brother leaned closer to Jane, clasping her hand in his.

Miss Bingley huffed, unaccustomed to not being the queen in her household. "Still, there are those who worry about your case, saying it is the first stage of illness. I do not believe it, but I only repeat what I have heard."

Elizabeth knew what she was about. "And what do they say?" she asked.

Smoothing her skirts, fluttering her hand over her heart as though the news which must have delighted her was disturbing, Miss Bingley said, "Only that amnesia is a disease of the brain and the longer you go without remembering, the more unlikely you are to ever recover. Sadly, once the disease has taken hold, it has no choice but to worsen."

Elizabeth laughed. "I am to go insane, then? How fortunate for the unattached females with designs on Mr. Darcy."

Miss Bingley must have felt the cut, but so confident was she in Elizabeth's fate, she met her eyes boldly, saying with all gravity, "Quite." She was a slow learner.

Jane's gentle voice cut through the tension as sharply as a saber. "If your intention in remaining as a guest in our residence is to pursue Mr. Darcy, the true love and betrothed of my sister, a man who loves her so fully he is willing to wait for her to recover, then you are not welcome at Netherfield Park." Her icy eyes glared, heightened by the burn in her cheeks.

Elizabeth had never seen Jane so angry, and she had to admit that the evidence of her sister's strength was reassuring. She had feared that between Miss Bingley and Mrs. Hurst, they would attempt to take over Jane's life. Apparently, Elizabeth had worried for naught.

She watched Mr. Bingley. Would he support his sister or his wife?

His complexion deepened a few shades, and when he finally spoke, his voice shook. "I am ashamed my wife had to say what I ought to have said, Caroline, but I stand by her. Darcy is my best friend, and Elizabeth is as much my sister as you are. I will not allow you to interfere with their happiness."

Miss Bingley huffed and puffed. "As Mr. Darcy interfered with yours and Jane's?" She turned to Elizabeth, a sneer twisting her features. "Did you remember that little gem? How could you possibly forgive a man who interfered with the happiness of your own sister?"

Mr. Darcy had been too honest with her about their first meeting to doubt he would honey-coat his past wrong against Jane. Whatever he had done, he had made right. "I agreed to marry him, and I trust my own judgment better than yours."

Such a lovely shade of burnt orange Miss Bingley turned; so complemental of her gown. "But he objected to their union! He purposely separated them."

"And yet, they are married and appear to be quite

content with each other. Really, I must thank you, Miss Bingley, for dredging up Mr. Darcy's past sins. Any gentleman humble enough to own to his mistakes and take action to correct them is deserving of the highest esteem."

Miss Bingley's face pinched again, but this time it was not in sympathy. Elizabeth recognized this look. Outright hatred.

"After all of my efforts... after all my sacrifices ... everything I have done—"

Mr. Bingley jerked around to face her. "What have you done? You will tell me this instant."

She waved him off. "Do not trouble yourself, Charles. It is nothing."

He did not budge. "Mr. Bennet told me the carriage was sabotaged. Someone intentionally damaged their conveyance to prevent Darcy's union with Elizabeth. For all we know, her life is in danger, and Darcy has charged me to help him protect her. Lord help me, Caroline, if you had anything to do with that carriage accident, I will march you back to Netherfield Park and pack your trunks myself."

Jane's eyes doubled in size, but her shoulders squared and her back straightened. "Is this true? The carriage was disabled?"

Miss Bingley fumed. "How could you possibly think I would stoop so low? I am a lady."

"Who is no comfort to anyone here," Bingley finished for her. "I think it best for everyone if you packed your things and departed with the Hursts this afternoon." He received a supportive nod from Jane, who regally kept her cool composure and looked every inch the mistress of Netherfield Park. Elizabeth was so proud of her, she would have clapped if the gesture would not have been exceptionally inappropriate.

Their father joined them just as Miss Bingley rose, her posture stiff and her lips pressed firmly together, assuming an air of dignity the shame of her complexion belied.

Bingley expressed his apologies. "There is a matter we must see to without delay, but I will call again later with Jane." He ushered his sister out to their waiting carriage.

Papa called after him, "Only if you and Jane agree to return to dine with us along with Mr. Darcy." He regarded Jane with a big smile and a twinkle in his eye. "Well done, my dear. I will no longer fear others taking advantage of your kindness."

He had heard everything. Elizabeth was glad.

Squeezing Elizabeth's hands, Jane followed her husband to the carriage with promises of a prompt return.

Peace prevailed in the parlor again, and Elizabeth sought to pass the time as well as she could with a book.

No sooner had her father settled into his favorite chair and snapped open his newspaper than Mrs. Hill entered the room. "Mr. Bennet, might I have a word?"

Papa lowered his paper and looked about. "There is nothing you cannot say in front of Lizzy. What is troubling you, Mrs. Hill?"

"It is the new footman," she said, wringing her hands in her apron. "He is never around when I need him, and when I send him to fetch Mr. Hill, he never manages to find him. I thought that given sufficient time, Thatcher would gain experience and perform his duties more efficiently, but a month has passed." She shuffled her weight, took a deep breath, and added quickly, "And, now, I have reason to suspect him a thief."

Papa set his paper aside. "What has gone missing?"

"The fine, lace tablecloth — Mrs. Bennet's favorite — is missing. I washed it after the wedding feast and hanged it out to dry, and now it is gone."

"I well know that tablecloth." Papa frowned, addressing Elizabeth, "I tried to convince your mother to allow me to use it as a netting for my beekeeping wardrobe, and that was all I heard about for above a week." He turned to Mrs. Hill. "Have you told Mrs. Bennet it is missing?"

"Not yet, sir."

Elizabeth heard his exhale. "Good. Good. That is the wisest. There would be no peace in this household otherwise. Let us give it a couple of days and see if it turns up. In the meantime, I will speak with Thatcher."

"Thank you, sir," Mrs. Hill said, then hobbled away to attend to her tasks.

Papa picked up his paper, commenting under his breath, "When it rains, it pours."

A sabotaged carriage, an interrupted wedding service, Lydia's sudden appearance, Mr. Collins' sighting of Mr. Wickham, Miss Bingley's threats, and now, Mama's treasured tablecloth was missing. Elizabeth wondered — and dreaded — what other excitement awaited.

CHAPTER 21

*D*arcy continued to the inn, not eager to cross his aunt but risking an encounter for the information he required. The innkeeper and barmaids were the best sources regarding the comings and goings in and around Meryton — if not through an eyewitness than through the gossip over cups which always made its way there.

The innkeeper, however, while eager to inquire how best to satisfy the demands of his difficult guest, had nothing to share about Wickham.

With a pause and a glance at the stairs leading to his aunt's rooms, Darcy decided not to engage with her in battle while a foe ran free over the countryside.

He inquired next at the stables, but while the proprietor admitted to seeing Wickham the day of the wedding, he was also certain he saw Wickham leave for

London on the back of a farmer's cart shortly afterward.

Next, Darcy asked at the shops. Wickham was incapable of entering a village without running up debts. Several mentioned seeing him with Mrs. Wickham, and a few added their relief when they had then observed him leaving on the road to London soon after.

Mr. Collins must have imagined seeing Wickham.

"Thank you," Darcy said, smacking his gloves against his hand and turning to leave.

The haberdasher fiddled with the position of his spectacles on his nose. "Pardon me for saying so, Mr. Darcy, but there are plenty of places a man can stay to escape notice if he sticks to the countryside and avoids the main roads and hedgerows. Wickham was stationed here for months and could easily go unperceived."

Of course, the man was right. Wickham had done the same in London when he had "eloped" with Lydia. It had not been easy to find them, and only Darcy's knowledge of Wickham's habits and favorite haunts and constant lack of funds had led him to the hovel in which they were hiding.

Perhaps Mr. Collins' observation was useful after all.

Across the street, Darcy saw Anne and Mrs. Jenkinson leaving the apothecary's place of business.

He crossed the street. "Good day, Anne. Are you

well?" What he really wanted to know was if Aunt Catherine had calmed enough to come to her senses, but he was grateful he inquired into his cousin's welfare when he noticed how frail she appeared.

Shading her ghostly complexion from the sun, she said, "Mother is well, thank you, Darcy. Mr. Jones gave me a bottle of his fortifying tonic. It is my hope that it tastes much better than that dreadful stuff Mother's apothecary makes."

Darcy could not recall the last time he had heard Anne speak more than a fragment of a thought. He encouraged her to continue. "Oh?"

"Mr. Jones told me he adds bilberry juice to make the tonic more palatable. It sounds quite delicious." She clasped her hands together and looked down at the ground, as though expecting reproof for over speaking.

Even Mrs. Jenkinson looked uncomfortable, shuffling from foot to foot, her eyes darting everywhere and landing on no one.

Darcy was at a loss. Fortifying tonics and calming draughts were not his areas of expertise. Would that Mrs. Bennet were here. She was an authority on the subject.

Finally, Anne spoke, her voice so soft, Darcy struggled to hear her. "Mother has charged Mr. Collins to ascertain the state of Miss Elizabeth's health."

Darcy gritted his teeth. He ought to have known that Mr. Collins' concern for his cousin had nothing to do with her welfare and everything to do with his attempts to ingratiate himself to his patroness. "He is spying for her."

"She swore she would never set foot at Longbourn after her last … exchange … with Miss Elizabeth."

How could he forget his aunt's rudeness? On one hand, her conduct was shameful. On the other, her meddling had ultimately given him reason to hope … besides granting him increased patience for the Bennets' frequent breaches of propriety.

Anne leaned against Mrs. Jenkinson as though she might faint. Her eyes were too large for her small face. She looked frightened.

Darcy reached out to steady her. "Allow me to see you back to the inn."

She shook her head. "No. There is more you must know. Mother means to send for a doctor from the asylum. At the first proof of instability, she will write to the director about having Miss Elizabeth committed."

Hot fury shook Darcy. "She has not the authority."

"She will call her sanity into question, suggesting that she is a danger."

"Elizabeth is not mad."

"The mind is fragile, its workings little understood. People fear what they do not understand. If Mother calls into doubt Miss Elizabeth's sanity, if she gets others to question her welfare, if she convinces an asylum doctor to confirm her own assessment…"

Cold dread raced through Darcy, chilling him to the

bone. "Then it would not matter whether Elizabeth is sound or not. The damage would be done. Even if I could sweep her away from Hertfordshire, I could not prevent word from spreading, from ruining her and bringing ostracism upon her family."

Darcy squeezed his eyes shut and wrapped his arms around his chest. If only Elizabeth's amnesia had not been so publicly revealed, he could have covered over her injury. But there had been too many witnesses, not all of whom would protect Elizabeth's interests as he did. Mr. Collins, for one, would blab the news all over the kingdom. Miss Bingley would saturate society with her venom.

His pulse throbbed in his head. He pressed his palms against his temples, trying and failing to contain his fear. What had she said in front of Mr. Collins? Had Elizabeth revealed any weakness his aunt could use against her? He looked wildly about. God help Mr. Collins if he appeared.

"I am so sorry, Darcy. Mother will do anything to keep you from marrying your lady. I will keep watch over her to ensure her letter is not sent. It is the least I can do."

The softness in Anne's tone, her offer of help, calmed him enough to abate Darcy's murderous thoughts toward Mr. Collins. He lowered his hands, clenching them at his sides. He had always compared his aunt's shocking behavior to that of Mrs. Bennet and her youngest daughters, but this was far beyond the pale. This was cruel. Calculating. Malicious.

"Elizabeth is not insane," he said, needing Anne to believe him. Needing to strengthen his own belief.

"What matters is what the doctors believe."

Darcy scoffed. "They believe amnesia is one step from madness."

Anne nodded.

"Do you think they are right?" Darcy asked, his tone sharper than he had meant it to be.

"I hardly know what I believe. But I am convinced that you are happy with Miss Elizabeth, and I would never agree to marry you knowing that we would forever live afterward with regret." Her voice trembled.

Darcy had never heard his cousin speak with so much passion. It shamed him to realize he had never before asked her opinion. "What about you, Anne? What do you want?"

"I am resigned to being unhappy. I am ill suited to be anyone's wife, and I would have been miserable had Mother succeeded in having her way, knowing that you were capable of loving another. Perhaps, given different circumstances, I might have been allowed more freedom … the liberty to better myself…" Her sentence trailed off, her gaze far-off, as though she were in another time or place.

Anne would never be happy until she was free of her mother's influence.

Darcy felt wretched for Anne, and even more so

when she proved herself stronger than she gave herself credit for at that moment by smiling.

The clip clop of hooves and a familiar voice explained her change of expression.

"Darcy! Anne! What the devil are you doing standing out in the street?" Richard dismounted, his booming voice contrasting with the dark circles rimming his eyes and his dusty boots. Lord love Richard. He must have gone to a lot of trouble to arrive so soon. The tension coiling in Darcy's shoulders loosened. There was nobody else he trusted more than the colonel.

Nodding at Darcy, Richard bowed at Anne and Mrs. Jenkinson. "You will never guess whom I saw at the club two nights ago. Do you remember Patrick Gibbs?"

Darcy did not recall the name, but the blush blooming over Anne's face said that she did.

"The navy has been very good to him," Richard continued. "He is staying in town seeing to some business matters before he returns to the comfortable little estate he purchased."

Anne's blush deepened. "He deserves any good fortune which finds him." Clearing her throat, she added, "We ought to return to the inn before Mother wakes from her nap. She will be cross if we are gone."

Darcy nodded. "We will call later."

"Not today, I beg. Mother went to bed with a

headache. Any attempt to reason with her would be futile and make her cross."

Which would only make Anne suffer. Darcy did not wish to add to her troubles. "Very well. I will call on the morrow."

After seeing Anne to the inn, Darcy led Richard to the stables where his horse waited, brushed and saddled.

"I came as quickly as I could, Darcy. Have you written to Georgiana?"

"The same day I wrote to you."

"Good. My mother says she has never seen Georgie more excited. She has been preparing Pemberley to receive its new mistress, her new sister."

His words jabbed Darcy's heart. "I wrote, but I did not explain in detail the cause of our delay. I did not want her to worry needlessly."

Richard met his eyes. "Needlessly? Do you wish to know why I did not arrive earlier?"

Darcy did not, but he was certain to hear it.

"I inquired amongst the doctors and surgeons in my circles, those close enough to inquire quickly, good men with a great deal of experience on and off the field. And all of them are of the same opinion." His pause added weight to what would come next. "Without exception, they agree that amnesia is one step away from insanity. I hate to say it, Darcy, but your Elizabeth is in grave danger."

Every muscle in Darcy's body tensed. He had

already lost Elizabeth once. He refused to allow it to happen again. He urged his horse onward, turning off the road before they reached Longbourn or Netherfield Park.

"Where are we going?" the colonel asked.

"Lucas Lodge." Darcy tightened his grip around the reins, the leather pressing into his palm and dulling his skin, tension stabbing through his numb body like a painful pulse warning him. Warning him not to loosen his hold lest he shatter into a million pieces.

CHAPTER 22

*A*nne held her breath and tiptoed past her mother's rooms.

"Anne! Anne, is that you?"

Sighing in defeat, Anne sucked in a lungful of air and resignation and walked into her mother's room.

"Good afternoon, Mother. Did you rest—"

"You were gone too long. Where did you go?"

Anne sat in the chair beside the bed. "Only to the apothecary's."

Mother narrowed her eyes — ever suspicious, always unhappy. "All this time? I have been awake this quarter of an hour."

"I inquired into the ingredients of the tonic, and Mr. Jones was kind enough to explain." Anne felt it best not to tell her mother she had seen Fitzwilliam and Richard. "I apologize if I took longer than you expected."

Her mother huffed. "It is no matter. I was able to attend to some correspondence while you were away." The smugness in her expression gave Anne pause.

"To whom did you write?" she asked, eager for an opportunity to intercept if Mother had, indeed, written to the asylum director as she had threatened.

"What an impertinent question! I hope I have raised you with better manners than to inquire so directly after another's personal affairs..." Mother chastised Anne for a solid five minutes on the matter, during which Anne's thoughts wandered to more pleasant pastures.

Richard had said that the navy had been good to Patrick. Mr. Gibbs. He had an estate, a cozy one, he had said. Anne hoped it was near Bath. She preferred Bath to all other places. So many fashionable people to watch, and so many events to observe, Anne could pretend she was allowed to participate. Mrs. Jenkinson had sneaked her the most delicious toasted cake from a tea shop there. If Anne tried hard enough, she could taste the sweetness on her tongue, feel it melt in her mouth.

"...Bethlem Hospital."

Anne snapped out of her reverie. "Bedlam? The palace for lunatics?"

"Do not refer to the hospital by that vulgar name. It is a respectable institution established in one of the finest buildings in London."

"The foundation is unsound. Not to mention the

horrors that ensue within its crumbling walls." Anne had seen images of the front gates, guarded by two grotesque statues made of Portland stone. Their names: Raving Madness and Melancholy Madness. She had also seen etchings portraying the barbaric treatment of the patients on the other side of the palatial facade. Surely, if Anne was aware of these atrocities, her mother was not ignorant.

"Nonsense," her mother huffed. "I insisted that the director send his finest physician."

Anne's heartbeat galloped. "Whatever for?"

"I do not trust Mr. Collins' account—"

"He was here?" Anne blurted boldly.

"Do not interrupt, Anne. It is most unbecoming in a young lady of your standing in society. One would think you had been too often in the company of that … that dreadful, manipulative girl."

Who was being manipulative? Anne dared ask only in her mind. Aloud, she said, "I was not aware Mr. Collins had called."

"You were away a long time."

Of course. It was her fault. Could she have prevented Mr. Collins from betraying his own kith and kin had she been present? Anne chewed on her lips, deeply troubled. Think, Anne, think. For once in your life, make yourself useful! Intercept the letter.

"What did Mr. Collins say?" she asked, probing for any useful information she might share with Darcy.

"That girl appears to be in excellent health, and he

noticed nothing untoward. But he let slip one detail of tantamount importance when he relayed that she still had not recovered her memories of Darcy. According to my discussion with Mr. Jones yesterday, she is now in grave danger of her condition deteriorating. The asylum doctor will know what to do with her."

"Where is the letter?" Anne asked.

"Mr. Collins posted it for me already."

Anne gasped. "Mother, that was presumptuous of you. I beg you not to interfere." If the post coach had not left already, she might be able to retrieve it before it was too late.

"And see you unmarried while Darcy attaches himself to that headstrong girl with a scandalous family? She will sully the Darcy name. I am only doing this for your benefit and that of our family. Darcy does not see it now, but he will thank me later."

Anne struggled to find the right words, her shock at her mother's aggressive coldheartedness astounding. "But what of Miss Elizabeth? You would send her to Bedlam merely to prevent her from marrying Darcy? He would despise me, and you would sooner find yourself cut off entirely from his association. Do you not see what you have done?"

Mother waved off her concerns as she would an irritating fly. "You do not know what is best, nor how to carry it out, Anne. Trust your betters to arrange matters." Mother smoothed the coverlet around her,

163

her lips pinched, the tremor in her hand suggesting her conscience was not completely undisturbed.

Just as Anne began to harbor hope of convincing her mother to leave Miss Elizabeth be, the great lady added, "I am under no obligation to her just as she told me in no uncertain terms that she is under no obligation to please me. She brought this upon herself, and I daresay if she is to go insane, I am doing her a favor by ensuring she is in an institution which can provide her with the care she requires."

Anne clasped the edge of her chair. "She is not insane."

"You cannot possibly know that. You know I forbid your association with that scandalous lot. Mr. Collins confirmed she does not yet remember Darcy, which bodes ill for the fragility of her mind. It is only a matter of time before she breaks completely."

"You cannot believe that." Anne certainly did not.

"I would not have written to the director unless I did, and if you had any sense at all, you would thank me for looking out for your interests."

Anne could do no such thing. Rising to her wobbly feet, grasping the back of the chair to steady herself, Anne spoke as boldly as she was capable of speaking. "I want nothing to do with the ruin of a young lady my cousin deeply loves. Think of what he has done for her already. Think of what she has done for him. His character has softened considerably in recent months. Miss Elizabeth is the cause." Proof of that was the manner in which he had spoken with Anne only minutes ago. He had never inquired after her or shown any interest in her wishes beyond what was polite and expected.

Mother smoothed the covers again. "Calm yourself, Anne, or you will fall ill. If that girl is not diseased, then no harm will be done. However, if she is altered, then I am saving Darcy from attaching himself to a woman he will have to watch go mad, who would taint everyone she touched by association. It would have been cruel of me not to interfere."

Now that her mother had justified her behavior behind an image of self-righteousness, there was no dissuading her.

Anne crossed the room without a word of dismissal, nervous energy coursing through her limbs, propelling her to run to the post. Such a scene she must have given, curls hanging limp around her face, rushing like a ruffian down the street and barging into the office. Anne cared not.

"Has the"—she gasped for breath—"post coach departed?"

The man standing behind the counter with his pen poised over a ledger regarded her over his spectacles. "I am sorry, Miss, but it left about five minutes ago."

Anne's knees buckled under her, but another woman who had been waiting her turn to be attended reached out to catch her. "A chair for the lady!" she shouted. "Hurry!"

Recovering what strength she could summon, Anne

leaned against the woman's arm until she could lean against the back wall by the door she had burst through a moment ago. "Thank you. I am well enough. I apologize for interposing." As soon as her legs could carry her, she left.

She wanted so desperately to do something, but she had no idea what. She was already too late.

CHAPTER 23

"Mr. Collins, I must insist that you leave Hertfordshire at once." Darcy crossed his arms, the mere sight of the groveling toad stirring his blood and overwhelming Darcy with the desire to strangle the buffoon.

Richard moved closer, be it to restrain Darcy should he give in to his urges or to assist in his attack, he did not know. He did not really care.

The clergyman bowed, as was his wont. "Is my cousin much improved? I said as much to Lady Catherine when she inquired—"

Flashes of red colored Darcy's vision. He prayed God witnessed his tremendous restraint and would remember him with favor should his path ever again cross with Mr. Collins in this lifetime. Speaking through clenched teeth, Darcy interrupted, "She is as well as can be expected after the trauma of her accident and the betrayal of you, sir."

"Wha—?" Mr. Collins sputtered.

"How dare you crawl at the feet of Lady Catherine when she viciously opposes your own cousin." He could not call her his aunt any longer. She was as distant to him as a stranger.

"But—"

"Do you deny it? Just as you attempted to set Lady Catherine against Elizabeth when you prattled senselessly that we were engaged, interfering where you had no right and turning her into the target of Lady Catherine's animosity?"

"Mrs. Collins' heard word about your engagement in a letter from her family."

"You would blame your wife and her family for your indiscretion?"

"Lady Catherine inquired directly—"

"And you felt it imperative to answer to her? You are a man of the cloth, Mr. Collins. You would do better to answer to God."

Mr. Collins had sense enough to clamp his mouth shut.

Darcy, however, was not quite finished. "Did you or did you not agree to spy on Elizabeth for Lady Catherine?" He heard Richard gasp beside him, and when his cousin took another step forward, Darcy was certain where his inclination leaned. He would not hold Darcy back.

"It was hardly my intention—"

"Speak plainly, man," growled the colonel, his hand at his hip. He did not wear a sword, but the effect was the same.

Mr. Collins squeezed his eyes shut, too cowardly to face them. "Not a spy. A mediator. Like Moses."

"What did you tell Lady Catherine?" Darcy pressed.

"Only the truth. That Cousin Elizabeth does not yet remember you but appeared in every other way as healthy and sane as she ever was." He peeked through the slits of his eyes, raising his hand to his throat and sighing as though relieved to find his head still attached.

He ought to be grateful. Not since Ramsgate had Darcy felt so murderous. Only his care for Georgiana had restrained him from calling out George Wickham.

Stabbing his finger into the center of Mr. Collins' cravat, Darcy said, "If Lady Catherine acts against Elizabeth, if she does anything to distress her, I will hold you as accountable as I will hold Her Ladyship. Your punishment will be swift and thorough."

Darcy spun away from the clergyman to the horses and galloped off as soon as his seat hit the saddle, needing distance from that despicable excuse of a relative and determining to foot the cost of breaking the entailment on Longbourn to sever all ties between the Bennets and that deferential sycophant. It must be done. If there was a way — and in archaic legal matters, there always was — he would find it.

His blood cooled to a canter when Netherfield Park came into view and to a walk by the time they reached Bingley's gravel drive.

"You are decided to end all association with Lady Catherine?" Richard asked. He was perceptive.

"Had she attacked me, I would bear it, but she aims her strikes at Elizabeth. If I am unwilling to put my betrothed's protection before the wishes of my family, then I do not deserve her love and my vows would be reduced to a lie."

Richard nodded, dismounting and tossing his reins to the stable boy, his steps slowing as they neared the front steps. "You said in your message that she does not remember you." He stopped, his hand gripping Darcy's. "I hate to ask, but how can you be certain she loves you if she cannot even remember you?"

Because I love her enough for both of us. Because if she does not, I would feel her loss like a death. Because I refuse to give up on her while there is yet hope. And I will always hope for Elizabeth. Darcy continued up the stairs, the words too painful, his throat too tight to speak them aloud.

Bingley strode out to them, his arms wide. "Colonel! I am delighted to see you!"

They clapped each other on the back, their greeting dampened by the gravity Darcy could not shake. He strode toward the stairs, intent on his mission to write to his man of business regarding the termination of the entail.

"Darcy, a moment, please," Bingley called after him.

The colonel cautioned, "Best allow him to cool down. He came this close to bashing a brethren."

Bingley coughed and convulsed, waving his hand at them while he recovered from his shock. "All the same, you will want to see what was delivered while you were away. Sent from Dr. Chambers."

That caught Darcy's immediate attention.

"I had the porters set it in the front parlor," Bingley added, stepping into the room and handing the letter laying on top of the large, wooden crate to Darcy.

Darcy tore the paper in his haste to break the seal. Inside was a drawing of the contents of the crate, along with instructions regarding its use. His doctor's handwriting filled both sides of the folded paper, and tucked inside was another letter from a Mr. Giovanni Aldini, who claimed to be the inventor of the device.

He read the instructions while Bingley rang for a servant and Richard impatiently pried off the lid. Shoving the packing aside, littering straw over the Turkish rug, Richard and Bingley stood over the crate, jaws open and speechless.

Having seen the illustrations and read the meticulous instructions, Darcy thought he was prepared to see the mechanism.

He was wrong.

A thick leather strap held with a silver buckle protruded with wires like the legs of a squid he had seen as a boy at an exhibition. The strange sea creature had given him nightmares for months. This machine, which was connected to a coiled rod, was rigged to send electrical charges into the brain. Transcranial electrical stimulation.

Was *stimulation* a kinder word for *shock*? The rough leather straps, crude wires, and bulky, rigid rods belonged inside Bedlam, not Bingley's cheerful cream and yellow front parlor.

"This produces the 'spark of life?'" Darcy asked incredulously.

Richard swallowed hard. "What do we know of this thing? Of its ... creator?"

Bingley mumbled. "Blast if I know, but I have seen this before."

Darcy shuffled through the papers. "Giovanni Aldini is the creator. An Italian physician and physicist, former professor of physics at Bologna, and currently residing in London ... with strong ties to the Royal College," Darcy answered, repeating the first paragraph of Mr. Aldini's letter wherein he had established his credentials and handing the bulk of the papers to Richard for further examination.

"I remember!" Bingley exclaimed, snapping his fingers. "His uncle was the one who did all of those experiments on dead frogs. I never saw it myself; it was before my time, you know, but my uncles took an interest in his machinery." More finger snapping. "Galvanizing ... Galvinate ... Galvani! Galvani was the uncle's name."

Richard rifled through the papers, reading aloud,

"Dr. Luigi Galvani, Italian physician, physicist, biologist, philosopher, and member of the Academy of Sciences. Aldini's uncle."

"Ha! And sworn enemy of Volta," proclaimed Bingley, waving a finger in the air and very clearly enjoying his moment of superior knowledge.

Darcy's brow furrowed. Volta. He knew that name. "The inventor of the battery — Alessandro Volta?"

"One and the same." Bingley rocked back on his heels and up to his toes.

Richard raised his eyebrows. "You are quite the expert. What else can you tell us about this Aldini and his confounded contraption?"

Twirling to the door, leaning out and looking both ways, Bingley quietly closed the barrier behind him. "Just in case," he whispered.

Darcy and Richard exchanged a worried look.

"I do not wish to disturb Jane," he explained further, heightening Darcy's apprehension.

Rubbing his hands together, Bingley began, "Aldini's uncle discovered what he called 'animal electricity.' He did several experiments where dead frogs appeared to come to life when attached to his machine. As you can imagine, this caused quite a stir and earned him a bevy of critics and enemies.

"Ever the loyal nephew, and having taken an interest in his uncle's experiments, Aldini moved beyond frogs' legs to reanimate larger livestock. Given the opportunity to observe the grotesque, people flocked to his laboratory to watch. He was all the rage."

A shiver shook Darcy to his feet. Grotesque, indeed.

"But his story gets better!" Bingley declared.

Richard grimaced, Darcy groaned, and Bingley continued chattering like an excited schoolboy.

"He soon began experimenting on human bodies. He would go to the Piazza Maggiore, wait for the executioner, and cart his beheaded prisoner back to his laboratory. Is it not the stuff of a gothic chapbook?"

Darcy questioned the soundness of his physician for sending this monstrous device.

"Unfortunately for Aldini," Bingley continued, "his battery depended on body fluids to work, and the cadavers would be bled out by the time he reached his laboratory. He needed a corpse with a head."

Glancing at the door to make certain it remained closed, Darcy mumbled, "That was how he came to England? The promise of whole cadavers?" He shivered again, his stomach twisting.

"Exactly! Unlike our friends on the continent, who beheaded their criminals, England disposes of their criminals more … civilly. He would hang around"— Bingley chuckled—"Dear me, not *that* kind of hang."

"Of course not," Richard agreed dryly.

"He *dawdled* around the gallows," Bingley said, "befriending the executioners so that they would hand over the bodies once their feet stopped twitching."

Darcy shook his head at Bingley. Seeing how

animated his amiable, sweet-tempered friend became over the macabre forced him to see Bingley in a whole new light.

"What is the matter Darcy?" Richard teased. "Aldini only did what any self-respecting doctor in need of dead patients would do."

Bingley nodded. "That was how he chanced upon George Foster." He glanced at the door, dropping his voice. "I saw it myself, though my uncle swore me to secrecy. Said my mother would stab him with all of her sewing needles if I let it slip he had taken me with him."

Darcy had heard quite enough, but Bingley was on a roll.

"It was mid-January, just before the start of Hilary Term. I remember as clearly as if it were yesterday. The day was cold, but the room was stifling. Word had spread that the executed criminal was to be delivered to the Royal College of Surgeons. Quite a procession followed the porters inside. I had to stand on my toes to see anything. Strangers pressed all around, everyone staring at the body on the table. A few fainted."

Pulse racing, Darcy hung onto Bingley's every word. He had read about the spectacle in the papers years ago — Though the details had faded over time, who could completely forget such a sensational story? — but Bingley's eyewitness account was more enthralling.

"Aldini connected Foster to the machine, and I swear on my life that what I am about to tell you is the honest truth. Foster's jaw quivered and his face twisted and contorted. I nearly lost my breakfast when his left eye popped open and he looked straight at me. I swear I saw him take a breath before his hand raised into the air as though he proclaimed victory over death, then did a celebratory jig before the battery died … and he died … again. It was a miracle. That was what the doctors called it, and I believe them."

"That is quite a story," Richard said, rubbing his chin. "Chambers says Aldini has used this machine with great success treating melancholia and amnesia. He guarantees it is safer and less painful than other brain stimulation methods."

Bingley, much more subdued, cleared his throat and rubbed his chin, too. "If the battery could spark a man back to life for a time, it is capable of resurrecting Elizabeth's memories."

Darcy clutched his stomach. "I cannot expect Elizabeth to try this." He peered down at the unwieldy apparatus symbolizing Elizabeth's most promising treatment. This was the best modern science and medicine could do? He shook his head, voicing his decision before he changed his mind. "I will test it first."

Richard gaped at him. "You mean to strap that contraption to your head?"

"How can I ask Elizabeth to if I am unwilling to try it first? We have the instructions. It does not appear difficult." Darcy said, sounding more stoic than he felt.

Bingley took a deep breath. "Allow me, Darcy. I am

not near as clever as you are and will hardly notice if any damage is done if the machine malfunctions."

"You are a braver man — and a better friend — than, I, Bingley," mumbled Richard, studying the pages in his beefy hands.

Bingley was a good friend — the best — but Darcy could not accept his gallant offer. Elizabeth would never forgive him if his machine harmed her sister's new husband, nor would he be able to forgive himself.

No. He was decided. He would be the first patient ... or victim.

"Are you well, Darcy?" Richard asked for the twenty-sixth time since setting out from Netherfield.

Mrs. Bingley pressed her lips together and discreetly looked down. Once she realized what they were up to, and Bingley gave her a splendidly edited account of the machine and how it came to be in her parlor, she had insisted on joining them.

Bingley, too, watched him from the other side of the carriage. They had taken Darcy's horse away, forbidding him from riding the short distance. Which explained his foul mood ... in part.

He scowled. "If I were not completely well, we would not be on our way to Longbourn with that ... thing."

Bingley and Richard shared a look, their shoulders

shaking and their guffaws loud. Addle pated jackanapes. Darcy glared at them for good measure, taking solace in anger when his stomach tied in knots the closer the carriage drew to Longbourn. He had bigger concerns than his strong reaction to the incredible machine.

Would Richard find Elizabeth changed? Would she remember him?

Descending from the carriage, seeing the crate safely settled in front of the door, Darcy prayed for a miracle. Lively chatter and laughter burst through the door when it opened. Someone played the pianoforte, and judging from the liveliness of the tune, Darcy knew it was Elizabeth. What she lacked in technical skill, she more than made up for with charm and enthusiasm.

She rose from her piano stool as soon as they were announced, and Darcy waited with bated breath for her reaction. Did she recognize Richard?

Picking a path around the overly furnished room, she held out her hands, a warm smile reflecting in her rosy face. "Colonel Fitzwilliam! How wonderful to see you."

Darcy's breath exhaled in a slow hiss. How could Elizabeth remember the colonel, a man she had only met briefly at Hunsford, and not remember him?

CHAPTER 24

*E*lizabeth was ecstatic. Colonel Fitzwilliam wore plainclothes, and she had recognized him without the advantage of his uniform. She greeted him like the harbinger of promise he represented.

She heard Jane, Mr. Bingley, and Mama in the hall along with a great deal of scuffling, but Fitzwilliam entered the room then. It was difficult to pay attention to anyone else when Fitzwilliam occupied her every sense.

At first glance, Fitzwilliam looked much the same. Polished, pressed, and perfect. She breathed in his sandalwood shaving soap, felt the warmth of his gaze on her. She searched his face for memories. His hair was slightly rumpled, his eyes haggard. Had sleep abandoned him as it had her?

More than anything else in the world, she wished she could lie and tell him she remembered. That she was safe from danger, and her heart was wholly his again. Elizabeth believed herself capable of loving this man fully, but the past — their past — evaded her.

"I brought something for you," he said, gesturing out to the hall.

Jane peeked inside. "The crate is in the dining room if you wish to set up the machine."

"Machine?" Elizabeth asked.

"A transcranial electrical stimulator, to be precise," offered the colonel.

"Come have a look, Lizzy. Its appearance is dreadful, but I saw how it worked … the effects of it, at least … and found it quite"—Jane's vision swiveled to Fitzwilliam, and she had to bite her lips before she could continue—"remarkable."

The colonel chuckled. "Darcy would never have brought the contraption if he thought it could harm you."

Their defense of the thing made Elizabeth more cautious.

Jane waved her into motion. "Come see for yourself, Lizzy. Mr. Darcy will explain."

Elizabeth listened closely as they walked down the hall to the dining room. Apparently, the machine involved straps and electricity designed to stimulate the dormant memories trapped in her brain.

Terrifying … and tempting.

Fitzwilliam must have read her doubtful expression. He added, "It came recommended by my family's personal physician and has been used successfully to treat other patients suffering from inflictions of the mind." He pulled a letter out of his pocket and handed it to her. "This was written by the inventor. He enumerates his credentials, and he was kind enough to provide a list of cases in which he was able, with the use of this machine, to assist several individuals to full recovery."

She read the pages and studied the drawings, hesitation gripping her until she came up from her consideration and saw Fitzwilliam's anticipation plainly etched on his face. He had gone to so much trouble and expense for her. But she was nervous.

She could not yet bring herself to look inside the crate sitting atop the table, knowing her courage might falter unless she was firmly decided first. "It does not hurt?" she asked.

Mr. Bingley snorted, hiding behind his hand and receiving a rare — most likely, his first — disapproving look from Jane.

Nobody seemed eager to reply, which was strange. It was a simple question, and their hesitation was confusing as the scowl on Fitzwilliam's face and the poorly contained merriment of Mr. Bingley and the colonel led her to conclude that he was the brunt of their joke. She did not imagine Fitzwilliam was the sort of gentleman who enjoyed being laughed at. Few were.

Jane spoke. "From the little I observed, it is quite

harmless. Merely ... tickles ... is that not so, Mr. Darcy?"

He cleared his throat, pulling himself up to his full height. "Aside from the awkwardness of the strap, I felt no discomfort at all. To the contrary, in fact. It gave me a euphoric sensation."

Colonel Fitzwilliam guffawed. "I should say so! You smiled wider than I have ever seen and laughed longer than I have ever heard. Had you not been strapped down, you would have taken flight!"

Even Jane sniggered, but Elizabeth paid them no heed. Fitzwilliam bore their laugher heroically, embarrassment tinging his cheeks, and convincing her of her course in a heartbeat. "You tried it?" she asked. "For me?"

"I had to make certain it was safe." He shrugged, as if his thoughtfulness did not mean the world to Elizabeth. She would have kissed him right then, but there were too many spectators, including her mother, who would march them to the church before noon to marry at the slightest display of Elizabeth's growing affection.

She understood what it meant to feel cherished then. Fitzwilliam had shown her. "Thank you," she said through her smile.

He laughed. "I made a proper fool of myself, grinning and giggling like a fool."

"That was nothing!" Bingley dabbed at the corners of his eyes, his complexion bright red. "It was when you leaped about the front parlor, asking if the altitude of your jump was higher than before."

"All you needed to do was flap your wings to take off!" Colonel Fitzwilliam doubled over, laughing so hard he cried along with Mr. Bingley.

Jane hid behind her hands, but her shoulders shook.

Fitzwilliam must have given them quite a performance.

While Elizabeth loved nothing more than to laugh at the weakness of others, she could not laugh at Fitzwilliam. Filling her lungs with a deep inhale, she stepped forward and peered inside the crate. "I will do it."

Her words had the precise effect she had calculated. The teasing ceased.

But her defense did more than that. Fitzwilliam regarded her with appreciation … and pride. It was a heady sensation, and had Elizabeth not known that her thoughts put into action would not be understood as mockery, she would have given into the temptation to jump around the room, flapping her arms for good measure. She did not need a machine to feel euphoric, she only needed Fitzwilliam's approval.

Elizabeth did not know when he had gained possession of her hand. He brushed his lips over her fingers, tickling her skin and shooting sparks up her arm. Electric.

Dropping her hand and spinning away from her before she was ready, Darcy unpacked the crate while

Elizabeth leaned against the papered wall to steady herself.

Her father studied the papers, and Jane explained the function of the pieces splayed over the table waiting for Fitzwilliam to assemble them to Mama, Mary, Kitty, and Lydia, who had since joined them.

Elizabeth did not wish to be a spectacle, but she understood their curiosity. She silenced her reserve and allowed her hope to soar. If the contraption worked as Mr. Aldini claimed it had for so many others, it was certain to help her when she only needed to remember one person.

Papa pulled his chair out at the head of the table, patting the cushion. "Here you are, Lizzy."

Aside from a large strap the width of her forehead, the assembled machine was not as terrifying as she had feared. So long as she did not dwell on the many wires secured to her head through which pulses of stimulating shocks would flow between her and the rod which resembled a candlestick.

"That is the battery," Fitzwilliam said, pointing to the rod.

She nodded, gripping the edge of the chair and reminding herself to breathe.

Papa placed his hand on her shoulder. "Sit still, and relax, now."

Mama fanned her face, leaning against Colonel Fitzwilliam. He and Jane reassured her while her sisters looked on in awe. Lydia went so far as to fetch her nerve tonic should they require it. Elizabeth was tempted to ask for a drink.

Elizabeth heard the battery behind her hum, and before she could ask anything else about the machine or request more assurances from Fitzwilliam, she was filled with such a pleasant sensation, she exclaimed in surprise, startling the too many occupants in the room.

Fitzwilliam was at her side immediately, his fingers on the buckle.

She raised her hand. "No, please do not stop the machine. It only took me by surprise." More than that, she could not say. Closing her eyes, Elizabeth floated and flew, swooped and twirled. The tension in her body released from her shoulders, melting down her legs to her toes and leaving her as light as a feather and more content than she had believed possible.

Elizabeth yielded herself to the device, allowing it to stimulate the recesses of her mind where her memories of Darcy lay. She attempted to think back, to relive her first meeting with Fitzwilliam, but the happiness overtaking her only allowed for the most pleasant thoughts. So, she daydreamed of Fitzwilliam, attempting to discern whether her musings were mere woolgathering or actual recollections — she felt too well to care.

She could have remained thus all day, but eventually the humming of the machine came to a halt.

Only when her father's face loomed in front of her did Elizabeth realize how widely she grinned. She must look a fool, but it was a small price to pay for her memories.

"What a marvelous contraption," Papa said. "You did not feel any discomfort, I surmise?"

Fitzwilliam carefully lifted the headpiece from her head, and Elizabeth patted her curls into place. "Not at all. It was invigorating. I have never felt more calm or more contented. It truly is an amazing invention." She still gripped the sides of her chair, but her motive was drastically different. She would have floated up to the ceiling otherwise, as crazy as that sounded.

Papa fiddled with his spectacles. "Do you think this battery will last a few more uses?"

Mama pushed Elizabeth out of the chair, plopping herself down. "I am next," she declared, waving her feet in front of her to prevent Lydia from shoving her out of the chair to claim the next treatment.

Fitzwilliam stood near, watching, silent.

The colonel clapped him on the back. "Let us see if the contraption stimulated more than pleasant feelings. Do you remember the topic of your discussion with this man when you stayed in with a headache and Darcy called at Hunsford Cottage?"

Eight sets of eyes turned to her (thirteen counting the servants standing just outside the door jostling for position).

Elizabeth smiled, her gaze fixing on Fitzwilliam. "We discussed…" Like a heavy door, her mind slammed shut, leaving her in the dark. She squinted her eyes, praying her tongue would continue where her mind was unable. "We discussed…"

Her heart lurched into her throat, her stomach dropped, and she crashed to the ground, scraped, bruised, crushed.

She closed her mouth, pressing her icy fingers against her burning eyes, her disappointment cruel after the heights to which she had allowed her hope to soar.

CHAPTER 25

*D*arcy clutched his fist into his stomach. It was still there, churning nauseatingly.

The machine had not worked.

Pinching his eyes closed, Darcy saw a picture of Elizabeth's emotions, displayed transparently on her beautiful face, transforming from elation to dismal disappointment. What he would give to forget that look. To turn back time and spare her another defeat.

Guilt battled with his need to comfort. He could not look at her, but he needed to offer his touch.

Her hands wrapped around his, warm and forgiving. "I will try the machine as many times as it is safe to use. Until the battery dies."

Darcy's chest tightened, too small for his heart. Raising her palm to his lips, he tenderly kissed her exposed flesh, felt her tremble, shared it. Her body remembered what her mind had erased, and Darcy grasped onto that small shard of gleaming hope with all the enthusiasm of an unrequited lover.

Placing her hand in the crook of his arm, he asked, "Care to join me for a stroll by the pond?"

She tugged him toward the door in reply, accompanied by the sound of Mrs. Bennet's glee.

"Papa will thank you for introducing us to Mr. Aldini's stimulator, if not for my sake then for my mother and sisters," Elizabeth teased.

HIs smile came easily. "My purpose is to please."

She tilted her chin up, gravity overwhelming coquetry. "What if I never remember? What then?"

"You will."

"You have said that before, but we cannot be so certain now. Too much time has gone by, and every minute that passes lessens my chances of ever recovering my memories of you … and increases the likelihood of madness."

Her words punched him in the gut, grabbing his insides and twisting. His step faltered. He could not breathe.

Elizabeth stopped, reaching up to stroke his cheek with her fingers. "I wish to deny the possibility as much as you do, but we must think rationally. I could not burden you with such a prospect."

"And I cannot do without you," he turned to face her, stepping closer and closer and closer until she was in his arms and all he could smell was the rosewater in her hair. Her fingers tickled a trail from his cheeks to the back of his neck, pulling him closer still, standing on her toes. Closer.

Darcy was powerless to resist. He captured her lips, and Elizabeth leaned into him, her fingers tangled in his hair, their hearts beating in harmony. She reciprocated his affection with an enthusiasm that left Darcy discomposed. Sky blended with grass, night seeped into day, and the only certainty was the woman he held in his arms.

They stood toe-to-toe, catching their breath, Elizabeth's hands pressed against the lapels of his coat. "You will have to marry me now, Fitzwilliam."

His breath caught in his throat. She had been calling him Mr. Darcy since their wedding day. If a kiss was the cure, why had he not kissed her sooner? "Elizabeth?" he asked. It was all he could ask.

She shook her head slowly, sinking down to the bench by the pond. "No memories yet, Fitzwilliam, but I consider myself most fortunate to have experienced a first kiss twice." She pushed against him, teasing, "Do not tell me we have not kissed before, for I would not believe you."

He had no desire to correct her … or lie. They had enjoyed numerous conversations — and several stolen kisses — under the willow tree. "I am relieved. For a moment, I thought you were trying to call off our engagement, and I would have had to object."

"Like Lady Catherine?" Her eyes glinted mischievously.

"I can be persuasive."

She hummed. "I believe that. But I will spare you the effort. I would be the worst fool to deny myself more of your kisses."

A pony and cart rambled down the lane, turning down the path to Longbourn.

Elizabeth popped up to her feet. "That is Dr. Sculthorpe! Fluffy, white whiskers and a jolly, round face. It is him! He has not changed at all."

Darcy followed her to the house, trying not to resent the doctor's poor timing when he was their best, and last, recourse.

Mr. Bennet waved from the door, meeting his friend by the cart. "Sculthorpe, my good fellow! It has been a long time."

"Too long!"

"I hope you had a pleasant trip. Are you well?"

The doctor's cheeks shone like freshly picked and polished apples. "There will be time enough to catch up, Bennet. Where is this daughter of yours?" His eyes landed on Elizabeth as Mr. Bennet introduced Darcy to the physician.

Sculthorpe bowed elegantly. "The forgotten betrothed. I am glad you are here, sir, as I shall require your assistance." He clucked his tongue, his stomach bobbing up and down as he chuckled. "Ah, Lizzy, you must have hit your head very hard to forget such a fine gentleman. Fear not, dear girl, we will soon put you right."

Darcy liked him immediately, but experience (and his own nature) made him cautious. "Where did you attend medical school?" he asked.

"The University of Edinburgh, many moons ago. And a stint at St. Bart's."

"Highly regarded institutions," Darcy owned. "Have you enjoyed a burgeoning practice since?"

The doctor's stomach shook again. Up down up down up down. "Perhaps not as burgeoning as my peers." He fell in beside Darcy, following Mr. Bennet inside the house, adding, "While I believe much experience is to be gained from a regular medical practice, I admit to a weakness of curiosity. A good deal of my time is spent pursuing the reasons behind popularly accepted treatments." He stopped outside the door. "You see, Mr. Darcy, just as you are skeptical about me — and justifiably so — I do not so easily trust common methods unless they can be proved scientifically. My investigations and findings have put me in high demand at the universities that invite me to present lectures. But, alas, I am an old man, and find it more comfortable to settle at Cambridge and continue my experiments from my nearby residence. As you can understand, this does not allow much time for me to attend to patients."

Darcy had one more question, then he would be satisfied. "What is your opinion on Bichar's Law of Symmetry?"

The same twinkle Darcy had often observed in Mr.

Bennet appeared in Dr. Sculthorpe's eyes. He leaned forward, lowering his voice. "Hogwash. Trite twaddle. A pretty theory which defies all common sense. Do you know, Mr. Darcy, how Bichat perished?"

"No."

"Of a head injury."

Mr. Bennet and Elizabeth had turned to listen in the entrance. They both gasped, as did Darcy.

The doctor continued, "And yet doctors continue to spread his nonsense, bashing their patients over the heads and collecting a fee for their exertion when any mean-spirited drunk would perform the service free of charge."

Darcy could not contain his laugh. This man was marvelous.

"I am grateful to have avoided such a painful outcome. Mr. Darcy would not let Mr. Jones near me once he suggested the treatment," said Elizabeth.

Smile reaching his eyes, Dr. Sculthorpe smacked Mr. Bennet on the shoulder. "I see you are to be blessed with a son-in-law with an active, highly functioning mind. I applaud Lizzy's choice and your good sense being willing to part with her for such a gentleman."

Darcy bowed his head. "I apologize for my distrust, but this has been difficult enough on Elizabeth. I am desperate for her to remember me, but I will not compromise her welfare."

Dr. Sculthorpe greeted the Bennets assembled in

the drawing room. Mary and Kitty curtsied prettily, uttering the usual pleasantries.

Mrs. Bennet curtsied deeply, her manners calm and pleasant, a lady completely at ease in the world. "Dr. Sculthorpe, we hope you will stay with us as long as Cambridge can spare you. I am certain Mr. Darcy will enjoy your conversation as much as Mr. Bennet, and I have had the decanter in his study topped off in the expectation you will keep the gentlemen company and help my Lizzy. Hill will carry your things to the guest room with our new footman," she gushed. Nary a word referencing her nerves or the vexation of housing another guest. Not one anxious comment about her unmarried daughters or Elizabeth's injury.

Lydia slipped in behind them, floating into the room with a vacant smile, followed by the rest of their party.

After introductions, Dr. Sculthorpe commented on Mrs. Bennet. "I do say, your nerves have experienced a remarkable improvement."

"It is that wonderful machine Mr. Darcy brought us from a famous doctor in London," she beamed. "We will not need nerve tonic so long as we have it."

Mr. Bennet gestured to the hall. "Would you like to see it? Elizabeth tried it shortly before you arrived."

Far from scowling in disapproval, Dr. Sculthorpe rubbed his hands together. "I should love to see what is responsible for the peace that has settled over your house, Bennet."

Darcy knew the moment the doctor recognized the machine. He gasped like a child in a toy shop, rushing over to the table to pet each piece. "This is Aldini's latest machine! I have been badgering him for months to send me one. How on earth did you get him to part with this? You say it has already withstood three uses? I had heard he found a way to improve the life of the battery."

Darcy made a mental note to have his man send a special token of gratitude to his physician ... and, if Aldini could be persuaded to part with another machine, to send one to Cambridge.

The doctor was too excited to wait for replies. "One of his first patients was a farmer suffering from melancholia. And there was another, a woman who fell out of bed and could not remember her children the following day." He looked regretfully at Elizabeth. "I wish I had been present to observe your first treatment. I have only read the accounts but have yet to witness one."

"Do you have any objections to observing my second treatment on the morrow?"

He rubbed his hands together. "I would be delighted. Now, if you please, I should like to converse with you for a while in a setting where you are most comfortable."

Darcy appreciated his haste.

Elizabeth said, "If my father does not mind us disturbing his bee skip drawings and research, I can think of no better place than his study. I will ask Mrs. Hill to bring in a tray. You must be hungry."

"To the contrary, Lizzy. I stopped at the inn to refresh myself before continuing here. I did not wish to waste any time once arriving. I will, however, accept a strong cup of coffee."

Mr. Bennet led the way to his study, closing the door behind them.

Dr. Sculthorpe's questions were conversational. He asked Elizabeth about her sisters, Jane's recent marriage, of the books she had read and her favorite passages, her opinion of her neighbors ... which led to an entertaining account of Mr. Collins and her shock at learning that her best friend had agreed to marry him.

She poured coffee while the doctor continued his inquiries, his ease belying the intensity with which he took note of every comment and reaction.

Elizabeth answered with her usual wit and charm. One would never suspect she suffered from amnesia. Darcy, too, began to doubt.

Until the doctor asked about him.

She looked down at her hands, her humor gone and her wit failing to snap a clever retort.

"I see," said the doctor. Looking at Darcy, Lizzy, and Mr. Bennet individually, making certain he had their full attention, he continued, "You must understand that the mind is such a brilliantly engineered mystery, it might take some time to uncover the pieces lost."

Elizabeth's eyes teared. Her voice sounded strangled. "How is it possible for me to forget my betrothed?"

Dr. Sculthorpe nodded his head gravely. "I have personally witnessed cases where certain events or periods of time are forgotten. These cases are rare, but they do exist. Remember the mother I mentioned earlier who forgot her own children?"

"Do they ever recall their memories?" she asked.

"Some do. Some do not. I will not give you false hope. Our limited understanding of the mind limits your options for treatment. However, I will share an observation. Those who have recovered were the ones who carried on with their lives."

"What about insanity?" she pressed.

"A threat heartless doctors use to scare patients into complying with their dubious treatments and harmful methods. Or of the ignorant who place their confidence in them.

"The brain is a difficult field to study. It requires volunteers on whom to perform their experiments, and how better to accomplish their need than to encourage patients to offer themselves willingly? They surely would not do so otherwise! Nobody in their right mind would. So many minds ruined. It makes me ill to contemplate.

"These scrupulous doctors would love nothing more than to lock you up at Bedlam. You are a tempting subject, Lizzy. A sound mind such as yours would allow for experiments that have been out of their reach." He shook his head, ridding himself of his frown. "But I digress. I apologize."

Mr. Bennet said, "It must be a subject dear to you to speak with such passion. Much like my bees are to me."

Dr. Sculthorpe chuckled, his humor restored. "Then you understand. I thank you, Bennet. You always were one to enjoy deeper conversations and lively debates."

Redirecting the conversation before it settled on Mr. Bennet's beloved insects, Darcy asked, "What do you suggest to help Elizabeth?"

Looking between them, the doctor answered, "Time is a great healer. Lizzy only requires more of it."

"Is there anything I might do to help things along?"

The doctor rubbed his chin. "Now that you mention it, there is. I suggest you spend as much time as possible with each other. Emotional attachments are remembered first, then come habits, then come the specific memories of events and people. Allow Lizzy plenty of opportunity to remember, but above all, be patient."

Elizabeth stifled a laugh. "Patient? You do not know what you ask of me."

Darcy felt the same.

Mr. Bennet sighed. "There, you see? Not all is lost. We have merely been looking at this from the wrong perspective. You cannot remember the past. What of it? Mr. Darcy is here and still very much in love with you. And consider the depth of your concern, my dear. You know he is important to you, otherwise you would not trouble yourself to remember him."

Kind words, but Darcy craved hearing the words she had said when she had accepted his proposal. Those three words on which he had gladly cast his fate.

The doctor rubbed his hands together. "A love match! How delightful! I have never been so fortunate to fall in love more than once. No woman of my acquaintance could surpass my craving for knowledge. However, you are in the unique position of falling in love twice — with the same man!"

Darcy felt as though he had been given a gift. A new purpose. From this moment on, he would no longer fret over the forgotten past. A far more important task awaited. He had a lady to woo.

CHAPTER 26

*W*ickham paced behind the carriage house. Would Darcy never leave? His call stretched far beyond the limits of propriety.

Figures moved on the other side of the window, and the entrance door squeaked as it swung open. Finally!

Pressing himself against the side of the outbuilding, waiting with bated breath, Wickham watched Bingley emerge with his bride, followed by the colonel. They walked to their waiting carriage, the colonel entering last and closing the door behind him.

No Darcy.

The carriage jolted forward, leaving without its fourth passenger.

Wickham smacked his fist against the brick. He would have to adjust his plans yet again. He would set the accident into motion when the household was asleep.

At dawn.

Thus decided, he waited until the stables were empty and the servants otherwise employed to grab an empty feed sack from an abandoned stall. He located the ladder, which he would return to retrieve once darkness fell.

Just an accident. Of the sort that befell people every day.

～

TOO STIMULATED FOR SLEEP, Wickham set out an easy hour before dawn, the lace tablecloth he had snagged from the line draped over his shoulder and the thick leather gloves from the gardening shed covering his hands.

Excitement heightened his senses better than the finest snuff. Every sound was crisp, clear; his vision was that of a cat, discerning shapes and shadows in the darkness.

Cautiously, he crept into the shed, the hoe balanced on top of the ladder hefted over his shoulder, and returned to the edge of the orchard, where the apple trees met the grove. The hive was quiet … for now.

Leaning the ladder against the tree Mr. Bennet had so conveniently led him to yesterday, Wickham draped the tablecloth over himself in imitation of Mr. Bennet's veiled hat and began climbing. One hand on the rung, the other holding the empty feed sack and hoe.

He would have to be quick. And precise.

Positioning the burlap under the bottom of the buzzing orb, Wickham leaned against the ladder, wielding the hoe like a sword. He could not afford to miss. Lifting his arm, his attention concentrated on his target.

Whack! Thump! The hive buzzed to life, and Wickham struggled not to lose his balance on the upper rungs of the ladder while closing the sack. Flinging the hoe to the ground, he grabbed the burlap with both hands, ignoring the angry, displaced insects hovering between the tablecloth and his exposed skin.

Heart racing, he swatted at his face before grabbing his tools and sprinting back to Longbourn.

Flinging the hoe into the garden, he blinked past his swelling eyes and burning cheeks to the side of the house.

Almost there. Almost done.

He leaned the ladder under the window and climbed. Forcing himself to calm down, he shoved his fingers under the framed glass and lifted slowly. Up up up it slid until the opening was large enough.

In one swift motion, Wickham hurled the contents of the sack inside the room and slammed the window shut. Too loud. He had to run.

Gripping the sides of the ladder, he slid down, hurling the tablecloth off him once his feet hit the ground and shoving it under a pile of hay in the shed. Flinging the ladder on top of the mound, he spun on his heel and fled to the fields, arms flailing around him until he entered the hovel.

Stings prickled his leather gloves. His hands shook so violently, it took several attempts to remove them. He could hardly believe what had happened. What was bound to happen.

Gently, he pressed his cold fingers against his eyes and cheeks, cooling the burn and soothing the swelling. He had not escaped without injury, but such was the way of an accident. A few stings would not kill him. He imagined how hundreds more of them would feel pierced into a lady's delicate skin.

Such a tragic accident.

CHAPTER 27

*E*lizabeth startled awake with an ear-shattering slam.

An insect buzzed by her temple, and she swatted at it. A buzz that did not belong in her bedchamber crescendoed, pushing all but one thought out of her mind.

Bees.

Another bee buzzed by her face, then two, three, more than she could count.

Her pulse galloped, choking her with panic.

Calm. She needed to calm herself. Bees reacted to aggression.

Shaking her head to discourage the bees from landing on her, she shrank under her covers, pulling the blankets over her and tucking the edges under firmly.

Relax. Relax and listen, she repeated to herself over and over.

She was not dreaming. The beehive in her bedchamber was not a figment of her imagination. Her father had told her that bees react to panic and abrupt movements. She needed to maintain calm and act sensibly — difficult when she felt an insect crawl down her bare arm. Muttering an apology, she wrapped her fingers around the blanket's fabric and squished the intruder, praying that it was not the queen for her father's sake.

She could shout for help.

As soon as she thought it, she knew the plan was not a good one. Whoever opened her door was certain to get stung, and the house would be infested with bees.

If she could slowly make her way to the window, she could open it and the bees would leave. She would give them plenty of time — an hour? Two? — then she would cross her room to the door and pray she had waited long enough to lift her covers.

If only her bed were closer to the door or to the window, her decision would be much easier. But her bed was in the middle, the window to the right, the door to her left.

Where was the hive? Logic told her by the window. Between her bed and the window, where someone had tossed it. On purpose.

Someone really did want her dead.

Fear squeezed the air out of her lungs, coiled in her stomach. She could not breathe. Could do nothing with the heavy blankets stifling her. She kicked her feet free, a prick and the throbbing of flesh on her ankle recalling Elizabeth to her senses.

To remove the blanket meant certain death. But she could not endure this panic and uncertainty for hours.

Risking a few more stings, she wrapped the blankets as firmly as she could around her and lowered herself to the floor. Inch by agonizing inch, she shuffle tucked shuffle tucked over to the door, feeling for the familiar grooves through the blankets. When she found the crack between the frame and the wall, she leaned against it and pounded her fist, praying the maid or Mrs. Hill would hear the muffled sound.

Elizabeth pounded until her arm fell heavy at her side, and her longing to inhale fresh air overwhelmed her.

Pressing her ear against the door, she listened. Nothing.

Calming her heart and inhaling what stagnant air she could, she pounded more. Until her body was slick with sweat.

Gasping in the stifling heat trapped with her, she listened again, crying out when she heard Mrs. Hill's heavy footstep approaching. The latch rattled and the door pressed against her, but Elizabeth leaned harder against it. "Mrs. Hill, please fetch Papa—"

"Miss Lizzy? Are you well? I cannot hear you, and

something is blocking the door." Another shove Elizabeth braced herself against.

Shouting through the covers, Elizabeth repeated, "Fetch Papa! Only Papa! There is a beehive in my room."

That, Mrs. Hill heard. She exclaimed all the way down the hall to the tempo of her swift staccato steps.

Elizabeth exhaled, leaning limply against the door, her relief draining her more than the door-pounding.

Another few minutes passed before her father tapped on the oak barrier. "Lizzy, I am here. You say there is a beehive in your room?"

"Yes. Do not attempt to open the door," she shouted.

A moment of silence, then, "I will have to extract the hive from outside. Can I reach the hive from the window?"

"I cannot see past the blankets protecting me." She wrapped her hand around her throat. Her voice would give out soon.

"No matter, my dear girl. Stay where you are. Do not move. I will extract the hive."

She waited and waited. And waited. Hours passed, or what felt like hours, when finally, she heard a thud from the other side of her room. The ladder. She thought she heard her father grunting and imagined him reaching for the hive, protected with coarse, white canvas and gauzy bridal lace. Her hero.

He mumbled the entire time, his soft voice soothing his precious subjects of study and her nerves … until her fear abated, allowing space to return to more sinister realizations.

Fitzwilliam had been right to worry about her. Papa was right.

A few stings were nothing, but hundreds were deadly.

This assault was directed at her. In her bedchamber. The carriage sabotage, while seemingly impartial, must also have been meant for her.

To keep her from marrying Fitzwilliam? Who despised her enough to want her dead?

She pondered, the buzzing dwindling as the minutes ticked. For all Elizabeth knew, a day had passed since the slam of her window startled her awake.

A tap vibrated her door. "Lizzy, I have put the hive inside my experimental skips. It is not how I hoped to attract the swarm, but the queen is alive, so there is a chance they will accept their new residence."

Was that what had taken him so long? Elizabeth rolled her eyes. "Is it safe?" she asked, her voice hoarse.

"You will need to allow me inside to look."

Elizabeth inched away from the door, feeling the edge press against her and hearing the brush of her father slipping through the narrow opening, then the click of the door to the passage closing. Still, she waited to remove the blanket. "Is it safe?" she repeated.

"If you are calm, I would say so. There are only a dozen or so more bees remaining to find their way through the window. Did you suffer many stings? I brought wax and liniment."

Slowly, she pulled the blanket over her head, her first breath tasting like heaven and reviving her wilted limbs.

Papa held the melted candle over the feverish red bumps on her feet, pouring the wax and blowing on them before peeling away the trapped stingers. The liniment wreaked of camphor, but Elizabeth would have bathed in it for the relief it provided.

"You were fortunate," he said. "Only five stings. Do you feel any others? I can send for Mrs. Hill to help you."

"No. That is all of them." She had had plenty of time to feel for painful bumps.

He cupped her chin in his cold hand, not saying anything, just looking at her.

Tears burned Elizabeth's eyes. She tried to blink them away, feeling foolish for crying now that the ordeal was done.

Papa released her chin, wrapping his arm around her shoulders. "It would seem that Mr. Darcy was wise to be cautious. First, the carriage. And now, this … this savage attack, this … brutal attempt to murder."

A violent shiver shook Elizabeth from head to toe, and she burrowed into her father's side, seeking solace. Sanity. Safety. Was she willing to risk her life to marry a man she could not remember?

She knew the answer the instant the question crossed her mind.

Yes.

Elizabeth did not understand how her heart remembered what her mind held under lock and key. She was not certain it mattered anymore, and Elizabeth was too weak to deny admitting what she had known all along.

She had never stopped loving Fitzwilliam Darcy.

CHAPTER 28

*D*arcy was happy to see Dr. Sculthorpe's cart sitting beside the Bennets' recently repaired carriage in the shed. The doctor had not yet departed, which meant he could oversee Elizabeth's electrical stimulation to ensure there was not an element they had overlooked.

Why did he trust the doctor? His credentials were as impressive as the other "experts" Darcy had investigated, but Dr. Sculthorpe's conclusions stood in stark contrast to the notable doctors and scientists' understanding — the very men who offered no better treatment than bashing his betrothed on the head.

That must be it. Dr. Sculthorpe was their only other option. If his theory was right, Elizabeth would suffer no permanent damage.

But if he was wrong…

Darcy clenched — his jaw, the reins, his resolve to woo Elizabeth.

"Darcy? Do you mean to sit there atop your horse all day, or are we to call?" Richard stood by Hill, Longbourn's door open to receive them.

He shook his head and dismounted. "Sorry. I was lost in my thoughts."

"I had not noticed."

Darcy wanted to wipe the smirk from his cousin's face, but he must not give in to his aggravation. He was here to court Elizabeth, not beat his insolent cousin in front of her and her family.

Dr. Sculthorpe greeted them enthusiastically. "Gentlemen! We have been expecting you."

Elizabeth looked well, though there was a strain around her eyes. Her manners were more reserved than usual. She greeted and smiled sincerely enough, but something was … off.

Richard bowed gallantly. "We are ever at your service. Do you have any progress to report?" he asked jovially, elbowing Darcy so that he bowed, too.

The doctor chuckled. "Only that I am tempted to extend my stay if Mr. Bennet does not object…" He glanced at his university chum.

"Of course, you must stay, Sculthorpe. As long as you wish. The conversation has improved dramatically since your arrival."

A belly-bouncing cackle and, "I cannot take all the credit when it was Mr. Darcy who brought you that delightful machine." He rubbed his hands together. "I do hope I will be able to observe its use today."

Elizabeth said, "Say the word, and you can have the honor of strapping the contraption to my head." Her voice was merry. Too merry.

"Delightful! Simply wonderful! I say, Bennet, I have not been this entertained in years. One day in your household is more eventful than one of those horrible gothic novels."

They laughed. Darcy did not. Tension built inside him along with the suspicion that there was something the Bennets were hiding.

Mr. Bennet cleared his throat. "Have you met with any success discovering my errant son-in-law's whereabouts?"

Richard shook his head. "He has not visited his usual haunts, and everyone of whom Darcy and I have inquired denies seeing him. I am beginning to think the rascal really did depart for London, and Mr. Collins requires spectacles."

Nobody laughed. Something was definitely wrong. Darcy looked to Elizabeth for answers.

She smiled at him softly, and he felt her reassurance … which meant his instincts were correct. Something had happened. Something awful enough for her to hesitate in its telling. Something requiring guarantees of well-being before it could be told.

Mrs. Bennet sent for more tea, complaining about their absent footman and shuffling her daughters around so that Miss Kitty was forced to relinquish the chair beside Elizabeth. Her ability to arrange circumstances to her daughters' favor so quickly was admirable, and when she offered him the chair, Darcy was pleased to accept.

Once the tea was brought in and steaming in their respective teacups, Elizabeth began, "It has been a rather eventful morning for us. First, I will assure you that I am well."

In Darcy's haste to set the tea on the table, he sloshed the scalding liquid onto the saucer.

She rested her hand on his forearm. "I am well, and I need you to listen calmly before I will continue."

He nodded his head, his foresight of what was to come offering little consolation and feeling anything but calm and growing increasingly agitated as Elizabeth told them about a second attempt on her life — for Darcy was now convinced that the carriage accident had been directed at her.

When she described the bee stings, he looked her over from head to foot, only then noticing that she wore wraps on her feet where slippers — or her favorite half boots — ought to have been.

He would kill the fiend who did this.

She squeezed his arm, having not removed her hand during the whole narrative. "I do not think Lady Catherine could have done this, but who else hates me enough to murder me in my bed? Miss Bingley departed for London, and it seems that Wickham is away as well." Her brow furrowed. "And even if he were here, why would he stretch his hand out against *me*?"

All eyes turned to Lydia, who shrugged. "How should I know?" She rubbed her stomach and asked for another slice of cake, earning the footman another demerit in Mrs. Bennet's accounts when he was not there to wait on them.

"Where is he off to?" she mumbled.

Darcy knew she referred to the missing footman, but he was more concerned about the missing ne'er-do-well, Wickham. There were too few suspects to dismiss him so readily. He caressed Elizabeth's hand and stood. "The colonel and I will ride over every inch of the countryside. Perhaps your neighbors will assist us."

Mr. Bennet rose. "I will accompany you."

"If it is agreeable to you," Darcy replied, "I would be much easier of mind if you would stay with Elizabeth. We dare not leave the ladies without protection with a murderer about." He glanced at Mrs. Bennet, but she did not flutter and sway. Nor did she produce her fan or complain of nerves. She had not even opposed Mr. Bennet's offer of assistance.

Mr. Bennet sat. "That suits me better than having my bones rattled and my organs jostled out of their proper place. But do you really think Lizzy is still in danger so long as she stays indoors and away from the windows? The villain could easily assume the worst, negating the need for any further attack."

"I am not tempted to walk on these swollen feet," Elizabeth said. "I think I shall stay indoors today." As though it were a choice.

Darcy loved her spirit, recognizing how shaken she must be to agree to stay in when she always preferred the out of doors and expressing herself in such a way as to dispel his anxiety.

Heavy boots squeaked over the floorboards, and Mrs. Hill appeared, dragging the poor, wincing footman with her by the ear.

"Mrs. Hill, shall we speak in the kitchen?" offered Mrs. Bennet in a shocking display of propriety.

"I dare not release my hold lest he slip away again. Neglecting his duties sneaking around the house, he was, and the state of his livery." Mrs. Hill's frown deepened as she glared at his grass-stained stockings, sweat-drenched shirt, and dust-coated shoes.

Twisting himself out of her grip, the footman stepped forward. "I found Mrs. Bennet's tablecloth, sir."

Mrs. Bennet sat taller in her chair, all attention. "Where is it then?"

The young man bowed his head. "I am sorry to tell you it is ruined."

Sinking back into her chair, the matron merely said, "Oh." No wails or fan-waving. Truly, that machine was a miracle worker.

Mr. Bennet raised his eyebrows, a glint of admiration in his eyes as he flicked his gaze away from his wife and back to the footman. "Where did you find it?"

Clutching his hands together, the young man replied, "You told me to keep an eye out after the carriage, so I took to walking about the house before nightfall. To ensure no strangers lurked about."

Mr. Bennet nodded, encouraging him along. "Is that when you found the tablecloth?"

The footman continued, "One night, I saw footprints and packed dirt behind the carriage house. It got me thinking."

"A fine occupation I always encourage," commented Mr. Bennet.

"I thought that maybe the man who cut the axle was the man I mistook for Mr. Hill the morn of the wedding."

Mrs. Hill gave up all pretense of pinching his ear, and Mr. Bennet kept his quips to himself.

"This morning, such a feeling of dread overtook me, I could not sleep. Not knowing what to do, but needing to do something, I swept the flagstones and filled the buckets. Mrs. Hill likes it when I do that."

Nodding her head, Mrs. Hill looked up at him proudly. Clearly, the way to her heart was through domestic work. "Please go on, Thatcher. Tell the Bennets where you found the tablecloth."

"A sound made me peek through the back door. That was when I saw a man running away from the house like the hounds were on his heels."

"Who was he? Did you see his face?" Darcy asked.

"It was Mr. Wickham."

Silence swelled in the room.

Lydia's mouth opened and closed, opened and closed, but no words spilled out. A truly miraculous machine.

"Are you certain?" Mr. Bennet asked, insisting no more on the tablecloth.

Thatcher clutched his hands together. "I am. He tried to carry on with my sister, see," he said before realizing that was not something one said in the hearing of the wife of the rake. Inclining his head apologetically, he added, "Before he married Mrs. Wickham, that is. Days before his regiment departed from Meryton. Whole days. Maybe a week."

Her flushed face twisted, and she crossed her arms tightly over her chest, her hands balled into fists, her lips pressing into a flat line. It was difficult to tell if she was mortified or enraged.

"Wickham was here," Darcy repeated to himself. To the footman, he asked, "You followed him? Did you find where he is staying?"

Glancing at Mrs. Hill, the young man continued, "I neglected my duties to follow him. I am sorry."

She patted his hand. "Do not fret over what is done. Where did you find him?"

"I followed him to an abandoned tenant hovel."

Richard jumped to his feet. "We must apprehend him immediately."

"He is not there. That is why I took so long to return."

"Then, where is he?" Richard demanded.

"I stopped following him once he reached the road. I ran after him but had to return when I grew too tired to continue."

Had Thatcher possessed the endurance of Pheidippides, Darcy had no doubt he would have run all the way to London in pursuit of Wickham.

Mr. Bennet gasped. "What would you have done had you caught him?"

Thatcher scratched his head. "I did not think that far, sir."

"Where was my tablecloth?" asked Mrs. Bennet, returning to the topic of her greatest concern. Miraculous the machine may be, but it had its limits.

"Under the hay piled in the barn. The ladder had been tossed on top of it. Mr. Hill never does that. I went to lean it against the wall and that was when I saw the lace. It was so soiled and torn, I almost did not recognize it."

Mrs. Bennet tightened her lips. "How vexing."

"I apologize for shirking my duties," finished the footman, clasping his hands in front of him and bowing his head like a man prepared to get sacked.

"Nonsense. You have been most helpful," Mr. Bennet said. "Mrs. Hill, I believe this answers some of your previous concerns regarding the lad. Make sure he gets a bath and a hearty repast. He must be exhausted,"

Mrs. Hill puffed like a pigeon. "I will see to the tablecloth and to Thatcher. He has done the family a fine service."

The young man beamed at her as she added, "You did well. Very well, indeed. Cook has a piece of plum cake for you in the pantry."

"Not anymore," a feminine voice whispered. Lydia.

Mr. Bennet chuckled. "Mrs. Hill will see that you get heartier fare, but I must ask you to take Mr. Darcy and Colonel Fitzwilliam to the abandoned hovel where you saw Wickham first. Perhaps he left a clue behind."

"Good idea," the colonel acknowledged.

It was a good idea, and had Darcy not been so reluctant to part from Elizabeth's side, he would have been more eager to agree with it.

His wooing would have to wait.

CHAPTER 29

*E*lizabeth settled herself inside her father's study, a long day ahead of her and a worn copy of *The Mysteries of Udolpho*. Radcliffe's gothic novel seemed appropriate, and given the profusion of extraordinary events in her own life of late, Elizabeth could not hope to entertain herself and pass the hours with anything less than an equally spectacular tale.

Joining the heroine and her father as they crossed the Pyrenees to the Mediterranean coast, anticipating her first meeting of her love, Valancourt, Elizabeth startled when her father touched her shoulder.

"Lizzy, Miss de Bourgh is here," he said, his expression as puzzling as his words. "She has come to call on you."

"Am I not staying indoors to avoid being seen? How am I supposed to receive callers if I am feigning to be dead?"

Papa scratched his chin. "Yes, that is inconvenient for her." He pushed his spectacles down, peeking at her over the rims. "Her manners are so agitated, I could not bring myself to tell her. She said her call is of an urgent nature, that she simply must speak with you."

"Goodness gracious." Elizabeth uncurled from her perch, setting the novel on top of the cushion to wait for her return. Pity it would not keep her seat warm. "How is our plan to keep me safe from Wickham to meet with any success if we cannot even properly fake my demise?"

"Miss de Bourgh arrived alone in a hired cart. Why would she defy propriety — and, no doubt, her mother — unless the reason for her call is of great import?"

Good points, all of them. "If you do not object, might I receive her here? With you and Dr. Sculthorpe?"

He raised his eyebrows. "She does not appear dangerous. If the lady is hiding some weapon on her person, I doubt her strong enough to lift it."

Elizabeth rolled her eyes. "If the reason for her call is so important, I would rather not be the only person to hear what she has to say. In case you have forgotten, I am not yet in full possession of my mental faculties, and I do not quite trust my memory well enough to relay the details to you later."

Papa did not laugh at her joke. Not even a smile. He patted her shoulder. "Patience, my dear girl. It will come. And perhaps Miss de Bourgh will help jog your memory."

She swallowed and blinked, regretting her poorly timed joke. "Then you had best see her in."

Miss de Bourgh did, indeed, appear agitated. Elizabeth soaked in her appearance and manners, from her drawn face and brittle frame to her cowed posture and apprehensive air. No memories resurfaced, but Elizabeth did not know if that was due to her amnesia or previous lack of conversation with the lady.

Too anxious for tea, Miss de Bourgh got straight to the point. "My mother wrote to the director of Bethlem Hospital. She has convinced herself she is doing you a service and sparing Darcy."

Sculthorpe cursed under his breath.

"Are you familiar with the gentleman?" Miss de Bourgh asked.

"It brings me no pleasure to say I am. We worked together for a time but had a falling out over methods. Dr. Slade is cold, unfeeling. He believes nothing should stand in the way of science. Not compassion. Not decency. Not human dignity."

"How convenient that I am no more, then," Elizabeth mumbled, explaining before Miss de Bourgh swooned. "I am not a ghost, nor have I gone mad. I am merely frustrated to be stuck indoors when I would rather enjoy the pleasant weather out of doors. We must allow my attacker to believe her ... or his ... latest attempt has been successful, and so I have ensconced myself in my father's book room." When her explanation did little to ease her caller's nerves, Elizabeth explained the calamities which had recently befallen them.

Miss de Bourgh's complexion paled, a feat which Elizabeth would not have believed possible had she not seen it with her own eyes. Blue and green veins crawled and pulsated under the lady's skin. "I realize my mother has given you no reason to sympathize with her and every reason to suspect she is behind these attempts, but I cannot condemn her nor deem her responsible."

Elizabeth was not so easily convinced. "Did she send her letter by post or messenger?" she asked.

"Post. Mr. Collins sent it."

Papa growled. "If Darcy does not flog his hide, I will!"

Charlotte's husband or not, Elizabeth would not spare Mr. Collins from either gentleman.

"Miss de Bourgh, you do well to defend your mother. Any loyal daughter would do the same," began Elizabeth. "However, please do not take offense if I have to wonder if she might have hired someone to interfere in her stead?"

The lady squeezed her hands together, her knuckles white. "My mother is strong-willed and overbearing, but she is not cruel."

Elizabeth was not so certain, but she would not

contradict the daughter when she had risked her mother's ire by driving to Longbourn.

"I know you do not believe me, Miss Bennet, nor would I if our roles were reversed. I have no better proof than my own word, which is as useless to you as it would be to anyone. I wish to be of assistance if I may in some small way, but I realize how unqualified I am in presuming to help you."

The tremble of sincerity in Miss de Bourgh's tone, the way she belittled herself as though she held no more esteem for herself than a frayed ribbon, stirred Elizabeth's compassion. "You do not give yourself enough credit. It took a great deal of bravery to hire a cart and drive here on your own to warn me when you have not been given leave to act independently." Elizabeth did not remember Lady Catherine clearly, but she sensed she was an imposing figure.

Miss de Bourgh smiled softly, her wide eyes glistening. "I dream of more independence." She pressed her lips together, her owlish eyes showing how deeply she regretted expressing her own opinion aloud.

Elizabeth could not allow for Miss de Bourgh to regret her boldness when she ought to be encouraged. Gesturing at the bookshelves surrounding them, she said, "Book rooms are for dreaming, Miss de Bourgh. You are in the safest place in the world."

Her caller nodded, the color of her knuckles warming to a pinker hue.

Papa took his cue. "It is also incomplete without a

cup of tea and a plate of cake. I will rouse Mrs. Hill to see what Cook has hidden from Lydia in the pantry." He caught Sculthorpe's eye and, in an effective-if-not-subtle gesture, he jerked his head toward the door.

Once they were alone, Elizabeth leaned forward, her voice light, conspiratorial. "What would you do with more independence?"

She caught a glimpse of color in Miss de Bourgh's cheeks, and for the first time, Elizabeth saw how she might have been a beauty had her health (or her mother) permitted it.

"I would take up residence in Bath and drink tea and eat cake every day at a fashionable shop where I could observe the striking frocks and outlandish styles of the ton. It is marvelous — like a living, moving painting." She blinked, looking down at her hands, the spell broken. "It is more colorful than the dark rooms at Rosings. My mother insists on drawing the curtains when I would rather see everything."

If anyone needed a reprieve from their mother, it was Anne de Bourgh. Elizabeth asked, "Do you know anyone at Bath?"

"No."

Phrasing her question so as not to be overly indelicate, Elizabeth asked, "Is there anyone who might be able to offer you a degree of independence?"

Miss de Bourgh blushed in reply.

Elizabeth was intrigued. Miss de Bourgh did know

someone — a gentleman she would wager. How very interesting. How very … hopeful.

Miss de Bourgh was so timid, so ill-used and abused, Elizabeth wished she could help her. Especially if she were to be truly happy with Fitzwilliam. Knowing his cousin withered away at Rosings would cast a shadow over the contentedness Elizabeth wanted with Fitzwilliam. She would rather see Miss de Bourgh happy … or, at least, free.

"A gentleman, perhaps?" Elizabeth pressed. Hearing no denial, she smiled, adding, "You cannot imagine how pleased I am to hear it, Miss de Bourgh. My conscience could not be at ease if I thought you held designs toward Mr. Darcy."

Her gaze shot up to meet Elizabeth's. "No! … That is to say, I could never agree to marry Darcy, knowing he loves another as much as he loves you."

Elizabeth warmed. Fitzwilliam had reassured her many times of his constancy, but it was quite another matter to hear another's observation of it. Such affirmation, so necessary and welcome, determined Elizabeth all the more to see to Miss de Bourgh's happiness.

"What of you?" she asked softly. "Is there someone you prefer? Someone of whom Lady Catherine certainly disapproves?" she added with a hint of merriment.

Miss de Bourgh smiled, as Elizabeth had hoped she would. Her hands lay open in her lap. "I used to think there was. We grew up together."

"At Rosings?" Elizabeth asked after Miss de Bourgh had fallen silent.

"Yes."

More silence. She was not easy to converse with, but with a mother such as Lady Catherine, it was possible that Miss de Bourgh merely lacked sufficient practice. Elizabeth attempted to draw her out, but Miss de Bourgh must have felt that she had said enough for one day. She uttered nothing more than farewells, forgoing tea and cake, saying she must return before her mother noted her absence.

Apparently, Miss de Bourgh had slipped some nerve tonic into her mother's tea to ensure her escape went unnoticed, thus reinforcing Elizabeth's heightened opinion of the lady. Miss de Bourgh was much bolder than she let on.

But until she was free of her mother, she would have no freedom. And, like most ladies of a domineering character, Lady Catherine was likely to disregard her own mortality and live longer than her daughter.

That left only one option. Miss de Bourgh must marry. And Elizabeth had a good idea whom she would ask for more information about the lady's mysterious gentleman.

Her father's study, normally a quiet haven for reading and contemplation, fluttered with activity as her mother and sisters returned from Meryton. They flitted in and out of the room, full of gossip and releasing themselves of the merriment they had suppressed with shows of grief. They had not gone so far as to claim Elizabeth deceased to the world, but they felt certain they had achieved their objective of suggesting that tragedy had befallen her.

They were tremendous actresses, well, except for Mary who was generally considered to be somber anyway. She said very little, but her participation in the scheme displayed a chink in her piety Elizabeth was relieved to discover. She decided that after Miss de Bourgh, Mary would be the next to benefit from her interference.

Lydia gladly plucked at the cake Miss de Bourgh left behind while Kitty informed Elizabeth about Maria Lucas' new gown of pink silk and the charming straw bonnets in the milliner's shop window.

Jane called not one hour after Miss de Bourgh departed, looking somber in a mauve gown.

"Mr. Darcy and the colonel asked Charles for help searching for Mr. Wickham. They said he had been staying at an old, flea-infested cottage. But, Lizzy, I do not understand it," Jane said.

Lydia shoved away the plate of cake, spilling her tea all over the surface.

"Have a care, Lydia," Mama gently admonished.

Jane continued her questioning. "Why should Wickham have anything against you? If anything, he would wish to take advantage of the connection you will give him with Mr. Darcy."

Lydia's lips were now pursed together, her nostrils flared as she sucked air through her nose.

"Lydia, calm yourself," Mama cajoled. "Fits and tantrums are not good for the baby."

Elizabeth watched her youngest sister's face crumple. "I will kill him! I will do it myself, I swear!" she wailed, collapsing against Mama's side, her weeping echoing amidst the shocked silence.

Mama whispered to Mary, "Fetch Dr. Sculthorpe. I daresay I succumbed to hysterics when I was with child, but it makes no sense to house a doctor if he cannot help her."

The doctor tried to soothe Lydia. They all did. But she was beyond the ability to reason.

"Does she have a calming tonic?" Dr. Sculthorpe finally asked.

Kitty lunged toward the hall. "I will fetch it!" she said, returning in short time with a spoon and the bottle of tonic of which Lydia had bragged about earlier to Mama.

Taking the bottle and balancing the spoon in one hand while consoling Lydia with the other, Mama poured the liquid like a seasoned master. Getting the spoonful into Lydia was another matter, though, and after several attempts with an equal number of spills, Mama huffed. "That is quite enough, Lydia. Hold still and open up."

Startled to hear Mama scold her so firmly, Lydia did as she was bid. Mama shoved what was left of the dose into Lydia's mouth, provoking a fit of coughs to which she smacked her daughter's back, saying, "That will do for now, I suppose. You will get more when you are calm enough to take it properly."

After a cup of tepid tea leftover from the dregs of the teapot, Lydia finally calmed.

Mama asked, "Dr. Sculthorpe, shall I give her more? I do not know what is in it besides bilberries. They are not harmful to her unborn child, are they?"

Dr. Sculthorpe indulged her concern, standing by Lydia and placing his fingers against her wrist. Next thing, he knelt on the floor in front of her, holding her chin up to look into her eyes. Her pupils were so large, her eyes looked black. "You say you do not know what is in that tonic?" he asked.

"No," Mama answered, her arm tightening around Lydia.

"Where did she get it?" he asked, lifting her chin and insisting, "Who gave this to you?"

More than alarmed, he sounded angry.

"A doctor from the north," Lydia said, her face turning red again, preparing for another bout of tears.

He turned to Papa. "Is there more cake or bread in the house? She must eat immediately."

Papa ran out to the hall, calling for Mrs. Hill.

The doctor turned to Lydia. "There, there. We will

fill your stomach, and you will be well. Would you say the spoon was only half-full, Mrs. Bennet?"

"I hardly know!"

"Pray try to remember. Your daughter's life depends upon it. This tonic is poison!"

CHAPTER 30

*M*ama's composure, which had held admirably steady up to now, burst. "Yes, a half of a spoon," she sobbed. "Perhaps a mite less"—sniffle—"Yes, I am sure of it, though I cannot understand why you should suggest such a dreadful thing." She clutched Lydia more tightly. "I do not know what I would do if my dear Lydia was no more." She rocked Lydia in her arms, both of them bawling.

"Now, now, I apologize for the scare," said Dr. Sculthorpe, adding cheerily, "If she took so little, I daresay the bread will soak up the poison, and she will be right as rain soon."

Papa returned, shoving the last of the cake in front of Lydia. "This is all there is."

Dr. Sculthorpe pulled a chair closer, holding the plate up when another bout of tears nearly sent the plate toppling to the floor. "Have a bite, love," he cooed, holding the plate under her nose. "It is delicious, is it not? Now, be a good girl, and clean your plate. Every last morsel."

Encouraged to indulge her sweet tooth, Lydia's hysterics surrendered to soft moans and chewing.

Once her mother's tears had dried and her wails had died down to the occasional hiccup, Elizabeth asked, "How do you know the tonic is poisoned?"

"Her pulse was too rapid, and when I saw how quickly her eyes had dilated, I knew she had imbibed belladonna."

"Belladonna?" Papa sank into the nearest chair, rubbing his temples. "Dear Lord, this is grave indeed."

Dr. Sculthorpe held up his hands. "Your daughter is of a … stout … disposition. I am of the opinion she will survive unscathed, but we will know for a certainty in an hour or two. The nightshade is deadly, but it works mercifully fast."

Mary, who had read as many books on horticulture as she had pamphlets with sermons, said, "Belladonna is taken from the Italian for 'beautiful woman.' It grew in popularity and use during the Renaissance. Women would extract the juice, dropping it inside their eyes to enlarge their pupils. Such is vanity — a fleeting striving after the wind."

The doctor nodded. "The berries' menace was known even in ancient Rome."

Mary added, "The empress Livia Drusilla was said to have used it to murder her husband."

Lydia stopped chewing, but Mama pushed the plate toward her.

Jane asked, "What should we look for over the next hour or two until Lydia is out of danger?"

"Aside from a racing pulse and dilated eyes, the worst cases provoke hallucinations and delirium along with convulsions."

Lydia shoved the plate away, her lips pressed into a firm, white line.

"You must eat your cake, Lydia," insisted Mama.

Tears pooled in Lydia's eyes, but she looked too angry to cry.

"Think of your baby," Mama added.

Squeezing her eyes shut, Lydia screeched, "There is no baby!"

"But your stomach—" Kitty exclaimed. "Your figure—"

Bottom lip trembling, Lydia sobbed, "George only brought me here to be rid of me."

Shocked silence filled the room before several voices burst forth at once.

How could you do such a thing?

Why did you lie to your husband? To Us?

Did you think we would not notice as the weeks and months passed?

What were you thinking?

Where is that ingrate?

Tears poured down Lydia's face, Kitty and Mama flanking her on either side, their arms around her waist, attempting to console her.

Again, Mama asked, "Wickham has always been so attentive, such a good husband. Why would you think such a thing?"

Lydia sniffed loudly. "George was distracted. There were nights he would not come home at all, or I would return from shopping early to find him home at the strangest hours. As it turns out"—sniff sniff—"he was carrying on with the maid."

Papa handed her his handkerchief.

Lydia buried her face in the soft linen for several minutes. Then, drying her eyes and leveling her shoulders, she continued, her grief yielding to spite. "I dismissed her, of course. George was angry with me, and he rarely came home after that. I thought … I thought that if I told him I was pregnant, he would pay more attention to me. That things would go back to how they were before we got married."

Kitty whispered, "You must tell them the rest."

Elizabeth sucked in a breath, dreading to hear more.

Voice raw, Lydia began, "I was convinced I had grown rather clumsy. I suffered many accidents — little things like tripping over carpets, falling down stairs, and walking into doors."

Elizabeth clutched her stomach, nauseous in

sympathy for her sister and hatred for her useless husband.

"However, I am beginning to think that George provoked these 'accidents.'" She blew her nose.

Kitty added gravely, "She has bruises all over."

What sort of man inflicted harm on a woman who he thought bore his own child? A monster. A sick, detestable monster.

"Why did you not say anything sooner?" asked Jane, tears flooding her eyes as she leaned over to take her sister's hands. "We would have helped you."

Mama cooed and coddled. "I always said that George Wickham was no good, did I not? All that soldiering. It incites men of weak character to violence."

"He hates me! He abandoned me, and now he is trying to kill me!" Lydia flared.

"He does not hate you. You are imagining things." Mama turned abruptly to the doctor, plastering her hand against Lydia's forehead. "Is this a hallucination?"

Lydia swatted her hand away. "I am perfectly sane — only sick from so much cake."

Papa rose to stand behind her. Placing a hand on her shoulder, he said, "You may stay here as long as you like, Lydia. If Wickham dares show his face, I will run him off myself."

"Not you, Mr. Bennet!" screeched Mama. "You would be honor-bound to call him out, and you would be certain to die in a duel. Let one of the other, younger men run him through."

He chuckled. "It is a consolation to know you are not so eager to be rid of me."

"To the contrary! I intend on many more years in your company."

"Some men may take that as a threat, my dear."

"Oh, you know what I mean."

As much as Elizabeth enjoyed the flirtatious banter between her mother and father, something Lydia had said troubled her. "Aside from the poisoned tonic, do you have any other reason to think Wickham was trying to kill you? Assuming he went to the trouble of bringing a hive to Longbourn, why did he not put it in your room?"

Lydia hiccupped. "He asked me to wave from my window. By the time we arrived, I thought for certain you had married and would depart for London … and I had planned on occupying your bedchamber." She shrugged. "It is much larger than mine."

The curtains billowing outside her open window. Mrs. Hill *had* closed her window. Elizabeth had not imagined it after all.

The bees, the tonic … Elizabeth's mind reeled. "Have you taken any of the tonic before today?"

Lydia thought for a moment. "My first night, I fell asleep on the couch and was carried to my room. Then, Mr. Darcy brought that lovely machine." Shaking her head, she said, "I have not needed it until today."

Elizabeth chewed on her bottom lip, talking aloud. "Belladonna is a common plant here. Wickham must have squeezed some of the juice into your bottle. Was there an occasion when he might have done so without you noticing?"

Lydia's eyes doubled in size. "When we recently arrived at Meryton. He left me at the inn while he disappeared for just over an hour." She put her hands over her mouth. "You do not think he is responsible for the carriage, too, do you? He said he only wanted to make certain you were away."

Wickham could have done more than poison his wife's tonic in that time. But why? Elizabeth forced herself to concentrate on what she knew, on the facts. The carriage did not fit — not yet — so she focused on the tonic. "I do not know yet. He must have hoped you would take your tonic and die in your sleep. When that did not work … he had to think of something else."

Papa frowned. "Thatcher said someone has been lurking behind the carriage house."

Again, another connection to the carriage. It *had* to have been Wickham. *But why?* The question would not go away.

"It is most likely," Papa continued, "he observed me tending to my bees and stole Mrs. Bennet's tablecloth to imitate my protective clothing." He exhaled deeply. "I must write to his commanding officer immediately." He locked Lydia's bottle of nerve tonic inside the cabinet. "There is enough evidence to condemn him."

Dr. Sculthorpe agreed. "Let us hope the young men have had success with his capture."

Elizabeth prayed as much, while she also feared for Fitzwilliam's life. A crazed man capable of murdering his expecting wife would not submit to an easy capture.

CHAPTER 31

*D*arcy hated to admit defeat, but short of tracking Wickham all the way to London — leaving Elizabeth without his protection, and thus as repulsive a prospect as giving up his pursuit — it was time to turn back to Longbourn.

"We will find him, Darcy," Bingley said, his unflagging faith and perpetual optimism annoying when nothing had gone right that day and so much had gone wrong in the days prior.

"Thank you, Bingley." The terseness in his clipped tone, when his friend had meant to encourage, moved Darcy to add, "This can hardly be how you had wished to spend your first week of matrimony."

Bingley grinned. "My wife treats me like a hero for forgoing our wedding tour to help her sister. I would say the delay is well worth my while." He blushed furiously, making Darcy regret he had said anything at all beyond a simple expression of gratitude.

Richard chuckled. "Well played, Bingley. It is my observation that the more firmly a husband establishes himself in his wife's good graces, the easier it is for her to forgive him when he inevitably bumbles awry."

Darcy grumbled, tapping his heels at his horse's side. He was in no mood to speak of matrimonial felicity when he was regrettably ... miserably ... unmarried.

"Come, Darcy," called his jolly cousin. "We are merely attempting to extract you from your brown study before you return to your lady love."

Richard was correct, but the afternoon had been replete with frustrations. First, the empty hovel with no clues other than a few boot prints which could have belonged to anybody. Then, they had gone to Lucas Lodge to secure more help, and Sir William's offer of Mr. Collins' assistance meant that the clergyman had not departed as Darcy had incited him to do the day before. What was Sir William thinking, offering his useless son-in-law's help? Mr. Collins could not open his mouth without giving offense or lulling his audience into a stupor.

But that was not the extent of Darcy's grievances. He had made the mistake of calling at the inn where his aunt informed him she had followed through on her threat to write to the director of Bethlem Hospital. Her interest, she claimed, was to do her duty by "that girl" in securing her the treatment necessary for her recovery. In reality, she held no qualms in having Elizabeth committed to Bedlam to be poked at and experimented on and studied like one of Galvani's frogs. Lady Catherine's moral obligation extended also to him and Anne, whose interests she boldly defended.

Darcy had objected.

She had retaliated with spite. "Are you so ungrateful when my only consideration is for your peace and prosperity? Do you really believe you could be happy attached to a woman doomed to insanity? I swore to your mother on her deathbed that I would watch over you in her stead."

Bringing his mother into the argument had been too much. "With such delusions you suffer, you will be hard put to direct the doctor's attention to Elizabeth. He would sooner have *you* committed."

It had been necessary to point out the presumptuousness of her interference, but he ought to have done so with less threat and venom. His harsh words haunted him.

Lastly, and worse of all, Wickham had escaped. Darcy had sacrificed a day of wooing to chase after that ingrate for naught.

Elizabeth met them where the drive to Longbourn met the road. She smiled, and even as Darcy slid to the ground, his heart soared, his disappointments assuaged.

"Did you leave Wickham with the constable?" she asked, looking between him and his companions.

"No. He could be hiding in London by now," Darcy replied.

She took his arm. "No matter. We will find him, and when we do, not even Wickham will be able to worm his way out of the consequences of his actions. The evidence is irrefutable." She told her audience about Wickham's indiscretions (no great surprise there), Lydia's injuries (deplorable, but again, not entirely unexpected), her faked pregnancy (what a relief!), and then, of Lydia's poisoned tonic. Horrifying.

"So, you see," Elizabeth concluded, leading her dazed audience into the house where the rest of her family and Dr. Sculthorpe were huddled together, "Wickham is the only one who would have poisoned Lydia's tonic, and when that did not work, he filched Father's beehive. And since his preferred hiding place was behind the carriage house, it is reasonable to assume he also sabotaged the carriage."

Richard flicked his coat tails aside, taking a seat. "The proof is there, but something does not quite ring true. Wickham is lazy. He is the first one to take advantage of an opportunity, but he has never been one to do the dirty work when he could get someone else to do it for him."

Darcy agreed. But a desperate man might go to desperate means. How desperate had Wickham been?

Dr. Sculthorpe drummed his fingers on top of his

belly. "This Wickham — does he, by chance, possess a grandiose sense of his own self-importance?"

"Absolutely," Darcy and Richard answered in unison, Darcy adding, "He presumes to have been the favorite of my father, a better son than I was."

The doctor nodded gravely. "Does he suffer delusions of grandeur, believing himself entitled and thus shamelessly exploiting others?"

"Yes." Darcy said nothing of Wickham's attempt to elope with Georgiana for her dowry, nor his many means of extracting money from the Darcys over the years.

Looking at Lydia, the doctor asked, "Did he constantly require praise and expressions of admiration?"

She shrugged. "Of course, but is that not normal? I quite like being praised and admired."

Dr. Sculthorpe smiled at her. "Of course, to a degree. Your father will have to recall our Greek studies, but I am certain he recalls a certain hunter renown for his beauty."

Mr. Bennet fiddled with his spectacles. "You refer to Narkissos?" After a confirming nod, he added, "He fell in love with his own reflection and was turned into a flower, the narcissus, for his vanity."

Dr. Sculthorpe tap tap tapped his fingers against his stomach. "Narkissos has since been used as a figure to represent the dangers of an exaggerated love of self. People possessed of such a character, if left unchecked, become so absorbed in themselves, so thoroughly selfish in their pursuits, they become callous and often lash out against anyone and anything depriving them of what they feel is their rightful due."

Darcy exchanged a look with Richard. The doctor had not met Wickham, and yet he had described him perfectly. "What can we expect from such a man? Is he truly capable of evil?" he asked.

"What can you tell me about your past dealings with this Mr. Wickham?" Sculthorpe asked, the drumming of his fingers slowing as he listened intently for a good half of an hour to the various accounts Darcy, Richard, and Mr. Bennet narrated. There were many from which to choose.

Several times, Darcy's gaze flickered to Elizabeth, praying their stories might restore some of her memories and fearing what she might add to their conversation if she did. Georgiana's greatest mistake was unknown to the majority in the room, and Darcy meant to keep it that way.

But, if Elizabeth remembered, she gave no evidence of it. She remained quiet, soaking in the conversation, only asking the occasional question.

"What do you make of him?" she finally asked. "Is he a danger still?"

The doctor clasped his hands together and sighed. "I am afraid this is only the beginning. He possesses the same peculiarities of some of the accused criminals I interviewed in one study. My aim was to discover if there was a connection — a family trait or characteristic, innate or learned — which could predict whether a man was more likely to commit a violent crime or not. I saw many of his kind.

"Years, or as I understand from your account, a lifetime of cultivated grandiosity and entitlement, of hiding his true nature behind a facade of charm... Most fell into two groups. One was proud, even boastful of their crimes. The others insisted on their innocence, convinced of their own lie until the rope dropped at the gallows. They were so accomplished at deceiving others, they deluded themselves into believing they were not responsible for their own actions, persuaded by their own twisted minds that their crime was nothing more than an unfortunate accident. They felt no guilt, no remorse, because they had committed no wrong. They would have been better off at an asylum — and I do not say that lightly."

Richard rubbed his side whiskers. "It is possible. If it is true, it makes Wickham a greater threat than we had supposed."

Elizabeth stood. "Not if we allow him to think he succeeded." Far from defeated, she sounded excited. There was a glint in her eye Darcy was familiar with, and had Wickham seen it, he would have been afraid.

"What do you suggest?" he asked, winning him a sparkling smile.

"We have already allowed the villagers to believe something dreadful has transpired at Longbourn. I say we use it to our advantage. We dress in mourning. We act as though Lydia has died and allow the gossip to spread."

"But he is pretending to have returned to the militia in the north. How will news reach him?"

"We pretend as though we have accepted his story and send a messenger to his regiment."

"That will take days. Up to a week," protested the colonel.

Darcy shook his head. "Wickham is impatient. He could not wait for the tonic to effect its course after one night, exposing himself to the dangerous task of transporting hundreds of bees in order to make another attempt. He will approach us sooner with a credible excuse."

"I will write to his commanding officer, detailing what we know so he can send an envoy to deal with him," Richard said.

"I sent a letter detailing the proofs over an hour ago," Mr. Bennet added.

Elizabeth clasped her hands under her chin. "All we have to do is bide our time and wait for the grieving widower to come to us."

That was the part Darcy did not like. "What about you? Wickham is not your only concern. Lady Catherine wrote to the director of the asylum. They will send someone."

That glint again. "As for that," Elizabeth said, not looking the least concerned, "there is a matter I must discuss with you and the colonel. I would like to know what you can tell me about a certain naval captain...."

Before Darcy could understand where her plan was directed, Dr. Sculthorpe rose. "It seems I must make a little jaunt to London. Miss de Bourgh told us the letter was sent in the post. If I leave immediately, I might delay them a bit ... if I am not too late."

"I cannot thank you enough," Mr. Bennet said.

"A pleasure," his friend bowed. "I do hope you keep me informed once the dust settles." Lifting Elizabeth's hand, he added, "And I expect to receive a full and detailed account when you are recovered, my dear." To Darcy, he said, "It has been an honor to meet you. Take good care of this one."

"I promise I will."

The doctor inclined his head. "And I am certain you will." That said, he took his leave.

Bingley spoke up. "So ... there is a murderer in our midst."

Mrs. Bennet fanned her face. "Whatever shall we do? We shall be murdered in our beds before the morrow."

Elizabeth cut her off before she agitated herself or anyone else further. "Which is precisely why we must act immediately. Mama, will you agree with the scheme? For my benefit? For Lydia's?"

It was interesting she did not seek his approval first but began with her mother. Had she learned enough about his character to recognize that of everyone in the room, he was most likely to oppose her disguise? Or was this simply proof that she did not know him still?

Mrs. Bennet replied, "I would do anything for the welfare of my girls."

Kitty agreed immediately. Elizabeth looked at Mary. "I know better than to ask you to lie, Mary."

Mary clasped her hands together and lifted her chin. "And I will refrain from uttering a falsehood during this deception."

Elizabeth was prepared with a counterargument. "Perhaps you may recall the account of Rahab who saved the two Israelite spies lives by … misdirecting … the men who would have killed them."

Lydia chuckled. "Rahab? The prostitute?"

Darcy clamped his mouth shut. Of course, *that* would be the one detail Lydia would remember of the entire account, of a lifetime of Sunday sermons and the many readings from Fordyce's sermons to which her pious sister had forced her to listen.

Elizabeth must have had similar thoughts. She rolled her eyes. "That is hardly the point, Lydia. The point is that Rahab was blessed when she and her family were saved from the destruction of their city because of her bravery in hiding the spies. Because of her deception."

Turning to Mary, Elizabeth appealed, "It is up to us to hide Lydia from her husband lest he make another attempt, a more successful one. Would you rather have the life of your sister on your hands?"

Mary shook her head. "You mistake my meaning, Lizzy. I did not mean to imply an unwillingness to participate. I merely meant to make it known that I would not purposefully lie if it could be avoided. Of all sins, taking the life of another, depriving another of their God-given gift, is a sin far worse than keeping silent or … misdirecting … the villain from his evil scheme."

"Thank you, Mary." Elizabeth turned to Lydia. "Your role is the most important of all. You will not be able to leave the house nor make yourself visible or heard until Wickham is caught. Are you willing to see this through?"

Lydia's face hardened and her eyes watered.

Darcy prepared himself for wails and tears and excuses for the behavior of her husband.

Her voice was blade sharp. "That no-good black-guard abandoned me when he believed me to be with his child. And now, I find out that not only did he merely wish to leave me, he wished to be completely free of me. I am so angry, I could … I could spit!"

"Not on the carpet, dear," Mrs. Bennet mumbled.

Finally, Elizabeth turned to Darcy. "You are too honest to submit to disguise. If you know of a better alternative, I know I am not the only one here who would be glad to hear of it. But, if this truly is our best … or only … recourse, I hope you will not think less of me for suggesting it."

Not only did she know his character, she sought his

good opinion. He could not disappoint her, and since Elizabeth's plan was sounder than anything he had thought up, he conceded. "My honor or your loyalty to your sister?" If she remembered anything about Georgiana at all, she would know Darcy could never make her choose between them. "Both values which must not be compromised. Therefore, on my honor, I will go along with your plan."

Mrs. Bennet turned to her youngest daughter. "You will have to stay indoors. I will instruct the servants to keep the curtains drawn. Kitty, Mary, you will walk with me into Meryton to purchase black ribbon and fabric for gowns. We will stop by Mrs. Philips' on the way."

Mr. Bennet mumbled, "That will take care of the gossip."

Mrs. Bingley added, "We will make a show of leaving." She rubbed her face, her skin reddening. "I will ask Mrs. Nicholls to secure mourning black for us." Pulling out a handkerchief, she dabbed her eyes and sniffed as she and Bingley supported each other out to their carriage.

The occupants trickled out of the parlor, and Darcy soon found himself alone with Elizabeth, Lydia, and Mr. Bennet, who promptly excused himself to check on his bees.

Lydia huffed. "I suppose you two will abandon me to stroll together in the garden." Her face hardened. "I will scratch his eyes out."

Darcy tried to imagine how she must feel, and just as quickly renounced any attempt to understand her. He did, however, feel he owed her an apology. "I never should have made him marry you."

Another huff. "What else could you have done? Come, Mr. Darcy, I am not an ignorant child. Not anymore. You saved my sisters from ruin and my family from scandal." Lowering her head and her voice, she added, "Wickham was my choice. You merely helped it to be an honest one."

"All the same, I am sorry it has come to this."

"You know, Mr. Darcy," she said, tilting her chin to the side, her expression sincere, "you are not as taciturn and stodgy as I thought."

Elizabeth laughed, and Darcy struggled to know how to reply. He had never sought Lydia's good opinion, but he found that he was happy to receive it. "Thank you," he said with a bow.

Tugging on his arm, Elizabeth said, "It has been an exciting day. I would like very much to sit by the pond."

Finally! Time alone to court Elizabeth was just the thing to remedy this topsy-turvy day. Tucking her hand at his side, Darcy smiled down at her, getting lost in her warm, chocolate eyes when Lydia's sharp voice interrupted. "The willow does not give as much privacy as you think."

Darcy thought his face would melt.

Elizabeth recovered quicker than he did. Turning to

her sister, she said in an admirably controlled tone, "Thank you, Lydia. We will keep that in mind."

The day kept getting better and better, Darcy thought bitterly. At long last, he had a few minutes with his Elizabeth, and he would not be able to kiss her after Lydia's revelation. The day's frustrations kept multiplying.

CHAPTER 32

*E*lizabeth loved how Fitzwilliam nestled her fingers between his, their arms swaying in unison. The sun warmed her, the breeze caressed her cheeks, and Fitzwilliam's touch kept her feet on the ground. It was as close to perfect as Elizabeth could expect, and she seized it. "I love you."

He pulled her behind the boughs of the willow, circling his arms around her.

She gasped. "Lydia will see us!"

"Would you have me release you to spare your sister's sensibility?"

"Hardly!" She snuggled against him, the silk of his cravat deliciously smooth against her skin.

They stood, holding each other, their problems forgotten for some time before she felt him kiss the top of her head. "I love you, Elizabeth." Releasing his hold, he dropped to one knee. "These past few days have been a trial, but it has only strengthened my affection for you, and you would make me the happiest man alive if you would agree to accept my hand in marriage … again."

She giggled. "I have already accepted."

"That was before. I am asking you now. Today, knowing what you know, feeling what you do, would you agree to spend the rest of your days with me? Please?"

That *please* would have changed her mind had she not already been so firmly decided.

Tracing her fingers along his cheeks, her knees wobbling when he leaned into her palm and sighed, it occurred to Elizabeth that if she was going to shock Lydia, she might as well do a proper job of it.

Sitting on Darcy's bent knee, she pulled him closer until her lips brushed against his. "Yes," she whispered against his warm skin, then pressed her lips against his, sealing her promise. Hot kisses trailed down her cheek, nuzzling at her neck so that she arched her back and shuddered a moment. She purred, as content as a cat stretching after a nap.

Fitzwilliam leapt to his feet, stepping away and holding her the full distance of his arms away. He gasped for breath, his cheeks flushed. "Forgive me, Elizabeth. It is not mine to take such liberties. Not yet."

"Then I suggest we marry as soon as it can be arranged so you may take as many liberties as you wish."

"A tempting prospect."

She sensed he held back. Arching her eyebrow, she prompted him. "But…"

He ran his hands down the length of her arms, sending delightful shivers curling through her. "But once we wed, I intend to give you my full attention — without distraction."

"I find no fault with your plan." Elizabeth could think of nothing more enjoyable than being the sole recipient of her betrothed's attention.

Fitzwilliam's smile made her melt — his caress left her breathless and weightless and completely secure of her place in his heart.

DARCY HAD THOUGHT he knew happiness, but his past experiences paled in comparison to this moment with Elizabeth in his arms.

His Elizabeth.

She had not yet recovered her memories, but it no longer mattered. She loved him.

He had won her heart a second time without all the adversities and misunderstandings enkindled by his pride and her prejudice. What was more, he had made peace with her family and her brilliant plan would, in time, promote peaceful relations with his. He had no doubt she would eventually win over Lady Catherine when he had been fixed on cutting off all association. Far from divisive, Elizabeth united.

She was magnificent.

He pulled away before the impulse to kiss her overwhelmed him again. Contenting himself with holding her hand, he looked at the most beautiful woman and wondered how he had been so fortunate to secure her love not just once, but twice.

CHAPTER 33

*T*ime both accelerated and crawled the following week. Accelerated whenever Darcy called on Elizabeth at Longbourn, which was more often and of longer duration than propriety permitted. As though Darcy would ever be tempted to adhere to society's strictures when his bride-to-be and her family endangered themselves to capture a madman.

His aunt, who stubbornly persisted in her claims despite the apparent success of Dr. Sculthorpe in detaining Bedlam's director, was another matter.

Seconds dragged through molasses in her presence, but he took solace in the knowledge that Elizabeth's scheme would offer Anne a choice. If Richard had been persuasive enough. The colonel had yet to return from London, and while he wrote to appease Darcy that all was well, his absence affirmed otherwise.

Sitting in Longbourn's cozy drawing room, packed with Bennets and Bingleys, he noted how the dreary weather mirrored the downcast, dispirited attitude of the occupants within.

"How much longer are we to continue in this state of boredom?" Lydia complained.

Mary lowered the pamphlet she had been reading. "There are many edifying occupations with which you may entertain yourself without venturing out of doors."

Lydia glowered at her sister. "I require others to entertain me."

Kitty said, with excessive cheer, "You could help me trim this bonnet."

"If I have to trim one more bonnet, I shall scream!"

"Calm yourself, Lydia," Mrs. Bingley soothed. "We must allow enough time for news to reach Mr. Wickham."

"Why do you not take a rest upstairs? Or you could use that marvelous machine again," Mrs. Bennet suggested.

Pounding her fist against her leg, Lydia said, "I do not get to have any fun. I could not even attend my own funeral!" She poked out her bottom lip so far a bird could have perched on it and crossed her arms. "Tell me again how well-attended my funeral was and how many ladies mourned with Mama in the parlor."

Elizabeth sighed. "You would have thought the king had passed." She tilted her chin and winked at Darcy.

He stifled a laugh. It was true that Lydia's death had been received with a great deal of exhibition, but her "mourners" were more curious than grievous, their explanation of her grotesque disfigurement from so many bee stings arousing more interest among their macabre neighbors than they had hoped to placate.

It had been quite a show despite their sincerest efforts to minimize attention. But too many wishes to see the lively beauty who had thoughtlessly tormented the less fortunate in looks, her indulgent parents brought low. Lydia had paid for her sins in their minds, but their forgiveness was half-hearted. They certainly would not forget.

Darcy hated disguise — even when it was necessary — but seeing how her neighbors sympathized for her family's benefit more than out of respectful remembrance for the departed stirred his pity.

Mr. Bennet chuckled. "It was a respectable attendance, but you will have many more when word of your resurrection spreads. I daresay you will have devotees calling from several counties."

Mrs. Bennet cheered. "We shall have to invite our neighbors to dine with us. A banquet to celebrate Lydia's return."

"I will not disagree, my love," said Mr. Bennet with a resigned sigh. "Perhaps they will more readily forgive us this deception once they hear the rest of the story ... and are fed from our table."

Lydia clasped her hands under her chin and giggled.

"Oh, how delightful! I do wish Wickham would hurry up!"

Darcy wondered if she understood what she said.

Mrs. Bingley looked at her with concern. "You *do* understand what will happen when he does finally arrive, do you not, dearest?"

Popping a grape into her mouth, one of the many condolence offerings left by a nearby family, she replied, "He will be escorted to his regiment to face trial."

It was apparent that Lydia's inability to foresee consequences was not limited to her own decisions.

Her father pressed. "Lydia, do you understand what will happen beyond his trial? He has attempted murder on at least three occasions, callously lashing out against the woman he married as well as his unborn child."

"Oh, but I am not pregnant."

"But he did not know that."

"I do not know why I should spare him when he tried to rid himself of me ... and our child. Had his aim not run so contrary to mine, I could endure it, but I very much wish to continue alive. Therefore, I have no option. He will face his trial, and I will accept the judge's decision ... whatever it may be." Lydia's chin quivered, but her voice was sharp.

"Eye for eye," Mary commented. Piety could be harsh.

"What will you do ... after?" Kitty asked.

Lydia sighed. "Since I have had so much time at my disposal, I have given the matter a great deal of thought."

Mr. Bennet's eyebrows shot up. "Really?"

She looked at their faces, giggling. "Do not look so shocked! I am capable of thought. Besides, I think you will approve of my conclusions. I am too flighty and fun-loving to be trusted with important decisions, and I am much too lively and handsome not to attract the wrong kind of attention."

Such a mixture of vanity and sense Darcy had never heard. He paid rapt attention as she continued, "I did not choose wisely with Wickham, but I could not bear to live alone too long. I should very much like to remarry, but I will rely on Jane, Lizzy, and Papa to help me select my next husband. I want what they have secured, so I will trust their judgment to help me."

Such a mixture of selfishness and praise. Darcy shook his head.

The conversation wavered between the profound and ridiculous until Hill barged into the room, chest heaving and hands fidgeting. "Mr. Wickham is riding up the drive!"

ELIZABETH LUNGED AT LYDIA, grabbing her hands as Kitty and Mary pushed her forward.

"All this sitting around, and I am to be denied witnessing Wickham's comeuppance?" Lydia squealed.

"Hush!" echoed through the room.

"Now is not the time, Lydia!" chastised Mama.

"You will spoil everything!" added Kitty.

Thinking quickly, Elizabeth put her hands on Lydia's cheeks. Looking into her eyes, she asked, "Do you promise to guard the strictest silence if we allow you to listen from the next room? The strictest silence."

Lydia nodded her head, pursing her lips together.

Dragging her sister into the next room, Elizabeth left Lydia with her ear pressed against the wall and her hands clamped over her mouth.

There was a knock at the door, but Hill waited until Elizabeth ran back down the hall and into the drawing room, where she struggled to control her breath and her heartbeat.

Soft mumbles and hesitant footsteps — slow and hushed, like anything somber — and Wickham appeared, red-eyed, disheveled, and donning a black armband. He looked so contrite, Elizabeth's palm itched to slap his duplicitous face.

One hand over his heart, looking pale and grave garbed in black, he asked, "Where is she? Where is my dear wife?" His voice cracked, as though he had wept his entire journey ... from wherever that had originated.

Wickham's patience in waiting until such a time as

he could have received the news and returned from his barracks impressed upon Elizabeth his desire to maintain his farce. It made him vulnerable.

She would exploit his weakness.

Mama leapt to her feet, fluttering her handkerchief and babbling incoherently about her tremendous loss and crediting the newly widowed Wickham with all the sympathy he *ought* to have felt for his dearly departed wife. Mama would have done well as a dramatic actress.

Wickham stepped inside the drawing room, his frown deepening. "Where is Lydia?"

Good grief, he did not expect them to display her body an entire week, did he? And in the summer?

"I had hoped—" Wickham's voice choked, and his eyes overflowed.

It had been many months since Elizabeth could conjure up any sympathy for the man, but his eagerness to see the evidence of his handiwork chilled her to the bone. Any understanding she might have extended him, had he possessed a modicum of good, burned in a flash as her anger rose.

Papa stared vacantly at the cold fireplace while Mama wept bitterly at his side.

Bingley slid forward in his chair, nodding in lieu of a bow, his snub genteelly covered over by his grieving wife who clung to his arm for support.

Mary and Kitty embraced each other on the settee,

their faces turned toward each other when they were not covered with their handkerchiefs.

Fitzwilliam stood beside Elizabeth's chair, wearing his usual expression (which lent itself well to the occasion. She would have to compliment him on it later.)

Elizabeth felt Fitzwilliam's tension seep into her muscles, saw the flicker of a smirk cross Wickham's face. What a vile man.

Swallowing her ire, Elizabeth gestured toward the chair closest to the wall where Lydia listened from the other side, determined more than before to be kinder to her sister for having to endure the touch and attention of the slimy eel.

Wickham sat slowly, with the caution of one prepared to bolt away at the slightest provocation. "Please, where is my dear Lydia? I take it you buried her already?" He dropped his head into his hands, running his fingers through his hair. When he lifted his head, fresh tear trails stained his cheeks.

Elizabeth wondered why he bothered with the militia when it was plain to see he was born for the theater.

"In due time," Papa said absently, reaching blindly to hold Mama's hand to his chest. Mama lost no time imitating Jane's pose with Mr. Bingley, and Papa soon found himself with his arms full. Had it not been imperative to maintain her act, Elizabeth would have smiled at the display.

Wickham shifted in his chair. "May I ask ... I must

know…" He ran his hand through his hair again, his voice tight. "How did it happen?"

His eyes were too grief-swollen to observe any remnants of his stings or the insect bites he must have suffered from the infested cot. But he could not disguise the infected, red dots on his hands.

"Bees," sobbed Kitty.

Elizabeth cleared her throat. "She grieved her separation from you since her arrival."

"I only sought her comfort and welfare, for her and our … child." He covered his face with his hands.

Elizabeth bit her tongue. Fitzwilliam's fists tightened.

Mama mumbled, "Of course. Of course. Every child seeks her mother when she requires greater care."

So intense had Elizabeth's concentration been on Wickham and the carefully choreographed scene unfolding in the room, she startled when an apologetic Hill announced another caller. "Mr. Collins, sir," he said, standing aside to allow the clergyman to pass.

Mr. Collins bowed and creaked, impervious to the interruption he had caused. What on earth was he doing at Longbourn? Why was he still lingering at Lucas Lodge, for that matter?

Ignoring Mr. Collins completely, Fitzwilliam cut through the silence. "What took you so long to arrive?" he demanded.

Knowing his words were certainly not meant for

him, Mr. Collins crept across the room and slinked into a chair.

Wickham's eyes hardened. "I came as soon as I received word. I rode as quickly as I could, but you more than anyone are aware of the distance."

"You maintain that you were with your regiment when you received word?"

"Have you become an inspector, Darcy?" Wickham scoffed. "Where else was I supposed to be?"

He was sticking with his story. Elizabeth was glad. The more he insisted, the more satisfying it would be to catch him in his lie.

"What happened to your hands?" Fitzwilliam asked.

"I am a humble soldier on insufficient pay. My lodgings suffer from unwelcome guests. Another reason I wished to remove Lydia from the unhealthy surroundings."

"You look agitated, Mr. Wickham," Papa said, calling for Mrs. Hill. "Pray fetch some of the nerve tonic my dear daughter praised before her premature demise. She would want him to take comfort in the elixir he so kindly provided."

Wickham squirmed in his chair. "That is hardly necessary."

"You are in denial, my boy. It is perfectly normal for grieving husbands to partake of something other than spirits to ease the pain."

Mrs. Hill returned, bearing Lydia's prettily painted bottle on top of a silver salver.

Wickham swallowed hard, his eyes fixed on the liquid sloshing half-way up the glass. He made no move to take the bottle.

Papa instructed, "Pour Mr. Wickham a generous amount. He is greatly distressed."

Mama took the tonic, shaking the dark liquid and moving closer to Wickham, the soup spoon filled to the top. "Lydia said you had this specially made for her." She held the spoon in front of him, poking his lips with the silver like a mother coercing a child to take his cod liver oil.

The room held its breath, its occupants on pins and needles as she prodded, and he squirmed away.

"Why do you not drink the tonic?" asked Mary, her question sounding like a scold.

Fitzwilliam's patience tired quicker than Wickham and Mama's little game of joust and jab. "Tell us why you refuse to drink."

With a huff, Mama dribbled the spoonful back into the bottle.

Wickham said nothing.

"Desist with this despicable disguise. You will not drink because you know it is poisonous. When your wife did not succumb to your scheme, you attempted to murder her in her sleep with a hive of angry bees." Fitzwilliam's sharp words shattered Wickham's defense. He blanched.

"Before this room of witnesses, we charge you with the murder of your wife and unborn child," Bingley pronounced.

Papa stood, pointing his finger at Wickham. "Along with the attempted murder of my Lizzy."

Eyes white with terror, Wickham looked about the room for a supporter, and found none. "I swear ... I swear on my own life ... I had nothing to do with any assault against Miss Elizabeth."

"You deny it?" demanded Darcy.

"I would never bring harm to anyone connected with you," Wickham insisted, rising to his feet.

Fitzwilliam released his hold on Elizabeth's shoulder, stepping closer to Wickham. "You are mistaken in your reasoning. Do you think I could treat Mrs. Wickham as anything less than my own sister? Any attack against Elizabeth's family is an assault against me, and my loyalty prevents me from sheltering you from the consequences."

Wickham's eyes widened. He held his hands in front of him, a flimsy barrier. "I swear on my life. I never meant to harm anyone. It was an accident."

An accident. Just as Dr. Sculthorpe had described the deranged criminals he had studied.

"I suppose the bees flew their hive into my bedchamber with no help from you?" Elizabeth asked.

"It was an accident. That was not meant for you."

"You confess you meant them for Lydia, then?" He fell into that trap much too easily.

Wickham bit his lips. Beads of sweat glistened over his skin. "I ... I—" He stepped closer to the door where

Lydia suddenly appeared, hands fisted on her hips, red-faced, and blocking his path.

"Lydia!" He stumbled backwards.

"Hello, George," she spat.

Recovering extraordinarily well, he opened his arms. "Darling! I am so relieved you are not dead."

Lydia launched forward, her palm striking against his cheek with a resounding smack. "You tried to kill me, you wicked scoundrel! I loved you! And what do I get for my affection? A man who would rather hang from the gallows than continue married to me — a man who swore he would always cherish and care for me. You swine!" She raised her fingers, poised to make good on her threat to claw his eyes out, when Wickham raised his arm.

Her bravado failed. Lydia immediately cowered, dropping and curling herself into a ball on the floor.

Everyone moved. Elizabeth and Jane dove to cover Lydia. Fitzwilliam seized Wickham's arm, twisting it behind his back until he squealed like a piglet. Mary called for Hill to send the footman to fetch the constable, if he had not already done so. Kitty and Mama fretted when they were not insulting Wickham. Bingley and Papa stood guard at the door, blocking any hope of Wickham's escape.

Elizabeth's heart ached for her sister, whose quickness shrinking into a smaller target bespoke of a great deal of practice.

Whether Wickham had meant to strike his wife

before them all or defend himself from her pointy fingernails, it did not matter. The way Lydia shook under Elizabeth, the tears she could not stop, testified to his guilt.

CHAPTER 34

*T*he next few hours pulled Darcy in all directions. Thank goodness for the Bingleys. They consoled and calmed while he ensured Wickham was secured in the gaol to await the arrival of his regiment's envoy.

Mr. Collins crept away, no doubt to inform Her Ladyship of their deception and the woes to have befallen his cousins of late. Darcy prayed they would all depart now for Rosings, for he had every intention of marrying Elizabeth on the morrow. Scheming saboteurs and murderous mates would not stop him nor alter what he set into motion after a brief call at the parish, upon which he continued to Longbourn.

Mr. Bennet held Lydia to his side protectively, and the way Mrs. Bennet looked upon her spouse with bold-faced admiration satisfied Darcy that the Bennet household would remain a calmer environment even after the machine's battery was exhausted. He could even imagine them staying at Pemberley without cringing and seeking ways to avoid their company.

The Bingleys returned to Netherfield Park, vowing to return shortly for dinner. Mrs. Bennet made certain to include Darcy in her dinner plans, an invitation which he gladly accepted for the excuse it gave him to linger in Elizabeth's presence.

Pulling her to the side, he relayed the details of his trip into the village and Wickham's conversation with the constable.

She worried her bottom lip. "He insisted he had nothing to do with the carriage?"

"But he admitted to the other offenses," Darcy countered.

"Yes, and rightly so. But not the carriage," she mumbled more to herself than to him.

"What troubles you?" He wondered if it was the same sore that bothered him.

She met his gaze fully. "I believe him. I do not want to, but I do."

Yes, that was it. As tempting as it was to blame all the troubles of the world on Wickham, Darcy could not in good conscience make potentially false claims against him. Wickham would face the consequences of his crimes. Nothing more.

The carriage did not fit. Wickham had the means, but he lacked motive.

"If Wickham did not cut the axle, who did?" he asked.

Elizabeth shook her head. "I do not know. But I suspect Lady Catherine knows more than she is letting on. I cannot help but suspect her continued presence in Meryton is more involved than an attempt to force you into a marriage with Miss de Bourgh. Especially when she has made so little progress on that front."

Darcy took a deep breath. He had hoped to avoid a confrontation with his aunt until Richard returned. That had been the plan. But something was keeping Richard away longer than expected, and Darcy wanted to end this sordid business as much as Elizabeth did.

"The hour is late, and I am spent, but I want to be done with this. Do you wish to accompany me to the inn?" he asked.

"Not this same evening! I am not so desperate nor improper as to call so late on a lady of the peerage," Elizabeth said.

Darcy cocked his eyebrow. Elizabeth clearly did not remember how that same lady had behaved indecorously toward her and the entire Bennet family, so that she might make her undue demands.

ELIZABETH SAT ACROSS FROM FITZWILLIAM, entertaining a conversation all their own with naught but gestures and glances.

Dinner was a joyous occasion, rife with laughter and discussion. The morrow would be difficult enough with Lady Catherine, but for now, they were merry.

Until a pounding at the door silenced their colloquy, and everyone sitting around the table looked at each other for answers nobody had.

Elizabeth's heartbeat pounded out to her fingertips, a sense of foreboding raising the hair at the back of her neck.

A scuffle, and then a tap step preceding an imposing figure swathed in stiff silks. Lady Catherine charged into the dining room with Mrs. Hill chasing behind her.

Something stirred within Elizabeth, but she could not put her finger on it. She had a sense she was reliving an event.

"I will have a word with you," Lady Catherine ordered, as though she were the Queen, and Elizabeth a chambermaid.

Again, that sense of previous experience for which Elizabeth could not account.

She had little inclination to acquiesce to Her Ladyship's demands, and especially less so when she saw the tall gentleman with sharp cheekbones and head-to-toe black watching her with hawkish eyes. He had yet to be presented — nor was he likely to be, given the rudeness with which Lady Catherine had interrupted their dinner — but his appearance and watchful bearing presented enough clues. He represented Bedlam. He was here for her.

Fear trembled through Elizabeth, but she squared her shoulders. She had nothing to fear. She was not going insane. What was more, she was in her home and surrounded by defenders who would not allow her to be carried away and committed.

Lifting her chin and arching her brow, Elizabeth set her napkin on top of her plate and rose from the table slowly, calmly. Turning to Her Ladyship, Elizabeth assumed her iciest tone. "I am surprised to see you here, and in this manner, Lady Catherine. Might I convince you to join me in the front parlor where our discussion will be less likely to upset my family?"

Fitzwilliam was at her side. "You do not have to meet her demands. She cannot expect you to receive her politely after such a ghastly display of vulgarity."

Elizabeth mumbled, "It would not be the first time."

Her breath caught in her throat, her mind catching up with her tongue as the realization of what she had impulsively said dawned. Something about Lady Catherine's unexpected, unannounced, unwelcome call had shuffled the missing pieces in Elizabeth's mind.

She felt Fitzwilliam tense, felt his gaze. He must have gathered that something significant had happened, but Elizabeth dared not admit to any weakness of mind before the asylum doctor nor encourage Fitzwilliam's hopes lest they lead to nothing more than one insufficient observation.

Still, there was no denying that Lady Catherine had jogged something in her mind into place, and Elizabeth was determined to take full advantage of the lady's call if it meant restoring her memories.

"Mrs. Hill, please show our guests into the front parlor. I will be along shortly."

Lady Catherine made it clear she did not approve of the delay, but Elizabeth did not concern herself with the grand lady's opinion when Fitzwilliam and her family needed to be appeased.

Once she ascertained that the doctor was out of hearing, she turned to them.

Fitzwilliam whispered, "Did you remember?"

Elizabeth grinned widely, her happiness far greater than her apprehension. She had a feeling she had triumphed over Lady Catherine once before ... if she could only remember how. But it was enough encouragement to continue. "A flicker, nothing more. Pray, do not get your hopes up, but I have every intention of seeing if Lady Catherine will fan the flames until our past is fully illuminated."

Papa warned her, "Take care not to show any signs of amnesia. I will not allow you to be taken away from Longbourn, but neither do I wish for Her Ladyship and the doctor to begin a campaign against you in the village. They could stir up fear and take the matter out of my hands, and I cannot allow it."

Elizabeth nodded. She was very well aware of what

could happen if she were presumed dangerous and her family incapable.

She and Fitzwilliam paused before the door Mrs. Hill had had the good sense to close, taking steeling breaths when a gentler knock tapped the entrance door.

Elizabeth looked at Fitzwilliam. Who could that be? At this hour?

Hill looked at Elizabeth, reluctant.

Elizabeth shrugged, "By all means, see whoever it is in." Why not?

It was Miss de Bourgh along with Mr. Collins.

Supposing their appearance had something to do with Lady Catherine, Elizabeth said, "We are glad you could join us, Miss de Bourgh. Will you join us in the front parlor?" Of her cousin, she said nothing, for Elizabeth was not at all pleased to see him.

Miss de Bourgh clasped her hands together, peeking up at Fitzwilliam. "You will not let my mother harm Miss Elizabeth, I know it. Had I known you were here, I would have been more at ease, but I will lend what little support I may. If you permit me to help."

Her gentle strength made Elizabeth happy she had interfered on Miss de Bourgh's behalf, though she feared that the delay in a reply bode ill for her scheme.

"Of course, you may help, Anne," Fitzwilliam reassured his cousin. "Your willingness to do so speaks well of you."

Mr. Collins bowed. "As Miss de Bourgh so elegantly

stated, I, too, am here to offer consolation and guidance where I may."

If he had hoped for equal praise, he was soon disappointed. Fitzwilliam glared at Mr. Collins, and Elizabeth pushed the door open before the clergyman was put in his place. A proper set down would take too much time when Elizabeth's memories tickled the edges of her consciousness.

Later, Mr. Collins. Later. You will get what is coming to you.

The four of them entered the front parlor.

"Anne, you are supposed to be in your rooms." Lady Catherine rose to her full height, towering over her own daughter, both hands grasping her cane like a scepter.

"Mother, I cannot allow you to continue in this heartless course. It is unlike you."

Elizabeth motioned to the chairs, but nobody sat.

Lady Catherine hissed. "Unlike me to protect the interests of my only child? An heiress?"

Fitzwilliam interjected, "Unlike you to undermine my happiness and Anne's prospects. I have defended you against any involvement in the carriage accident—"

Pointing her finger at Elizabeth, Lady Catherine spat, "An accusation made by *that girl*, no doubt."

"Your own stubborn spite accuses you," he said.

"How dare you accuse me of stooping so low over this insignificant chit. Can you not see how she is driving a wedge between you and your own family? Will you forsake me for a conniving fortune hunter out to ruin you?"

"Elizabeth is my family as much as you are, only I have *chosen* her to be such. Someone sabotaged her carriage, resulting in harm to her person, and I will not relent until I find out who is responsible."

Mr. Collins interrupted, "Was not Mr. Wickham accused of that crime … besides his many others?"

Neither Fitzwilliam nor his aunt heeded him, leaving Mr. Collins to wither into a corner where Elizabeth could only hope he would make himself unheard.

"You would accuse your own flesh and blood of such atrocities? I do not know you, Fitzwilliam Darcy."

"Mother! You know not what you speak," Miss de Bourgh plead.

Elizabeth sought to lessen the tension. Gesturing once again at the chairs, she said, "Please take a seat. Heated words will do nothing to mend the breach I am supposed to have caused."

"Silence!" Lady Catherine demanded, jabbing her cane into the carpet.

Taking a deep breath to compose herself, Elizabeth said, "You forget yourself. You imposed yourself on me. In my home. I am under no obligation to you."

"You unabashedly hunted my nephew, preying on him with your feminine machinations. You are nothing more than a grubby upstart willing to sell yourself to gain Pemberley."

Elizabeth forced a smile, the sting of Her Ladyship's insults placated by her own purpose. She was on the verge of resurgence. "That is hardly the case." She squeezed Fitzwilliam's hand, wondering when he had reached for her … or if she had reached for him.

"You have the audacity to deny you only accepted his proposal after you had toured Pemberley and its properties?"

"Yes. That is precisely what I suggest because it is the truth." Elizabeth was proud to say she had fallen in love with Fitzwilliam — the second time — with absolutely no memory of Pemberley. Any claims to the contrary had no leg to stand on. She knew it. Fitzwilliam knew it.

"Obstinate, headstrong girl! Have you no shame?"

Elizabeth's head reeled, the people and the room whirling as past spun into the present. She and Lady Catherine faced each other, Her Ladyship demanding Elizabeth give up her last thread of hope and Elizabeth refusing.

She remembered. She remembered all of it.

Elizabeth wanted to shout her triumph, to spin until she was dizzy. There would be time enough for celebration later. First, Lady Catherine. Calming her breath, Elizabeth said, "I am obstinate and headstrong. And my mind has never been more sound than it is at this moment." She looked at Fitzwilliam, her hands clasped with his in front of her lest she burst with happiness.

Recalling her words, delighting in her ability to repeat them, Elizabeth said, "You have insulted me in every possible way, and can now have nothing further to say." She rose, opening the door and losing some of her bravado when her mother and father stumbled forward into the room. Clearing her throat to keep from laughing, she added as commandingly as she was capable, "I must ask you to leave immediately."

Lady Catherine huffed and puffed and blew outcries and threats. "Only a girl out of her mind would treat me in this undignified fashion."

The Bedlam doctor, Elizabeth noticed, no longer watched her when he had a more volatile example to keenly observe. His gaze riveted on Lady Catherine.

"I demand you commit her!" Lady Catherine waved her finger at Elizabeth.

He rubbed his hands together, his voice docile, mollifying. "Without proof of madness, I have no authority to take her in. Tis a pity, for the director looked forward to a healthy subject recently displaying symptoms of mental degradation."

Lady Catherine's veins throbbed at her temples, casting a purple hue over her complexion.

The doctor continued in his complacent tone, "Of course, madness is not unique to the young, nor can those of the first circles escape its hold. If it bit King George, nobody is immune."

It was then Lady Catherine must have realized his words were not directed at Elizabeth, but at her. From mottled purple and red, she blanched white. "You cannot believe me mad!"

He merely observed her, his hands rubbing.

"Darcy, Anne, tell him I am not mad!" Her eyes were white and wide.

Reassurances proved nothing when Her Ladyship gave enough evidence to counter her and anyone else's claims.

Elizabeth intervened with a question. "How did you come to arrive today, sir? I was under the impression Her Ladyship wrote a week ago."

Finally, the man released his predatory focus away from his new target. "Dr. Sculthorpe called on the director as I was taking my leave. He informed us that your condition, since Her Ladyship's letter was received, had reversed in its entirety."

A lie for which Elizabeth was grateful.

"As you can imagine," he continued, "Dr. Slade's disappointment was severe. However, madness runs rampant, and when he received a second letter, more insistent and aggressive than the first, he sent me to investigate." Again, his gaze settled on Lady Catherine.

"You did not come for me, but for Lady Catherine? What proof have you to pursue this course?" Elizabeth asked.

"Not only have I heard it observed from her own relatives this very evening that she is not acting like herself, but I have personally noted her complete disregard for decorum — a vulgarity no lady of her position in society would ever overlook.

"The lady herself wasted no time explaining, in a convincing manner I will add, the attachment between Miss de Bourgh and her nephew." He nodded at Fitzwilliam. "However, I have yet to see any evidence that such a connection ever existed.

"Complete disregard for propriety and social norms, sudden shifts in temperament, untempered aggression aimed at an imagined foe, and delusions. I would say I have more than enough proof to suggest you charge Her Ladyship with the care of the asylum I represent. We will take good care of her there."

This was serious. Had Elizabeth possessed a more vengeful nature, she would have held her peace. But she could not be responsible for condemning the woman to shame and torment just to be rid of a bur in her boot.

To Fitzwilliam and Anne's claims of her sanity, Elizabeth added her own. "Her Ladyship is as sharp as I am, sir."

The doctor frowned. "I hate to return to the asylum empty-handed. If you will not release her to me, if you are certain my efforts to raise a case against her would waste more of my time, then is there anyone else you suggest? Someone young and recently of sound mind, or of the peerage?"

What a strange question to ask of them. As if they would betray anyone to the likes of him.

Papa moved to show the man the door.

"Wait!" exclaimed Lydia. "You said someone young? Would a soldier brought up as a gentleman do?"

"Lydia," Papa cautioned.

"Papa, I know what I am doing. If George faces trial as he is, they will sentence him to hang. As many times as I have said that I hate him, that I would kill him myself with my bare hands, I cannot send him to die like that. I would rather send him to the madhouse." Turning to the doctor, she added, "He is at the gaol, but you had better hurry before the militia carts him off."

He departed, and not one person impeded his withdrawal.

Mama sent for coffee, a kindness Lady Catherine was too unnerved to refuse.

Mr. Collins, however, was presumptuous enough to bid them good night, asserting that the evening had taxed Her Ladyship … as befit elegant females of her station. And so, Mama's hospitality was verbosely refused in the utmost display of pompous humility.

The depth of Lady Catherine's humiliation was evidenced in her willingness to lean against Mr. Collins' arm, availing herself of her rector's condescension. He must have been overjoyed.

Miss de Bourgh curtsied hastily, obliged to follow in their wake, though it was obvious she would rather stay. It was enough to make Elizabeth pity her, but not enough for her to dissuade Mr. Collins from taking Her Ladyship away from Longbourn.

A collective sigh rippled through the parlor as their unexpected guests gained the hall.

And a collective gasp echoed off the walls when, from the entrance door, they heard the sound of another knock.

CHAPTER 35

*A*nne held her breath, along with everyone else standing in the hallway and crowding the door from the front parlor.

"Dear Lord, who is it now?" Mrs. Wickham exclaimed.

Anne would never have expressed herself so … obtrusively … but her own thought had been similar.

The elderly houseman looked at a loss. He could not open the door without delaying their departure, but they could not leave unless he opened the door.

Another knock, more insistent this time.

"Open the door, Hill," Mr. Bennet instructed.

The houseman did as he was bid, and Anne heard several sucks of breath behind her, followed by several whooshes when they saw the colonel standing at the threshold.

"Richard!" Anne said.

He doffed his hat, clutching it in front of his chest, a wide smile planted on his face. "Anne, just the lady for whom we were searching."

"We? At this hour?" Anne's confusion grew when a shadowy figure shuffled behind Richard.

More Bennets filed out to the hall, the Bingleys peeking over their heads from the parlor doorway.

Richard bowed. "I apologize for the late hour, but I stopped at the inn with a friend from London and heard that my aunt and cousin had hastened away to Longbourn with Mr. Collins and an unknown gentleman. The innkeeper was greatly agitated, fearing both for his esteemed lodger and his friends here."

Mrs. Bennet was as eager to entertain the colonel as Anne's mother was resolved to leave. Mr. Collins, too, seemed eager to distance himself from his family when he ought to have been rejoicing with them rather than attending to his patroness.

Richard and the stranger in the shadows allowed them to pass, but Anne lingered. "You said you were searching for *me?*" she asked.

Her cousin stepped aside, and the gentleman behind him moved into the light.

Anne's heart leapt into her mouth, and tears clouded her vision.

"Come, Anne!" demanded her mother stiffly.

She ought to reply or move or do anything other than stand dumbly in place. But she could not take her eyes off the man standing before her or blink for fear he would disappear.

He was taller than she remembered, not as tall as Darcy but taller than Richard, and handsome. So handsome. His left arm was fixed to his side with a sling matching the color of his coat, and while his collars were high, they did not completely conceal the scars running up his neck to the side of his face. He stood widely, firmly, like a man accustomed to rolling decks and uneven wood planks.

"Patrick," Anne's heart whispered. What would he think of her? Embarrassed, she dropped her chin, turning to hide behind her bonnet.

"Anne, come before you catch your death of cold!" Mother said.

She did not feel the chill.

Patrick lifted her chin, swiping his thumb over her cheek when a tear escaped. "Annie," he said with a tenderness Anne had not heard in years. Not since her father had died and Patrick left to make his name and fortune. Not since he had promised he would return for her. An eternity ago. "I came back for you, Annie."

A sob escaped her. This had to be a dream. A cruel dream she would wake from any minute. Except his touch felt real and his nearness warmed her.

"I demand an explanation! Stand away from my daughter!" Mother protested.

Anne smiled. Her mother's anger was real. He was real.

Richard turned to Mother. "You do not recognize this gentleman? He is so much in demand in society, I had difficulty prying him away from their clutches. Not that I blame them for wanting to honor a celebrated captain whose acts of bravery have made the papers."

Mother huffed, quite recovered from her earlier shock. "I know everyone of consequence."

"Excellent, then you will have no difficulty remembering Captain Patrick Gibbs of His Majesty's Royal Navy."

Patrick doffed his hat, tucking it into his arm. "Lady Catherine. My mother sends her regards."

Several times Mother opened her mouth to speak. "Anne's nurse? You are the son of one of my old servants?"

Patrick treated her insult lightly, swooping an elegant, impertinent bow. "At your service, madam." He never had been intimidated by Mother.

Looking at Anne, he added, "I have risen in rank and have earned the respect of both my subordinates and my superiors. The Navy was good to me. I have won a fortune and am now in possession of a comfortable estate very near Bath."

Anne's stomach fluttered. "Bath?"

His smile deepened. "You spoke so often of the place, I could hardly purchase a residence elsewhere."

He really *had* thought of her. After all these years. Anne thought she would burst.

She yielded her hand to him freely, gladly, feeling like a maiden in the bloom of her youth. Pressing her palm against his heart, he said, "It took bodily injury to recognize how fortunate I was to be forced into retirement. Otherwise, I would still be aboard my ship instead of here with you. I have never been a man of superficial emotion, Anne. If you will allow me to court you, I will ask for your hand in marriage. It is my intention to love you every day for the rest of our lives."

Joy swelled in her throat, flooding her eyes.

He took her other hand, caressing them to his chest. "There is nobody else for me but you, Anne. If you will have me."

Mother shouted, "I object!"

Of course she did. But for the first time in Anne's memory, she paid her mother no heed.

"Yes!" she answered.

"No, you will not! You are engaged to Darcy."

Anne pulled her gaze from Patrick to her mother. "I have not, nor have I ever, agreed to marry my cousin when my heart has long belonged to another."

"Are you so selfish you will forsake your family? The position you were born into? What will society say?"

Anne smiled up at Patrick. She had never felt braver or bolder. "They will say I have made quite a catch, I daresay, but, really, Mother, I do not care."

"Obstinate, headstrong girl!"

Her mother compared her to Miss Elizabeth? Anne felt reborn. "That is the best, kindest compliment you have ever bestowed upon me. Thank you, Mama."

DARCY PUSHED AWAY from where he was listening at the window, allowing more room for Mrs. Bennet and her younger daughters to elbow each other for the best vantage ground. He had heard enough.

Elizabeth pulled away from the bunched crowd, wearing the expression of one smugly satisfied with her plan. She ought to be proud.

"You did that," he said, full of wonder for his bride's thoughtfulness for another when she had had sufficient obstacles of her own to overcome. "You know my aunt would never accept our union. She would have blamed you for separating me from Anne, and she would have made her life unbearable. She would have despised me, straining our relationship beyond reparation and isolating herself from anyone who supported my decision to choose you over her."

Elizabeth chuckled. "Lady Catherine will have to adjust her expectations."

Darcy shook his head, his grin widening. "She will come around. Eventually."

As quick as a shot, the curious onlookers scattered away from the window, sitting in the closest chairs and doing their best to look bored.

Richard entered the parlor, the glint in his eye communicating that their secret was safe with him.

The newly engaged couple followed, whom he proudly presented. Mrs. Bennet was in raptures at the sight of the gold epaulets on the blue embroidered coat.

Mr. Bennet teased, "If uniforms bring you so much pleasure, my dear, I shall have to find my white breeches." He patted his middle. "And, perhaps, make a trip to the tailor."

"A blue coat with brass buttons would complement them nicely," Elizabeth added.

Richard joined them, clapping Darcy on the back. "I apologize for the delay. I was not exaggerating when I said I had to contend with society's grasp, but the captain could not very well refuse an invitation to Carlton House."

"The Prince Regent?" Elizabeth gasped.

"He insisted the captain attend his ball ... and so, I had to wait." Richard looked about, saying absently, "Which reminds me ... I must speak to Bingley sooner rather than later, or else he will have quite a surprise when he returns to Netherfield Park."

"What have you done?" Darcy demanded. Bingley had displayed the patience and forgiveness of a saint, delaying his wedding tour, generously opening his residence to Darcy, and riding all over Hertfordshire in search of murderous husbands. He could not in good conscience allow for any more abuse.

Richard sniggered. "You will find out soon enough. Think no more of it when you ought to be dreaming of your wedding. When is the happy day?"

"On the morrow." Darcy would have preferred that moment, but even he must abide by the church's rules.

"Perfect. We will be ready." Richard slipped away to the Bingleys', leaving Darcy to wonder who the 'we' were.

Loathe to permit Anne to celebrate her good fortune, Aunt Catherine joined them in the parlor, her unexpected presence provoking several sideways glances and stilting the conversation.

"Lady Catherine, it would be my honor to see you to the inn," offered Mr. Collins. He mopped his face with a handkerchief.

Elizabeth stared at him, her expression curious, then settled, then narrow. "You are terribly nervous, Mr. Collins."

He fumbled his handkerchief, the damp linen dropping to the floor.

Extraordinarily nervous.

Darcy, too, narrowed his eyes at the clergyman.

CHAPTER 36

*E*lizabeth shook her head. Why had she not seen it before?

Granted, her mind had been occupied with the puzzle surrounding her delayed wedding and Wickham's artfully contrived appearance. She could hardly be blamed for failing to notice the significance of one vital piece.

"Why are you here, Mr. Collins?" she asked, giving him a chance to explain, a consideration she only extended him in honor of her long-standing friendship with Charlotte.

Mr. Collins stuffed his wadded handkerchief inside his waistcoat pocket. "You are my cousin." He clasped his hands behind his back and rocked on his feet, looking like the boy who got caught snatching the last biscuit from the pantry.

She arched her brow. "A sense of familial compulsion?"

"Yes. I have always held your family in high regard—"

"Really? As high a regard as your beloved patroness?"

He blanched, so that it became difficult to distinguish his skin from his shirt collar.

Elizabeth went in for the attack. "You have made it plain since your arrival that you place Her Ladyship's whims far above the welfare of your own family."

Fitzwilliam exhaled, pressing his eyes closed and shaking his head. He knew, too.

"Her Ladyship ... That is to say..." Mr. Collins began without finishing.

"You were eager to pin the carriage incident on Mr. Wickham, and when it became clear you would not have success casting the blame off yourself, you suddenly became eager to leave. Why is that, Mr. Collins?" Elizabeth asked.

Several gasps pronounced the silence. Now they knew, too.

Mary's scornful voice added to Elizabeth's accusation. "Did not the Lord chasten the false Pharisees, calling them the offspring of vipers and of their father, the Devil? It is an abomination for a man of God to act deceitfully, and even worse for you to put the vainglorious whims of your patroness above the will of God.

You will receive just payment for your sins on Judgment Day."

The threat of eternal damnation, the same prospect he held over his parishioner's heads every Sunday, broke Mr. Collins. He lurched forward, hands pressed together in a plea. "I wished to please Her Ladyship and cause a delay. Only a delay. Nothing more."

Lady Catherine objected, as she was wont to do, but in this case, Elizabeth did not blame her. "I never asked you to do such a thing, nor had such a scheme entered my mind."

An idea took root in Elizabeth's mind — one which might benefit everyone. In her gravest tone, she said, "What if I had died, Mr. Collins? Your sabotage could easily be seen by a jury as an attempted murder. What if my father had been the victim of your interference? Anyone would assume your attempt was motivated by impatience to collect your inheritance and cast us out to the hedgerows."

Mama fanned her flushed face. "Appalling!"

Fitzwilliam nodded. "Indeed. The charges against you are grievous, Mr. Collins."

The colonel added, "An accusation of murder is enough to draw the Archbishop's attention. You would be stripped of your title and of your living, cast out of society with no hope of redemption."

Mr. Collins blubbered, "Anything ... I will do anything to ... rectify ... the situation. Only, please say nothing to the Archbishop."

Calm settled over Elizabeth as she seized the opportunity she had been seeking since her Mother's hope of bearing a son had shriveled and her nervous spells had begun. "There are only two things I require." She paused, securing Mr. Collins' full attention before continuing, "The first is that you dedicate all the devotion you currently grant to your patroness on your family, foremost of whom is the wife you have been neglecting by your continued presence here. You will strive to become a man worthy of her respect and admiration, fulfilling your duties in such a way as to raise her whole family in the esteem of the rectory in which you reside."

Hunsford had the potential to provide handsomely for the Collinses. A rector's position was not a lowly one, and if Mr. Collins made himself more agreeable, he would reap the benefit of his parishioner's kindness along with the tithes and fees he received. Charlotte would suffer no disadvantage or discomfort.

Mr. Collins nodded vigorously. "I will. I swear it. I will depart immediately to Hunsford and attend to Charlotte."

A promising start, but Elizabeth was not done. "That brings us to my second requirement." She paused, feeling the impudence of her demand. "You will agree to end the entail on my father's estate, allowing us a common recovery and forfeiting your inheritance in favor of my mother and sisters."

He did not like that part of the agreement. Elizabeth

had not expected him to, so she added convincing incentive. "If you accept these conditions, I will agree to overlook your attempt against my life. Furthermore, I will not send a letter detailing your grossly immoral conduct to the Archbishop."

Mr. Collins sat down hard in the nearest chair. After some minutes, he said, "I have no choice. I must accede to your wishes."

Elizabeth inhaled and exhaled deeply. "On both accounts, Mr. Collins. If I hear you are neglecting Charlotte, the letter will get sent."

His face in flames now, Mr. Collins nodded.

Satisfied, Elizabeth said, "Very well, Papa will make arrangements with Uncle Philips first thing in the morning — before the wedding — so as not to delay your return to Hunsford."

Mr. Collins nodded again, quite speechless.

Mama, on the other hand, had never been more pleased. "Bless you, Lizzy. I always said you could not have been born so clever for nothing."

Clever? Elizabeth was not so certain her cleverness was not more of an impediment than a gift. She had thought herself an excellent judge of character until Fitzwilliam challenged her prejudice against him. And, more recently, she had feared that without her full memory, he would lose interest in her … or worse … stop loving her.

Foolish thoughts for one praised for her cleverness.

Elizabeth would never stop cultivating her mind;

she would always enjoy deep conversation and witty banter. But she had learned the strength of her heart, and the strength of her love for Fitzwilliam Darcy ran far deeper than his position and property, encompassed far more than their matching intellects and shared interests.

Having lost a piece of herself for a while, Elizabeth now understood the meaning of love.

Fitzwilliam was her heart — her missing part.

CHAPTER 37

*E*lizabeth opened her window, appreciating the puffy, white clouds in the azure sky, and closed her eyes to better take in the sweet aroma of the bloomed roses scenting the air. The day was perfect.

Mrs. Hill hummed a merry tune as she flitted from one room to the next, her footfall pausing outside Elizabeth's bedchamber. "You look absolutely stunning, love," she said, frowning when her appraising gaze reached Elizabeth's worn half-boots. "Except for those."

Chuckling, Elizabeth pointed at the pair of slippers with shimmering satin rosettes by the door. "It is only for the short walk to the church. You can hardly expect me to ride in the carriage."

Mrs. Hill exclaimed, "Gracious, no! Not until after the ceremony! Then you may ride in as many of Mr. Darcy's fancy carriages as you like." She crossed the room to close the window, a sad look flickering in her eyes. "Last time I shall have to do that for a long time."

"I will tell Lydia. I have it on good authority she plans on moving her things into here this same afternoon."

The prospect cheered Mrs. Hill, and just in time for Mama to clap her hands in the hall. "Mr. Bennet, girls, let us not delay a second longer."

Elizabeth had been ready the better part of an hour, her stomach full of butterflies both anticipating her second wedding day and already wishing it was over so she could finally be Mrs. Elizabeth Darcy.

Which reminded her…

Running over to her pillow, Elizabeth slipped the signature-filled paper from under the cover and tucked her sentimental memento in a bandbox set on top of the trunks she would next see at Darcy House in London.

Papa and Mama waited outside the entrance, their arms held out to her. Kitty, Lydia and Mary, who offered to carry Elizabeth's slippers, walked behind them like sentinels.

"We are taking no chances today," Mama explained. "I do not intend to release my hold, nor will your father, until we can hand you directly to Mr. Darcy."

Thankfully, their jaunt to the church was uneventful. Nary a twisted ankle.

Sliding out of her half-boots and into her slippers, Elizabeth watched as Lydia flounced inside the building, enjoying the surprised exclamations of those who had not yet heard of her miraculous revival. Of Wickham's fate, Elizabeth gave no consideration. Not on this day.

Today was a special gift, one of those rare days when dreams came to life, and Elizabeth would soak in every joyous moment to remember always.

True to their word, her parents did not release their hold on her arms, which was as well, for she was not prepared for the sight awaiting her when Kitty opened the double doors. Packed pews and hordes of happy faces. Faces Elizabeth did not recognize, but who she knew must belong to Fitzwilliam's side of the family. So many of them.

Elizabeth smiled when she saw Georgiana sitting by a stylish older couple who nodded their approval.

Lady Catherine sat beside the gentleman with Captain Gibbs on her other side, looking unhappy but subdued between the large gentlemen. She would cause no trouble.

Elizabeth's eyes teared. She had not realized how badly she wished for Fitzwilliam's family to celebrate their union, to welcome her into their family, until she saw them giving visible and irrefutable evidence of their support and acceptance.

It was perfect. And when Fitzwilliam vowed to love her, comfort her, honor and keep her in sickness and in health; and, forsaking all other, keep only to her, so long they both shall live, Elizabeth trusted he would keep his word as he had kept every other promise. As she would.

She was — at long last! — Mrs. Elizabeth Darcy.

Heart so full, her eyes blurred, she felt Fitzwilliam tug gently on her finger. "Look, please," he whispered to her.

Elizabeth looked down at her hand, and the tears flowed freely, spilling over her smiling lips. The gold and garnet ring Fitzwilliam had slipped on her finger was a forget-me-not.

EPILOGUE

*D*arcy handed his horse to the stable boy, relieved to return home after a long day with his steward. A quick wash, then he would find Elizabeth.

The butler met him at the door with a letter in his hand and a knowing smile.

It would be another Love, Lizzy note. Perkins never looked so pleased to deliver any other correspondence but the precious missives he delivered from Darcy's wife.

Carefully unfolding the paper, Darcy read:

I MAY BE FOUND in my sitting room penning hundreds of Thank-You notes at my writing desk ... in case you wanted to find me.

.   .   .

Love,

Lizzy

HER "L"s swooped over the page, swirling upward in smiling flourishes. Much like their author, who smiled often and flirted relentlessly with her adoring husband.

His bath could wait a moment longer. He needed to see her.

Elizabeth sat with her back to the door, facing the window. Sunlight shimmered against her hair. Darcy's breath caught in his throat. He had dreamed of Elizabeth so long, there were times he still, after a month of marriage, believed she was a vision.

She spun around then, and she wrapped her arms around him and kissed him until his doubts dissipated. She was real and here with him.

Cradling his cheeks in her palms, she lowered from her toes. "You are my hero for interrupting me when you did. My fingers are in danger of petrifying against the quill."

He looked past her to the towering stack of envelopes waiting to be posted. "My family will think no less of you if you take your time."

She shoved him. "You would continue to distract me as you have been doing the past month!"

He grinned, wrapping his hand around her waist, and lowering his mouth to her neck. "I can think of several other, more agreeable ways to pass the time."

She wiggled out of his grasp, laughing. "Not today, Fitzwilliam Darcy." Then, twisting her lips to the side, amended, "Not this moment at least. I am determined to thank your relatives and friends who have sent gifts and hearty welcomes before the sun sets. Besides,"—she hopped on her toes—"I am in possession of such delicious news. I was sorely tempted to ride over the fields in search of you hours ago, and I would have done so were it not for all these letters I must write."

Tugging his hand, she led him to the settee by her writing table.

"I heard from Jane. She said that Georgiana invited Mary to stay with her and the Matlocks in London." She bit her lips and looked at him through her thick eyelashes.

He chuckled. "If you are scheming something, you may be assured of my cooperation."

Darcy loved how her eyes glistened and danced.

"I am glad to hear it, and I will not abuse your trust. What I was thinking of was perhaps inviting Mary to Pemberley so that she and Georgiana might continue their friendship. You saw how they were at the wedding feast."

"Inseparable." He had noticed, and it had been a pleasant surprise to see how Mary encouraged Georgiana's confidence while benefiting from her experience at the pianoforte.

"Excellent! I will suggest it to Georgiana when I next write." She counted on her fingers. "That was the most pressing matter, but there is more." Her expression went somber. "Jane's letter was rushed as it contained some startling news. Wickham is dead."

Darcy stiffened. "What happened?"

"As you know, the Bedlam doctor traveled with him to convince his commanding officer that he was insane and in need of the treatment at the asylum. However, Wickham had suffered so many bug bites and bee stings, one of them, too long unattended, became severely infected. He developed a fever, and by the time they lanced the festering wound, the poison was in his blood." She rubbed Darcy's arm. "I am sorry."

"I am, too. How is Lydia taking his death?"

"Jane said she is already in widow's weeds and grieving her situation in her best dramatic fashion. It will be difficult for her to flirt in head-to-toe black."

Just like that, she lightened the air. Darcy brushed his lips over her fingers in appreciation. "How do the rest of the Bennets fare?" he asked.

"Kitty has taken to heart the lessons to be learned from Lydia's rash conduct and poor choices. Jane says that she spends more time with Papa in his study, reading and discussing his bees. Papa is happy for her company, as the bees accepted his skiff as their own, and he needs her help to collect their honey."

"And Mrs. Bennet?" Darcy worried for her now that the battery of the stimulator had given out.

"Papa has extended his area of study beyond bees to batteries, and she is content in the knowledge that he is concerned for her welfare. That, and the security of Longbourn has restored her nerves marvelously. Which leads me to my next bit of news. I finally heard from Charlotte."

Now it was Darcy's turn to console Elizabeth. Taking her hands, he asked, "How is Mrs. Collins?"

She sighed. "You know how anxious I have been going so long with no word of my dear friend — anxious she would resent me for taking Longbourn away — but it was for naught. I ought to have known better."

Darcy breathed a sigh of relief.

Elizabeth continued, "She apologized for not writing sooner, but she has been feeling so ill, she could hardly sit long enough to attend to her correspondence until recently. She assures me she is much improved, and that Mr. Collins is generous in his attention. She only has to lift a finger, but he is at her side, eager to be of assistance."

"I am happy to hear it. What did she say about Longbourn?"

"She admitted she knew better than to set her heart on Longbourn, knowing I would find some way of securing it for my mother and sisters — a security Charlotte would have seen to had her mother and sister been in the same position and, therefore, one for which she can hardly fault her dearest friend."

Darcy pulled Elizabeth closer, settling her in the

crook of his arm. Kissing her forehead, he said, "You must be relieved."

"I am. Deeply relieved. Oh, I almost forgot," she said, twisting to face him. "I also received a letter from Anne."

"You have been busy today."

"She bears the best news. She is happy running her own home, truly content and at ease. The captain keeps her busy decorating, sparing no expense and plying Anne with as many pastries and chocolates as he can persuade her to take. She plans to invite us for a stay once the rooms are finished."

Darcy said, "Richard says Aunt Catherine is resigned to the match now that it is done. She sulks alone at Rosings, but she has been after the colonel to settle."

Elizabeth laughed. "He is to be her next project, then? I wish them both well in that battle, though I do hope Richard prevails."

"He is as bullheaded as my aunt."

"As you are?" she teased, tilting her chin up to look at him.

He kissed the tip of her pert nose. "I have only ever met one to equal me in obstinacy. Aunt Catherine was no match for her."

Elizabeth snuggled into his side. "Just think, none of this would have happened had I not lost my memory. Anne would still be miserable at Rosings, Lady Catherine would have cut ties with us, Wickham would be your brother, and I would have wondered for much longer if your choice in me was worth the trouble it generated between our families.

Darcy felt likewise. "Not every lady receives three proposals … from the same man," he teased.

She nestled into his side, spinning her ring around her finger, her breath tickling his neck. "And not every lady is so fortunate to fall in love twice … with the same man."

Elizabeth did not finish her correspondence that evening. Darcy might have felt guilty for distracting his wife, but he was remorseless.

For Darcy had learned the importance of memories worth recalling, and he would give his Elizabeth as many pleasant remembrances as there were minutes in the day.

Can't get enough of Darcy and Elizabeth? Read on to find your next book!

Can curiosity and crimes lead a young lady to the altar? Join Elizabeth Bennet as she finds out!
Read all the standalone books in the Mysteries & Matrimony series!

Follow Fitzwilliam Darcy as he overcomes various challenging roles on his path to love.

Read all the standalone books in the Dimensions of Darcy series!

Darcy and Elizabeth form a formidable investigative team as they work together to bring enemies to justice and forge unbreakable bonds with their newfound family.

One-click the complete Meryton Mystery series!

A hidden letter that rocks the Darcy cousins' world. Will it ultimately lead them to their own happily-ever-afters?

One-click the complete Darcy Cousins series!

THANK YOU!

Thank you for reading *Forget Me Not, Elizabeth*! Of all the stories you could read, I'm honored you chose mine. I hope you enjoyed it, and I'd love to hear your thoughts in a review.

Want to know when my next book is available? You can:

* Sign-up for my newsletter
* Follow my Author page on Amazon
* Follow me on social media.

ABOUT THE AUTHOR

When Jennifer isn't busy dreaming up new adventures for her favorite characters, she is learning Sign language, reading, baking (Cake is her one weakness!), or chasing her twins around the park (because … cake).

She believes in happy endings, sweet romance, and plenty of mystery. She also believes there's enough angst on the news, so she keeps her stories light-hearted and full of hope.

While she claims Oregon as her home, she currently lives high in the Andes Mountains of Ecuador with her husband and two kids.

OTHER BOOKS BY JENNIFER JOY

Single Titles

Earning Darcy's Trust

Love Never Fails

Win, Lose, or Darcy

Sweet Contemporary Romance

Written in the Stars: Starlight Terrace Proposals #1

Made in the USA
Middletown, DE
28 August 2021